THE PASSIONS
OF CHARLES KINGSLEY

SALLY ARMSTRONG

Grosvenor House
Publishing Limited

This book is published by
Grosvenor House Publishing Ltd
Link House
140 The Broadway, Tolworth, Surrey, KT6 7HT.
www.grosvenorhousepublishing.co.uk

A CIP record for this book
is available from the British Library

ISBN 978-1-78623-515-2

Also by the same author:

Racers

Vintage Champagne on the Edge of Space.

Lives of great men all remind us
We can make our lives sublime,
And, departing, leave behind us
Footprints on the sands of time;

Henry Wadsworth Longfellow 1839

CONTENTS

PREFACE

I have been asked many times over the five years of completing this book why I chose to write a novel about Charles Kingsley. My initial knowledge of him was from childhood when I owned a copy of one of his novels, '*The Water Babies*'. As I started to delve into his life story, I discovered that here was a man who had led such an exemplary life, had such dedication and conviction that ultimately he left a lasting mark on the world.

He stands amongst the great novelists of Victorian England - Charles Dickens, William Makepeace Thackeray and George Eliot, yet his humanitarian work is also hugely important. With his deep religious beliefs, his life was dedicated to improving the conditions of the sick and poor, the plight of the young chimney sweeps and petitioning for the working classes in the cities and factories across England. His great love of nature, geology, history and above all his family also play a part in this story. His causes and passions were many.

In his fifty-six years of life he was active in so many areas that I have admittedly, left out certain historical events and I hope the Kingsley historians will make allowances for this. This is a story about a charismatic man with overwhelming dedication and devotion to his countrymen, a truly likeable man of the people and a man with many passions.......

Sally Armstrong. 2019

PROLOGUE

Rain. And more rain. Another dismal day in the city.

From the inside of his shop, the hunched up passers-by appeared as shadowy ghost-like figures. The shopkeeper had lost interest in the crowded pavements. Looking up from his accounting, the tinkle of the doorbell filled him with expectation. He glanced at the wall clock. Twelve-thirty. Hopefully here was his first customer of the day. The rain always dampened trade and judging by the poor state of dress of the man standing before him, he deemed him not to be a potential customer but one of those idle trades people who come in to shelter from the rain.

'Can I assist you?' he asked, peering over the wire rims of his glasses.

The man before him bore his hat so heavily over his forehead that the shopkeeper could barely see his face. Before making a reply, the man removed his sodden hat, which to his onlooker's disapproval, dripped water onto his polished wood floor. The man stared back at him with wistful eyes and smoothing his damp hair with an equally damp hand, announced seriously.

'Yes, I hope you can, sir. I am looking for books by the Reverend Charles Kingsley.'

The shopkeeper's eyes grew wide in surprise. Perhaps he did have a customer after all. Although shabbily dressed in a threadbare coat and worn, muddy boots, the man had a bearing about him. The shopkeeper detected his demeanour was one of pride, not to be mistaken for arrogance.

'And which title would you be looking for? There are many,' he said matter-of-factly.

'I was hoping you might advise me, sir.' The man clutched his hat in his hands with a degree of nervousness.

'We have some of his books in the window. The rest are over there on the shelf by the door.' The shopkeeper pointed to a smart collection of volumes. His love of books and indeed the works of Charles Kingsley melted the stiffness in his voice.

'Now let me see,' he said leaving his post behind the heavy wood desk and, forgetting his customer for a moment, ran his fingers along the long row of leather-bound volumes. 'We have nearly all of his works in stock. Although, we are down to the last two copies of *'The Water Babies'*. Mm- I have to order more, he said to himself.

'They are most popular.' He turned to the man. 'And since his death, they have become even more so. Such a shame, such a talent has left us.' He shook his head. 'I believe he was a most kindly man and did much to help the unfortunates.'

'He did indeed, sir, and I was fortunate to have met him.'

The shopkeeper appeared not to have heard his comment but concentrated on his stock. 'Here we have his first book, *'A Saints Tragedy'*, then the popular, *'Alton Locke'*, *'Yeast,'* *'Hypatia'*, *'Hereward the Wake'*, *'Glaucus,'* *'At Last – Christmas in the West Indies'*... Ah and '*Westward Ho!'* Now there's a good adventure story.'

The man's eyes followed the shopkeeper's fingers as they skimmed across the many volumes. He noted that adjacent to them, and as many in number, were the works of Charles Dickens and William Makepeace Thackeray. Who would have guessed the young Charles Kingsley he had met all those years ago would become so famous? He delighted in telling his children the story of their meeting and he hoped that today he could make a purchase they could share and treasure together. The choice bewildered him. His knowledge of literary works, indeed his knowledge of reading was scant. If he had to admit to it, he had read but two books in his life. But he had saved up enough money to start a collection of books to enrich his children's lives, unlike his own destitute beginnings. Which is the reason Jim Hatchett found himself at the bookshop at no 6, Lion Street in London.

Somewhat wary of the shopkeeper's intimidatory manner, he was loath to touch any of the volumes. Instead, he enquired. 'Which one would you suggest is suitable for my children?' And myself, he omitted to say. He was most anxious to read one of Charles Kingsley's books but not the more intellectual tomes that he had heard were a part of the author's acclaimed works.

'My choice would be '*The Water Babies*'. It's a magical tale about a chimney sweep -'

A pink flush spread across the man's already ruddy cheeks. He was about to volunteer the information of how he had started off his working life as a sweep's boy but something stopped him. He was reluctant to share this piece of his life-story with the formidable stranger.

The shopkeeper removed the volume from the shelf and hesitated before handing it to his customer. The man quickly disposed of his hat on a chair and self-consciously wiped his hands on his coat.

'Thank you,' he said as he held the volume in his hands and opened it reverently. The book was illustrated with drawings of a naked little boy swimming with underwater creatures, of dragonflies and fishes. It promised an insight into a magical world. He closed the volume.

'I will take it, thank you.'

The shopkeeper gave him one of his rare smiles. He didn't mind that he had initially misjudged the man. Obligingly, he wrapped the book with great care in brown paper and then seeing the rain still splashing against the windows, enveloped it in another layer before tying in with string and hoping that it would keep the book waterproof.

The man counted out two and sixpence to the shopkeeper. He would inevitably receive a scolding from his wife for spending their 'shoe money' on such a triviality, as she no doubt would describe it. Nevertheless, he already had his response ready. Like Charles Kingsley, he believed a child's education was of the utmost importance. Despite his poor start in life, it hadn't stopped him leaving the evil trade as a sweep's boy to become a wheelwright near Eversley in Hampshire. He had made a decent living for himself and family. And now he wanted his children to do the same but through learning to read and write.

As he clutched his prize and headed out into the rain, the book firmly tucked under his coat, he smiled with anticipation. He could now tell his children they owned a book by the famous Reverend Kingsley whom he had met in Clovelly, Devon all those years ago.

EARLY YEARS
1831

Barefoot and dressed in knee-length shorts and brown cotton shirts, three young boys bounded across the shoreline, splashing in the shallows as they raced towards the rock pools, with buckets and nets bouncing in their hands. The sun was at its hottest on this June day, lessons were over, and for the first time, Charles had been given permission to take his younger brothers, Herbert and George, down to the beach unaccompanied by an adult. Gerald, the youngest sibling by three years, had accepted an invitation to go pony riding with friends on Exmoor.

The morning lessons given to Charles by his father, the Reverend Kingsley had been a fear-fuelled two hours. On entering his father's study to recite his studies of Latin verbs, he had forgotten his declensions and stammered out a poor attempt. His father had lost his temper and, in a fit of frustrated rage, Charles had taken his punishment with a sound slapping of a ruler on his outstretched hand.

But the young student was taken aback when, instead of having to remain in his bedroom and re-learn his homework, his father had relented and suggested he and his brothers go to the beach. Charles had not been privy to the heated, whispered argument between his parents.

His mother had implored her husband to be gentle with her delicate child and had gone so far as to suggest that his harsh treatment towards him had resulted in the stammer that Charles was now developing.

'The child has such a sweet nature and is so sensitive he cannot take your admonishments. His stammer gets worse by the day and your strict discipline will not help matters.' Mrs. Kingsley had wrung her hands in despair; her husband had rarely seen her so forlorn. He could not deny she had a love for her eldest child, now eleven years of age that he could never match.

The rector gave his wife one of his stern looks of disapproval. 'But my dear, it is imperative we bring up our children to learn the virtues of hard study. If, when they fail, it means punishment, then so be it. I am in no mind to change my views on this.'

But Mrs. Kingsley had persisted. Upon seeing her downcast yet sweetly innocent face, her husband relented. As a rare concession, he would allow Charles to forgo his homework and allow him and his siblings to go to the beach, much against his own strict beliefs on child rearing.

The boys raced down from the Rectory as far as the steep, narrow street of Clovelly that led to the quay and shoreline. Charles ran on ahead whilst Herbert waited for George, aged five, and on his first trip to the beach with only his older brothers for supervision. As they approached the top of the cobbled street, Charles took on a more adult role. He strode importantly with the other two following behind imitating his marching steps. At a very young age it had been instilled in them to act as children of a 'man of the cloth' and with the utmost propriety. So, bidding a polite 'good afternoon' to the passing local villagers, they sped on as fast as decorum would allow.

Their time on the beach passed all too quickly. They filled their buckets with different species of shells, seaweed, tiny shrimps, and hermit crabs. Charles had screeched with delight when he came across a bright red sea anemone lurking at the bottom of a rock pool and had pulled out his sketchbook to record its size and shape. Despite his young age, Charles knew the name of every type of shell, seaweed and shellfish.

He loved discovering new specimens and adding them to his already extensive collection stowed carefully in glass boxes and labelled both in English and Latin.

They paused in their hunt for seashore bounty to watch the fishing fleet prepare for their night's work. The fishermen had already launched the twelve boats at the circular stone quay and were hoisting their brown sails. Fishing was the main livelihood in the small village and, as a close-knit community, not a day went by when the locals, young and old would gather at the beach to see them off or await their return in the morning.

The Kingsley boys carefree joy of scavenging contrasted strongly with the serious routine of the fishermen, some as young as Charles as they made last minute inspections of the nets and adjusted the rigging on the home crafted masts.

Charles waved to his young friend, one of the village boys as he approached his fishing boat. Despite the planked hull's construction of strong timber, Charles wondered about its robustness when faced with the Atlantic storms that occasionally rolled into Bideford Bay. He had seen how the sea, without warning, could suddenly change its mood and turn into a seething, angry cauldron with such power it could scoop up a child from the shoreline and into its depths.

However, in Charles' eyes, a night at sea was without doubt a huge adventure. Excitedly, he quizzed his fishing friend about their evening ahead; what was their expected haul of fish, and how far were they were sailing.

'You are so lucky to be out at sea amongst the stars tonight. I wish I was coming with you,' Charles said earnestly, running his hands over the wooden deck.

'Why don't you come wit' us?' the boy replied. 'I'm sure me Dad could use an extra pair o' hands. The wind is set t' rise this evenin' and we'll need all hands t'reef the sail.'

'When are you leaving?' Charles glanced at the sun now dipping towards the horizon. The sea glinted gold in its shimmering light and with its mirror calmness looked even more inviting. The clear sky promised an excellent night for star watching. Charles was very tempted. He pictured himself riding the bow of the boat in the waves glistening with phosphorescence, hauling in the catch under a brilliant moon and returning home as a proud member of the fishing fleet with a token of herring as a reward for a hard night's work. The fantasy faded as he visualized his father's reaction. He would never allow him to go on such a wild adventure. His dream of joining the fishing fleet would have to wait for another day.

His young friend smiled at him. He could see by the faraway look in Charles' eyes just how much he wanted to go with them.

'We're off when me Dad's back with the basket for us supper. You've time t' change and put on some warmer layers,' the boy suggested.

'Come on Charles. We've more rock pools to explore before we go home.' Herbert was calling from some distance away. He was knee-deep in a rock pool, his arm extended with a trailing piece of brown seaweed, and holding onto George who was impatiently tugging at him to go for a paddle in the sea. Reluctantly, Charles bade his friend farewell and promised to be at the quay when the fleet returned early the following morning.

'And God take care of you,' he called as he waved goodbye.

The Kingsley boys left the picturesque scene of the fishermen at work on their boats, their women folk hurrying to the beach with baskets of food and the older men looking down at the preparations from the high circular quay. It was a centuries old everyday scene. Weary after their beach-combing, the boys climbed back up the cobbled street to their home - an eighteenth century rectory standing amongst the trees and with a view of the sea from the large terrace. Five-year-old George found the walk back exhausting. He was panting heavily by the time they reached the entrance gates to the rectory.

'We're home now and you've behaved so well, George. I shall tell Mama you deserve to come again,' Charles announced as he laboured with two buckets, one of which was full of stones that George had taken a fancy to. At the side door to the kitchen stood a horse and a cart, laden with sacks.

'Look the sweep is still here. We must feed the poor horse before it leaves. He looks half-starved,' Herbert said grimly.

'He'll need some food if he's to take all those sacks of soot out of town.' Charles' sunburnt face creased into a frown at the sight of the horse's ribs protruding from his skinny body.

The three boys slipped in through the open front door. They pulled up suddenly as cries of shouting and swearing rang in their ears. They exchanged horrified glances. Such unseemly speech was unheard of in the normally reverent atmosphere of the rectory. Abandoning their buckets and nets in the front porch they followed the direction of the ranting to the front parlour.

'Git down now you lil heap of nothin' otherwise you'll be sorry,' rasped an angry voice. The sweep, a small bony figure of a man was standing by the fireplace. Scruffily dressed in a patched jacket and trousers caked with dirt, he bent over and shouted up the chimney from where the cries of a child could be heard.

'I'll tan your bleedin' hide if you don't git down 'ere this minute,' he threatened menacingly.

'I cean't I'm stuck,' came the muffled reply.

The boys stood rooted to the spot. They had heard of children cleaning chimneys but this was their first experience of seeing such a heartless practice. Across the hall, the door of the study slammed and the Reverend Kingsley strode angrily into the room. Mrs. Kingsley alerted by the noise came scurrying down the stairs having left her youngest, Charlotte of three years, asleep in the nursery.

'What is all this commotion about?' she enquired anxiously, smoothing her ruffled hair after she had been abruptly woken up from her afternoon nap.

The Reverend was equally upset. 'Mr. Gormley, I will not have you using such language in this house and particularly in front of children.'

'But there is a child up the chimney,' George piped up 'and he's stuck.'

The sweep straightened up, alarmed at the Reverend's admonishment.

'Cuse me, Sir, but this boy is new to the job and 'e's not so agile as me last one. As you can see he's 'avin some difficulty comin' down.' He changed tactics to placate the Reverend. 'Are you alright boy?' He now addressed his charge with a tinge of sympathy.

'No. I cean't move an' I cean't breathe no more.' The little voice broke down choking and sobbing.

'This is abominable,' the Reverend snapped. 'Does this normally happen?'

'No Sir.' The sweep shook his head deferentially and, with an evil sneer, showed his yellowing broken teeth. It wouldn't do to upset this comfortably off client. He would more than likely miss out on a handsome tip.

'Right,' the Reverend said, pushing past him. 'Out of my way. We must do something and quickly. How can we assist you?' he called to the boy up the chimney flue.

The sobbing stopped. 'Blimey Sir. I dunno. Me bum's stuck on this ledge.'

'Mind your language, boy,' the Reverend whispered as he cast an eye towards his wife who in shock had clamped her hands over her mouth.

'Can *I* help?' Charles asked.

The Reverend moved aside to make way for him and Charles peering up into the blackness saw one blackened foot dangling within his reach.

'Shall I give you a tug?'

The Reverend gave a loud harrumph and Mrs. Kingsley was so worried about the idea of a child suffocating in one of their chimneys, she grabbed hold of young George and Herbert and led them hastily out of the room.

'Do be careful Charles,' she implored as she left with George clutching his mother's hand and his petrified face swivelling towards the sweep.

Charles stretched up into the chimney flue and caught hold of the foot attached to a stick thin leg. The boy's master by now had lost interest in all this maundering of the boy. If he'd had his way, he would have taken his well-used stick to dislodge his errant apprentice and given him a good jabbing with it. A heavy soot fall landed on top of Charles and he felt around for the other foot. Taking hold of both he gave a sharp pull, then another. With a cry of pain and more soot falling, the small boy landed in the grate, like a small wounded bird dropping from its nest.

Charles, feeling the hero of the moment, was hastily escorted to the kitchen pump by his father and with cook heaving away at the handle, received a dunking of cold water to remove the worst of the soot. The sweep's boy too frightened to talk and fearful of the consequences from his master, cowered in the corner of the kitchen slurping noisily on a bowl of soup.

Much to his surprise, the Reverend had also insisted the cook clean him too before he was allowed into the kitchen. So there he sat having had his first dousing of water in many a month and feeling strangely different. The sweep meanwhile, was loading up the cart, muttering under his breath about the punishment he would meter out to this new half-witted boy.

The distressing incident left the Kingsley children in shock. Over a family tea later that afternoon the Reverend refused to discuss the matter.

'It is the way that chimneys are cleaned and has been so for many years,' he said matter-of-factly. 'Let this be an end to it. Your mother is most upset by the incident.'

'But there must be other ways to clean a chimney? It's terrible to send a small boy up there,' Charles opined.

'If you are so concerned, young man, then I suggest you invent another method for cleaning chimneys, isn't that right Mother?' His father was deeply irritated that his eldest child insisted on pursuing the conversation in front of his younger siblings.

Later that night over prayers in the nursery led by Charles, he asked God to forgive the sweep for treating a small child in such a way. He gave thanks that he and his brothers were fortunate enough to have a happy home and with enough money to provide for them all.

'Amen,' chorused Herbert, George and Gerald.

'And please God, may we never have to go up chimneys,' George added who was still very upset after the event.

Storm and Riots

Charles awoke to the sound of the oak tree branches outside his bedroom window thrashing wildly in the wind. He found the noise of the high winds around the house comforting. He would have thought no more of it and gone back to sleep had a sickening thought not struck him with a terrible ache in his chest. He leapt out of bed and drew back the curtains with such fury he woke Herbert who shared his room.

'What is it?' Herbert whispered as he joined Charles on the window seat.

'The fishing fleet is out in this storm. Please God help them,' Charles cried.

The boys, wide eyed, peered out into the blackness of the night. The wind whooped and whistled around the walls of the house as the moon appeared from behind a massive cloud. Through the snatches of moonlight they could see in the distance the boiling sea, its white caps lit up into wild breaking foam. They could hear the roar of the waves as they pounded the beach despite it being some distance away. It seemed the boys kneeled on the window seat for an age watching the storm that showed no signs of abating. Terrified, they could only imagine what was happening to the fishermen struggling in their small boats to sail to the safety of the shore.

'I'm sure they'll be all right,' Herbert murmured nervously. 'They probably sailed for home the moment the wind got up. Don't upset yourself Charles. There's nothing you can do.'

Charles reluctantly dropped from the window seat and wiped away his tears. 'You're probably right.' he agreed.

But as he thought about his young friend and all the boys and men, who were fathers, brothers, sons and husbands to the village folk, it struck home how dangerous their work was and who knows what his fate might have been if he had insisted on joining them?

At dawn, the household awoke to a loud banging on the front door. Charles, who had dropped off into a fitful sleep, was unaware of the commotion at first. But then he heard his father's anguished voice and his heavy footsteps. There were voices in the hall, urgent voices, pleading, cries and women sobbing. Charles and Herbert dressed hurriedly and raced downstairs just as the gathering group left for the beach. They followed the crowd down the street and by the time they reached the quay most of the Clovelly inhabitants had gathered there. Women were wailing, their arms wrapped around each other. Anxious men were hurrying down to the beach.

Then Charles saw the wreckage. Jagged pieces of planking were the sole remains of the boats. There were splintered sections of masts, and tattered, torn sails strewn along the shoreline. What at first sight looked like sacks of fish in the grey light of dawn were, to the children's horror, washed up bodies rocking back and forth in the shallows. Charles realised that amongst all the carnage would be his friend, the young fisherman. Word spread quickly. Only four of the twelve boats had survived the gale that had unexpectedly blown in.

Four days later the Reverend Kingsley led a line of hastily built coffins of different sizes out to the graveyard of the Church along with the whole village of mourners. Out of the twenty four lost, six had been young boys. Charles, along with the multitude of villagers, looked on at the devastating loss of life in their small community. The rooks circling above cawed mournfully. The trees bowed their branches in the rising wind as if to pay homage to these brave men. The Kingsley household was subdued for weeks to come and Charles never forgot the fragile line that separates life and death.

* * *

Life at Clovelly was as idyllic as a young boy could wish for. Charles now had a new brother, Henry. His sister Charlotte was three and apart from the strict discipline of studying with his father, Charles enjoyed a happy family life. After their morning lessons, the boys spent their afternoons, sailing, riding on the moors and cataloguing new discoveries of the seashore.

Charles, however, was aware something was amiss by the sudden change in his mother's mood. Her normal gaiety was replaced with reserve. All became clear a few days later when their father summoned the two boys to his study.

'Charles, Herbert -I-or rather *we* have decided that a proper education is required of you now, and after the summer holidays you will be starting at a preparatory school in Bristol. It has a good reputation and has so much more to offer than a quiet life here.'

'But Father,' Charles had turned pale, and forgetting his father's strict rule about not interrupting him, he blurted out, 'Father we are happy with our studies here. We learn so much from you and ...'

'Silence, boy. Life is not all about happiness. It's about facing life's challenges and you are of an age where you must start to take charge of your life and learn independence.'

Herbert burst into tears. 'But who will look after our ponies?' he wailed.

'They will be well looked after by the young groom.'

'But I don't want to leave Mama.' Charles' lips wobbled as he tried to restrain his tears.

The two boys left the study mute with shock and in the following days and weeks, mother and sons shed many tears. After the joys and freedom of a summer by the sea, two nervous and fearful boys set off by horse and carriage to

Clifton Preparatory School along with their trunks and a package of small boxes for collecting wild flowers and insects. A change of scenery would not impact on their love of nature.

The happy bubble of family life they had enjoyed as youngsters was soon shattered by the harsh realities of life outside. The Headmaster informed the boys there was great unrest in the neighbourhood. The school stood on a hill above Bristol and the city life below was entirely different to their quiet sanctuary. There were riots, he told them, and the poor were starting a revolution and killing people. He therefore forbade anyone to leave the school boundaries.

'What are the poor rioting about, Sir?' Charles stood up and asked the Headmaster as he was about to leave the classroom.

The class of ten boys was getting restless. It was time for their morning break and this new boy, Kingsley, had developed the annoying habit of always asking questions. And with his irritating stammer, it always took such a long time. The masters were showing more patience with him than his fellow pupils. This occasion was no exception. The Headmaster explained in a louder than normal voice to get the attention of the boys fidgeting restlessly at the back of the room.

'History is in the making, Kingsley. Not only here but in towns and cities across the country. There had been moves afoot in Parliament to pass a bill to increase the voting rights of the people. The working classes are of the opinion this will improve their wages. It is a sad state of affairs, however. This bill was not passed and now the underprivileged are growing mutinous. We are living in difficult times. So be warned- we do not wish for any pupil's life to be put in danger.'

Charles was deep in thought as he took a walk the following afternoon. It was a miserably wet day and Herbert had decided to stay at school. Curiosity was nagging at Charles to glimpse a side of life the headmaster had so vehemently warned him about. Cushioned as he was in his middle-class upbringing, he had little idea of the abject poverty of city life. Despite the headmaster's warning, he set off down the hill, excited yet fearful. He found himself near the docks.

There were cries and a multitudinous roar of shouts, like a baying of hounds. It was one of the most evil sounds Charles had ever heard. Suddenly afraid, he crouched behind some crates and grew rigid with fright. Glancing around the narrow alley, he saw hovels far worse than he had ever imagined. Rotten wood held together by planks served as doors. Windows were no more than gaping holes, their glass panes long gone. Charles dreaded to think what lay behind these piteous exteriors. Vile smells assailed his nostrils. Beside him were piles of human and horse excrement. Decaying rubbish was heaped up in the recesses of the alley. As the enraged mob approached, he saw how poorly dressed they were - the children, shoeless and in filthy rags. Mesmerized, Charles was drawn to follow the crowd to the main square, and, taking cover behind a horse and cart, he watched as the crowds ran amok, breaking into and plundering the shops.

Just when he thought it was safe to leave, he heard the raucous laughter of two stragglers from the riot. Two burly and bloodstained men had stayed behind to finish off one of the Customs House Officers who had tried to resist the looting of the warehouse. They had left him for dead. Fired up as they were, and spotting the smartly dressed schoolboy beside the cart, they bellowed at him.

'What's a toff like you doing in these parts? Come to watch the blood sport 'ave you?' Their guttural laughter rang in Charles' ears and sounded like a death knell.

Wielding their bloodied sticks they gave chase. Charles broke into a sprint, dodging rubbish, turning corners and running as fast as his legs would allow. Finally, he found the road back up to the school and, having lost his pursuers, he stopped to catch his breath. His heart was pounding and his body trembling. As the distant roar of voices grew less, he stumbled back up the hill to the school, the vivid images and sounds of the riot reverberating in his head.

He crept in through the empty main hall, relieved to find the rest of the school was in the refectory having tea. Herbert was waiting for him in the dormitory. His mouth fell open as he saw his brother caked in mud, bedraggled and ashen faced.

'Where have you been all this time?' he demanded, jumping up from his bed and rushing over to meet his brother. 'You look an awful mess.'

Charles removed his wet coat and sat down on the bed, wiping his wet cheeks with a trembling hand. The full impact of his escape hit him as he tried to stem his tears. He sat silently for a minute taking in deep breaths.

'You have never seen such a disturbance,' Charles stammered.

'Where?'

'In the city.' Charles stared at his brother with hollow, scared eyes.

'But the Headmaster told us…'

'I know what he said but I had to see it for myself,' Charles hissed.

'Tell me what did you see?' Herbert edged closer so he could hear his brother's whisperings. 'I was close to the mob, too close, but I hid when they passed. Hundreds of them, there were, armed with sticks and hammers and knives. They were shouting and screaming like wolves. The sound alone was frightening enough. They were breaking into shops and looting them; carrying off anything they could lay their hands on. A group of men were drinking from bottles of spirits they had stolen and were quite drunk. As I ran through the square, houses were being set on fire. Furniture was being thrown out onto the streets and I saw people jumping out of windows, their clothes alight. It was the most awful, terrible scene you could ever witness.' He turned to his brother, his eyes wide with excitement. 'It was a scene from hell.'

Herbert clamped his hand over his mouth. 'Oh I wish I had seen it too. It must have been so terrifying.'

'It was, and I don't think I shall ever be able to forget it, and you are far too young to have seen such evil and cruelty.'

'Don't tell the Headmaster whatever you do, Charles. You will be in such big trouble,' Herbert said slipping an arm around his brother's shoulder.

His protected and happy childhood had not prepared Charles for such violent, bloody scenes. His world of beauty, peace and innocence had, in a few hours, been shattered.

Later that night, the boys in the dormitory crept out of their beds to see the ravages of the rebellion below. Huge flames licked the night sky and a heavy pall of smoke hung over the city. There was little sleep for the boys as they witnessed the event. It fuelled their imaginations with bloodthirsty scenes of the rioters climbing the hill and attacking the school. After the first lesson of the morning the Headmaster gathered the boys together to announce that Her Majesty's soldiers had quelled the riot and many of the perpetrators shot dead.

The boys could talk of little else for the rest of the week. They gleaned terrible stories from the carter who called with supplies to the school. The Mansion House, the Customs House and the Bishop's Palace had all been set on fire and reduced to ashes. The jail had been broken into and the prisoners released. After the looting of wine shops, casks of brandy had been wheeled out onto the street and broken open. Children and adults alike stooped to drink the liquid when the spirit caught alight and many who were in its path were, as the carter described it 'instantly transformed to blackened corpses.' Nightmares replaced the sleepless nights of the children up on the hill.

Loss

After the close brush with the riots of Bristol, Charles and Herbert were moved to a school near to the Lizard in Cornwall. The boys were thrilled at the prospect of returning to the coast and countryside. Helston Grammar School, named the "Little Eton" of England was set in the pretty town of Helston and was close to lush meadows and fields around the River Cober. After lessons the pupils were allowed to indulge in outdoor pursuits and Charles and Herbert spent long hours around the estuary collecting wild flower specimens. Charles was never happiest when he was close to nature, and Herbert too shared the inquisitive mind of his brother.

At first, the Kingsley boys impressed their classmates with their knowledge of Natural Science. However boredom soon set in with Charles's constant spouting of facts.

'Kingsley knows too much,' one boy remarked out of earshot. Charles was explaining the life cycle of the butterfly after a trip to the meadows one summer's afternoon. The pupils were logging their wild flower collection in their notebooks whilst Charles was pinning a dead butterfly to his collection in a glass case.

'These have complete metamorphosis,' he explained as he bent down to study the Red Admiral in front of him. 'It's strange how a transformation from a caterpillar to a beautiful butterfly takes so much energy and yet these beautiful creatures have such a short life span, sometimes as short as a week, maybe a month, depending on weather conditions, of course.'

He looked up hoping to have an attentive audience. The boys were drifting out of the classroom.

'Oh, give it a rest, Kingsley,' one snapped as he walked past him. 'We're off to play cricket but don't bother turning up. We won't need you.'

Charles was shell-shocked.

'Take no notice of him. The boys are only envious because you know so much more than they do,' Herbert said gently, wrapping an arm around his brother's shoulder.

'But that last bit about cricket hurt.' Charles blinked trying to stem the tears.

'Don't take it so seriously,' Herbert commiserated. 'Your cricket might not be up to first team standard but you are by far, a better athlete. Give them a two hundred yard sprint and you can see them off any day.' He gave Charles one of his impish smiles.

Charles was not thinking about his athletic prowess but being excluded from cricket touched a raw nerve. He desperately wanted to be popular amongst his schoolmates.

'Am I really that much of a 'know-all,' Herbert? I can't help myself sometimes.' Charles's face was piteously sad. 'I want to share my passion of everything that God has made. We live in such a beautiful world and there is so much to learn.'

As he bent down to examine Charles' butterfly collection, Herbert could only admire his brother's enthusiasm for nature. 'There are no prizes for guessing what you will do when you grow up?' he chuckled.

Charles thought for a moment, his face brightening. 'A geologist, perhaps. Or maybe a botanist. Can you imagine travelling the world and compiling the largest collection of plants ever? How exciting would that be? What do you see yourself becoming when you leave school?'

Herbert looked up and stared at him blankly. 'I've never thought that far ahead. I know Father would like me to achieve some high qualification such as a lawyer or a professor. But I'm not cut out for any of that, not being terribly bright.

I'm not sure what I will achieve. I can't see into the future, like you can.'

Herbert's face suddenly turned serious as he gazed into the distance. 'I'm not sure what the future holds for me.'

During those days of collecting the flora around the river estuary, Charles forgot the ugly scenes he had witnessed in Bristol. He was back to a comfortable existence.

'Dearest Mama,' he wrote soon after their first few weeks in their new school. '*Herbert and I are very happy here at Helston. We are adding to our already impressive collection of plant specimens that I shall list in Latin – for Father's benefit as well as my own! Nature is my passion and we are to be so fortunate to live in this beautiful environment. We stargaze on clear nights, we watch the moon rise over the mirrored glass of the river, and on mornings such as this, it is a pure delight to stroll under the oaks by the riverbank as swans and ducks chatter idly amongst themselves. On Sundays we are allowed to visit the Lizard and when we are not searching for minerals, we stride out along the beach taking in deep breaths of fresh sea air. My life is complete. I have written several poems that I shall send to you. I hope you will approve of my efforts. Please send my love to the boys and dear Charlotte. Herbert is most excited that I shall be celebrating my fifteenth birthday soon!*'

But much to Charles' surprise, Herbert was not as settled at school as he supposed. One afternoon the Headmaster called on him.

'Where is your brother, Kingsley? We've been looking for him everywhere.'

'But I thought he was with Matron. He was complaining of headaches, Sir.'

'I don't wish to alarm you but could he have run away?'

Charles looked startled. 'Herbert? Run away? I don't think so, Sir.'

'Never mind, boy. It's just a suspicion I had.'

By evening there was still there was no sign of Herbert. After supper, Charles was summoned to the Headmaster's study. The news was not encouraging. Charles stood nervously before him, imagining dark thoughts. The Headmaster had informed the police and a search started in the local area. Thinking Herbert had skipped off for the day to avoid punishment for not handing in his homework was one thing. Staying out at night was quite another matter; a serious one and one that incurred a harsh punishment.

Charles spent a restless night, his mind churning over the dire possibilities of Herbert's fate. His brother had acted quite out of character and Charles' vivid imagination was already seeing his murdered corpse abandoned on the riverbank. Early the next morning, he determined to find news of his brother. The sight of a bedraggled figure halted his rapid descent on the stairs to the entrance hall. A policeman stood by his brother's side.

'Herbert, where have you been?' Charles demanded.

Herbert dropped his head onto his shoulders. 'I'm sorry,' he murmured.

'Get yourself off to the Headmaster's study *now*,' the policeman barked. 'You've got some answerin' to do.'

Charles could only look on as his brother was dragged away by the strong arm of the officer who, having spent most of the night searching for the scoundrel and now desperately tired, was not of a mind to show any sympathy.

As a punishment, the headmaster instructed Herbert to be locked up in a cold and sparsely furnished room and fed on bread and water. Charles sought permission to see him. From the dim light of a small window, he made out the listless body of his brother lying on a bed. A candle flame flickered from a draught. Charles gave an involuntary shiver as he drew close and saw his brother's face as pale as a winter moon.

'Herbert,' he whispered. 'You look in a bad way. What happened and why did you run away? Is it so bad here at school?'

Herbert tried to sit up but fell back on the worn pillow and stared at the ceiling. A thin blanket was all that covered his body.

'I fancied an adventure, Charles. I wondered what it would be like to be free. Like a grown up.' He turned his head so he could see his brother's reaction. Charles remained impassive.

'Well, Mama and Papa will not be too happy to hear of your adventure. Has the Headmaster called a doctor for you? You look washed out.'

Herbert nodded. 'He said I caught a chill. But to punish me I'm being fed on bread and water. And do you know when they caught me they put me in handcuffs? I felt like a criminal. And I feel very weak, Charles. My body aches. Do you think I will get better?' His face was so wretched that it moved his brother to tears. Charles embraced his hands that were burning with fever.

'Of course you will and all the boys wish you well very soon. They miss your jolly humour. And so do I. You must get better in time for the holidays. And I need your help with our gunpowder experiments.'

'I will try, but do you think you could ask for some food? A bowl of cook's soup would cheer me up.'

'Of course. No sooner said than done. I will find Aunt Betsy, the housekeeper right away. After that I have to go to class but I will call on you this evening - if I'm allowed to.'

Herbert gave a weak smile. 'Thank you, Charles or should I call you 'Cave' like all the other boys do?'

'Now you will be in trouble when you're well again! My mouth is not that big. Those boys exaggerate.'

They exchanged warm brotherly smiles. Charles's heart was fit to burst with love for his younger brother and yet he feared his condition was far worse than he had imagined.

A few days later, Herbert still languished in bed. Charles visited him once a day and they talked about the school news and cricket. Charles gave a scathing account of his performance in a cricket match and Herbert grinned as he recounted his short time in bat.

'I'm no match for these fast bowlers,' he complained as he watched Herbert sip on a bowl of beef broth that 'Aunt Betsy' had smuggled in. 'But I beat the cricket team in an obstacle course I set up. '

'An obstacle course? What did you do?' Herbert asked abandoning his soup.

'I devised a course where we had to run a mile down the lane, jump the widest part of the stream at the end, climb the tallest apple tree in the orchard which I had marked it with a red ribbon and then climb through the fallen trunk of that dead oak tree to the finish.'

Herbert saw the twinkle in his brother's eye. 'And did you win?' he asked knowing full well that Charles had seen off the competition.

'Yes. I didn't want those boys to think me a complete ass at sport. I had to retrieve my reputation somehow but,' and he gave a hearty laugh, 'you should have seen me when I crawled out of the old tree trunk. Naturally I was first through it and I disturbed a huge nest of wood lice and came out covered in the little devils. What with those and an assortment of very large sleepy spiders I looked like a walking specimen for the Natural History class. '

Herbert gave a weak laugh as his eyes glazed over with admiration.

'Charles, I've been such a booby. I regret what I did. Pa will be furious with me and he will never forgive me. And Mama will be so upset. What can I do? I have to see the headmaster tomorrow and that cane of his hasn't been near my derrière for a very long time. I can't face the thought.' Herbert sunk back onto his pillow and Charles noted his pallid complexion had returned.

'Herbert, you must not worry. You're not well enough yet to have the headmaster cane you or give you any other punishment. He would not be so hard-hearted as to consider such a thing.'

Charles turned to see Aunt Betsy bustling into the room. 'Well now, young man did you finish your supper?' She exchanged a worried glance with Charles.

Herbert gave a loud yawn. 'Oh yes, thank you. It was delicious but it's made me feel very sleepy.'

'You have caught a chill after all that sleeping rough. I hope you won't be of a mind to run away from us again. And I'll find you another blanket as soon as I've smuggled your supper away.' Aunt Betsy gave him one of her caring smiles.

'Thank you for feeding him,' Charles replied, trying to sound brave.

'I'll be in big trouble if I'm caught, mind, but we can't have young Herbert living off bread and water. He'll fade away in no time and besides, you need to build up your strength, don't you?'

Herbert nodded and gave a languid smile.

'Come on, Charles. The supper bell rang five minutes ago. You better hurry before it's all gone. I doubt if those hungry fiends will think to leave you any,' Aunt Betsy urged.

Charles gave his brother a rub of his tousled hair. Like his forehead that glistened with perspiration, his hair felt damp.

Had Herbert's fever returned, he asked Aunt Betsy when they had left the room.

'Don't worry 'bout it lad. The doctor will be here tomorrow to take another look at him. And I'll check on him a little later.'

The next morning the boys were aware of unusual activity in their normally smooth routine. The Headmaster was not present at morning prayers. There was a sense that all was not as it should be. A figure was seen scurrying down the corridor clutching a bundle of sheets. A panicky Aunt Betsy followed behind. The doctor's sudden and dishevelled appearance sent alarm bells ringing and hushed whispers amongst the assembly of boys. Had the Headmaster had a serious fall, someone asked.

By the time they had returned to their classrooms, rumour was rife. The Headmaster was nowhere to be seen and there was an abnormal amount of disruption. Lessons continued but neither the schoolmasters nor pupils had any appetite for learning. Either the Headmaster was seriously ill or maybe, someone suggested, he had died suddenly. The masters would not be drawn on the subject. Now the panic had spread to the pupils. Unable to concentrate on their lessons, they held their collective breaths and waited for something to happen, an announcement perhaps.

They dismissed the headmaster's demise as the boys heard his familiar stride along the corridor. It stopped outside the class taking History.

Opening the door, the Headmaster beckoned to Charles. His voice was as grave as his countenance. 'Come with me, Kingsley.'

Charles followed the Headmaster, his mind awash with terrible thoughts. Had his father or mother been taken ill? Herbert was on the road to recovery. It couldn't be him. The Headmaster led the way to the sick room. From the open door Charles saw his brother laying on the bed, a sheet covering his still body, his eyes closed and his inert face the colour of the whitewashed walls.

'I'm afraid your brother took a turn for the worse overnight. He was dead this morning when we came to check on him. I'm most terribly......'

But Charles heard none of this. He let out a heart-rending scream that even the pupils in the furthest classrooms could hear. No one needed to inform them it was Herbert who had died - and in such miserable circumstances. It was futile to continue lessons that morning. All the pupils were shocked at having lost such a popular schoolmate. Death overshadowed the school and left a heavy cloud of mourning and despair.

Charles was inconsolable. As he was prised away from his brother's dead body he wept uncontrollably. In the kitchens, Aunt Betsy was distraught with grief.

'What a way to give the poor boy the news,' she sobbed into her apron. Herbert was one of Aunt Betsey's favourite boys and to spring his death on that poor brother of his in such a way was, in her eyes, heartless.

'Young Kingsley loved that brother of his more than life i'self and for him to see his corpse like that and with no warning. 'Tis a shame the Doctor didn't diagnose his rheumatic fever earlier. They might have saved the boy.'

The rest of the kitchen staff could only nod in agreement.

Life at Helston was never the same for Charles after Herbert's death. He neglected his studies and brooded on the many experiences he had enjoyed with his brother. In class he would daydream about their expeditions -of gambolling like young foals through the meadows awash with buttercups and dandelions, of listening to the skylarks sending alarm calls to protect their nests, of hearing the first call of the cuckoo in April. All this was a bittersweet memory. The joys of discovering nature seemed to pale into insignificance without Herbert.

City Life

Charles grew more insular and, recovering from a mild bout of cholera, he consoled himself by writing poetry about love and death. He struggled to keep up with his studies and the Headmaster was obliged to write to his parents who took the matter in hand. Charles was recalled home. Before he left he said a final farewell to Herbert. He sought out his resting place in the churchyard and standing by the simple grave, he found it hard to come to terms with the tragedy of losing such a loving brother. At fourteen years of age, Herbert's life had barely begun.

Neither would he forget the first meeting with his father after his death. Did he imagine the rebuke in his father's watery eyes? Was Charles to blame for Herbert absconding from school? Charles would never learn the truth as his father refused to discuss the matter. In spite of herself, his mother tried hard to comfort him. Unlike her husband, Mrs. Kingsley was not afraid to show her emotions and in private, she and Charles wept many tears.

'Why did Herbert have to die?' Charles sobbed one morning after yet another fitful night's sleep filled with bad dreams. They were sitting alone in her bedroom that had become her sanctuary. Dressed in black mourning and isolated from the rest of the household, it was left to the children to visit her there.

'If only we knew, my dearest. God has called him so early in his young life,' she said as she took Charles in her arms and stroked his dark curls. Reaching for a handkerchief from her dress pocket she dabbed her son's tears away. If only her husband had shown more sympathy towards him and his traumatic discovery of the death, she thought to herself. It was harrowing enough to lose a brother at such a young age but to be shown his body without warning was so terribly callous. Charles had not been the same since returning from Helston.

Two weeks after his return, his father summoned Charles to his study.

'Charles, you're probably wondering why I have brought you home? The fact of the matter is- and I'm sure you are aware - your studies have suffered since....' He paused to reconsider his words, 'your studies have suffered of late and we have decided to employ the services of a tutor. According to your schoolmasters, your Greek and Latin studies have fallen behind, your mathematics needs much improvement and if you wish to enter university it is imperative that these are brought up to a higher standard. Understood?'

'Yes Papa.' Charles felt numb. His chest felt so heavy he could barely breathe. How could his father talk about scholarly achievements when he had just lost his son? How could he be devoid of remorse over Herbert's death? Was this really how a devout man of the Church dealt with loss, he wondered. He wanted to cry out all these thoughts but he knew it would cause a scene. His father would only lose his temper and upset his grieving wife further. It was too much of a risk. But Charles made a promise to himself. If he ever became a father, he would show such compassion and love for his children they would never want for his care and support.

'And we have a big change for the family.' The Reverend Kingsley proffered a smile. Charles was brought back to the present with a bang.

'I have accepted the position as Rector of St Luke's, Chelsea. We will be moving there in late summer. It will be a highly influential preferment for me and you will benefit by being near to the libraries and galleries and all that London has to offer. It will also provide a distraction from your.....' he coughed abruptly, 'our recent loss.'

Charles stared at his father blankly. If he had expected a positive response to the news he was wrong. Charles could not share his father's good fortune. He bowed his head to hide his bitter disappointment. It was devastating enough that he had lost a brother and was leading a solitary life at home, but at least he had Clovelly with its beaches, the moors and the village folk to pass the time of day with. Now all this was to change. He left his father's study with a heart near to breaking.

At seventeen, and the family having moved to Chelsea, Charles had no choice but to forgo the delights of nature. Despite the area being semi-rural, the Battersea marshes were a poor substitute for his walks along the Helston Estuary and beach combing at Clovelly. Much to his relief, his parents decided against a tutor and enrolled him at King's College, London. Although he shared his home life with the company of his younger siblings, Gerald, George, Charlotte and Henry, he missed his brother Herbert desperately. His panacea was to throw himself into hard study of Greek, Latin and mathematics, necessary subjects for entrance into Cambridge University. His two years of dedicated work paid off. Charles gained a first class in Classics and a second in Mathematics and was accepted into Magdalene College, Cambridge. A new era of liberation was about to begin.

NEW BEGINNINGS

Surrounded by cigar smoke and the ballyhoo of voices, Charles sat in the Common Room listening to the wild carousing of his drunken colleagues. A dozen students in a high state of intoxication sat around a large table littered with empty bottles. Some were using the tabletop as a resting place for their stocking feet. Watching them sprawled in their chairs and talking over each other, Charles wondered if this was how the next three years of student life would continue. He had never imagined it to be such a hedonistic and indulgent lifestyle. Coming from a quiet sober background, and as a devout churchgoer, this came as a shock and something he had not bargained for in such a hallowed place of learning.

He found his first few weeks difficult. His stammer and shyness held him back from mixing with the other students and he was ridiculed and shouted down when he tried to make a point in a debate. However, much to his good fortune, he struck up a friendship with one of the most popular students, Charles Blatchford Mansfield. With his handsome good looks and lithe body, Mansfield had a magnetic attraction that was admired by both sexes and was the envy of his peers. He and Charles were attracted by their differences in personalities and Mansfield instilled some much-needed confidence in his friend.

The door to the Common Room burst open and Mansfield, grinning wildly, his grey eyes flashing with excitement, bounded in with bottles of wine under both arms. Laboriously, and hampered by his inebriation, he opened one and poured himself a glass of red wine before offering it to the others. Then in a flash he leapt up onto the table and amongst the debris of bottles performed a handstand much to the delight of his fellow drinkers. There were roars of approval that grew more deafening as he balanced on one hand and picking up his glass, drank from it. As quickly as he had jumped up, he landed with both feet on the table and stretched out his arms and bowed to his colleagues. There followed a loud applause and raising his glass, he announced with one of his bewitching smiles 'A toast to our Queen!'

'To Queen Victoria,' shouted the students raising their glasses.

There were more cheers and, with the nimbleness of a wild cat, Mansfield sprang off the table narrowly missing the students around him.

One sole voice resonated above the rest. 'But not her bloody government.' Helmsley, an overweight figure with puffed out red cheeks, looked much older than his years and on this occasion, much the worse for wear.

'Not that again, Helmsley. Can't you give government bashing a rest for one night?' a student shouted.

Helmsley staggered up out of his chair and, with glass in hand, rested against the heavy mahogany table to steady himself. Even with all the drunken antics around him, the brouhaha stopped for a moment.

'Let him have his say,' one of the older students called out.

'Did you not read the article in *'The Times'* by Lord Melbourne?' Helmsley began, as he wiped the spittle from his mouth. 'The Queen, God bless her, enquired of him about educating the poor. And do you know what he replied?'

'By Gad, Ma'am what poor?' volunteered one of the group in a mocking voice.

There was a general titter and guffawing.

'Almost,' Helmsley continued. 'He said- 'Why *bother* the poor?'

'So why don't *you* get off your fat rump and go join the Christian Socialists?' heckled one of the party.

'Absolutely. Why don't you go and help those starving men you're always banging on about? Educate them? See how they feel about education when their bellies are empty!' said another.

'I will- when I've finished my degree,' Helmsley retaliated.

'Ha!' heckled a voice from the back. 'And then what? After you've finished your privileged education will you then not return to your family's estate in Dorset and make quiet noises like a mouse?' He made squeaking noises followed by laughter from the others. 'And then some 'big cat capitalist' comes along and stamps on your protests and offers you a well paid job in the City? These types don't like change. Life for them is as good as it gets and besides any reform will cost them money – more money in wages to start with!'

There was more jeering and Helmsley, deflated by their response, sat down and gulped wine greedily from a bottle. The revellers had lost interest in the speech making and returned to university gossip.

Then Charles stood up and mounted a chair. It took a minute or two before he grabbed the group's attention.

One student looked up and demanded. 'Have you something to say Kingsley or should we say stutter?' There was laughter all around.

'I ha...have j...just th... this to say.'

'Give the man another brandy,' shouted someone.

Charles paused and drew breath. In the half-light of the smoke-filled room his fellow students waited for him to speak. They could not deny he was an imposing figure of a man with his whiskery cheeks, prominent nose and piercing eyes. His tall slim body betrayed none of the athleticism of his taut muscles and stamina.

Charles cleared his throat. 'J-jest with me if you wish... but remember one thing m-my f-fellow students. I defend

Helmsley's argument. I swear I will *not* be one of those capitalists wh-whose only aim is to make their bank accounts fat whilst the poor starve.'

'And how do you intend to change the world?' demanded a sardonic voice. His audience was losing interest and there was idle chatter in the background but Kingsley persisted.

'Her M-Majesty's government is sadly blind to the misfortunes of our working classes, without whom we would be a nation of no c-c-consequence. The hard labouring of these people is what makes us a great developing country. The Government has banned the slave trade in the British Empire but lo-and-behold, we still have generations of slaves in our own country!' Kingsley was now rising to the occasion and was so carried away by his passionate beliefs that his stammer left him.

'Children as young as six years old are put to work in our cotton mills, our mines and our factories. These unfortunates are dying from overwork and malnourishment. Last week a child fell asleep at the loom in the cotton mill in Derbyshire and was crushed to death. Accidents like this happen far too often in the mills. I have on good authority the children who work in the slaughterhouses are so hungry they gnaw at the bones they crush for sustenance. Children are kept in attics working for tailors and seamstresses and rarely see the light of day. Even grown men would find it hard to keep up this punishing regime. And the abuse of these youngsters as chimney sweeps is yet another example of the huge injustice of our younger generation.'

Kingsley continued vehemently, remembering his own sad experience with the chimney sweep in his youth. His hawk eyes scanned the room and bored into the eyes of each and every one of his fellow students. His voice quivered with conviction. 'They are starved to stunt their growth so they remain small enough to climb up chimneys. Is that how we want to the youth of our country to grow up? They are no more than slaves! We must heed these children - children who should be receiving an education so they can aspire to a better life. It is our incumbent duty to lobby for change in their working conditions. How can anyone with a conscience in today's society accept the gross disparities between the rich and poor? Have we no shame?'

His speech was met with a long silence and the atmosphere turned serious. The students who had derided him earlier hung their heads. Kingsley's speech had a profound sobering effect on his colleagues.

'Well spoken, Kingsley. You have a nobleness of spirit.'

It was Mansfield who broke the silence and started applauding. Slowly, the rest followed his example. Even if Kingsley's speech came at an inappropriate moment, it was heartfelt, nonetheless. One of the students anxious to dispel the gloom of Kingsley's speech spoke up.

'So, Kingsley, how about saving your serious speeches for another day and give us some jape? What do you suggest, old man? We're getting bored and it's only just gone midnight. How shall we liven things up after your weighty speech?'

'Come on, Kingsley, how about some tomfoolery?' bellowed Helmsley.

Charles embarrassed by this sudden request and not wanting to disappoint his fellow students asked, 'W-w-would you have me to wager a bet with you all?' His eyes widened and his wide stern mouth broke into a grin.

'What do you have in mind?' asked a voice from the back. 'A drinking marathon? I'm well past that.' Loud guffaws followed.

'No,' Kingsley mused. 'I prefer outdoor pursuits. A r- race to the top of the oak tree outside the kitchen and I m-mean to the top!' He pounded the table with his fist. 'I'll wager a bottle of brandy to anyone who can beat me there.'

There was laughter, excitement and surprise amongst his comrades who thought this an excellent idea. That the shy retiring Kingsley would undertake such a challenge would prove what sort of a man he was. The men sprung into action as jackets, waistcoats and bow ties and other non-essentials were removed. Cigars and wine glasses were also abandoned as the group raced across the lawn to the tall, shadowy outline of the oak tree.

Charles joined in the sprint discarding his jacket at the base of the tree. As nimble as a monkey, he shinned up the trunk and grabbing hold of a sturdy branch, climbed from one to the other leaving the rest of the students struggling to gain a foothold. A few stopped at the first few branches and, realizing their advanced state of inebriation, hung on grimly before falling like ripe conkers onto the grass. There was much laughter and hilarity as they gave up, whilst others cheered for those struggling to climb in the darkness. But there at the top and clinging on to the highest branch, his white shirt catching the moonlight, was Charles.

'Long Live the Queen,' he called out triumphantly accompanied by cheering and clapping from below. Then Charles began a fast descent. Mansfield who was standing below heard the ominous crack first. A branch gave way under Charles' weight and there followed a tumbling of a body. It gathered speed as it fell through the foliage then came to a stop on the lowest branch ten feet from the ground. A groan was heard, then another, as Charles fell and lay limp at the feet of Mansfield.

'Well by Jove, what do we have here?' Mansfield asked, grinning at the prone figure beside him.

The others rushed over, anxious to see how badly hurt their new hero was. Mansfield bent down by Charles' side and whispered. 'Lay still, Kingsley. Let them think you've broken some bones and you'll have sympathy and more.'

'But I have,' Charles moaned. 'I can't move.'

'Someone fetch him a brandy,' ordered Mansfield. After examining his friend in the half-light of the moon, he lifted an aching Charles to standing position.

'Mm, you have some pretty bad scratches on that handsome face of yours. And your arm is bloodied but I don't think you've broken any limbs. You'll live.'

Sipping a draft of brandy, Charles made a slow recovery and a while later, aided by the support of Mansfield and Helmsley, he limped off to his rooms, wounded but proud of his achievement.

Kingsley had made a name for himself and gained a group of new admirers.

THE GRENFELL SISTERS

With his newfound popularity, Charles slipped easily into student life. Away from the harsh constraints of his parents, he experienced a freedom unknown to him before. His personality flourished and, despite his stammer that his colleagues now found amusing, he lost his shyness. As his close friendship with Mansfield developed, he indulged in pastimes of rowing, shooting, hunting, fishing, and inevitably, drinking.

It was during his first year at university that his parents moved out of Chelsea to a country rectory in Ipsden, Oxfordshire. The Reverend Kingsley had sought a brief respite of two months from the hectic London parish where the congregation numbered several thousand. Charles received a letter from his mother who, in great excitement informed him that four sisters, all in their late twenties and early thirties had relocated from Cornwall to a grand house called Braziers Park not far from the temporary Kingsley home. They were orphans of a recently deceased tin magnate in Cornwall, Pascoe Grenfell and his wife, the Honourable Georgina St Leger. His mother made no secret of the fact they had inherited a large fortune.

After a timely interlude to allow the new neighbours to settle in, and with Charles summoned home, Mrs. Kingsley issued an invitation to the Grenfell sisters for tea at the Rectory. She held onto a vague supposition that one of her sons might be attracted to these most eligible sisters. Her husband matter-of-factly dismissed the idea but was willing to receive the ladies in his home. Their attendance at Church would no doubt increase the coffers of his Sunday collection which was well below that of the parish he had just vacated.

The ladies arrived in their grand barouche and, Mrs. Kingsley bursting with anticipation, scurried to the front door, ahead of the disgruntled footman to meet them. Politely, the Grenfell sisters accepted her profuse welcome as they were led into the drawing room. Gerald rose from his chair and bowed effusively. Gerald Kingsley, Charles' younger brother was nineteen and on leave from the navy.

The Reverend Kingsley stood erect and aloof and gave his visitors the briefest of smiles. He considered all their flounce and ostentatious dressing to be against his Christian values. Introductions over, the sisters sat demurely on the pale green sofas as their carriage with four snorting horses was led around to the courtyard at the back of the house.

The drawing room was a pleasant, airy room with large sash windows that overlooked a drive lined with lavender and rose-beds. Beyond, lay a vista of the sleepy English countryside with sheep grazing in the fields. The peaceful setting outside, however, did not reflect the atmosphere in the drawing room. All were assembled waiting for the last of the party to join them. Charles, as usual, was late.

'Well, here we are,' Mrs. Kingsley announced, her face a picture of motherly satisfaction. She was desperately anxious to make her important visitors feel at home. 'I'm sure Charles will be here at any moment. He's been so full of enthusiasm to meet you. I can't think what has held him up. Did he say where he was going, Gerald?'

Gerald shrugged his shoulders 'No Mama. He went out on one of his rides after lunch and you know what he's like once he's out in the countryside convening with Nature. Time has no meaning.' Gerald did little to disguise his sarcasm.

The Reverend Kingsley coughed abruptly. 'This convening with Nature is all very well but punctuality is the politeness of kings,' he muttered under his breath. Despite his deep frown and pursed lips, he was trying hard to disguise his annoyance.

The drumming of his fingers on the armchair only served to emphasize his mood. He stood up abruptly and strode over to the window, hands behind his back, waiting for his son's appearance.

Mrs. Kingsley's polite questioning about the ladies new home at Braziers Park, soon relapsed into an awkward silence. Gerald, who was used to male company in his naval career, grew uneasy as he became aware of the four women silently assessing his virtues or lack of them. He had shown little enthusiasm at this invitation to meet the sisters.

The guests began to fidget, especially the youngest, Francis Eliza who found the silence amusing. She was trying hard to keep a composed expression. Her eldest sister, Georgina frowned at her disapprovingly. Henrietta found a stray thread on her elegant taupe dress and was giving it her full attention, whilst Charlotte decided to engage in conversation with the Reverend Kingsley. Much to his delight, she asked him about the paintings on the walls.

'The landscape with the river is beautiful,' she remarked. The Reverend's stern features melted into a proud smile.

'Ah,' he said amused. 'You have good taste. That is one of mine–the first one I have painted since our move here.'

The sisters gave approving nods and murmurs.

'And you, Gerald? Do you have your father's talent for art?' Charlotte enquired hoping he might contribute something to the conversation.

'Being heavily engaged with naval duties at present, I have no time for such pursuits,' he replied. Charlotte decided he had the unfortunate cold countenance of his father.

With an awkward silence settling over the room, Mrs. Kingsley hoped the distraction of a pleasant tea might help lighten the mood. The cook had made her husband's favourite caraway seed cake and shortbread biscuits.

'Well,' she said brightly. 'Let's start without Charles. I'm sure he's been held up for good reason.'

She went over to the marble fireplace and tugged on the bell-pull to summon the maid, all the while chiding herself that her son and husband sadly lacked the art of conversation. If Charles were here, it would be so different.

The maid made a welcome entrance carrying a tea tray followed by a younger maid laden with plates and refreshments. Mrs. Kingsley poured the tea into her Coalport china cups under the fractious gaze of her husband. With tea served, the girls relaxed and listened politely to Mrs. Kingsley's constant chatter. She was interrupted by the sound of horse hooves on the gravel. A horse and rider came abruptly to a stop within yards of the window, scattering gravel as it did so. The ladies were so startled they could not prevent their teacups performing a little jig in their hands.

'Thank goodness.' Mrs. Kingsley gave a huge sigh of relief. 'Here is Charles at last. I was getting quite worried about him.'

There was a heavy thud as the front door closed, a marching of boots echoed across the marble hall floor and the drawing-room door was flung open.

It was as if a whirlwind had entered the room and filled it with a magnetic energy. Before Charles had chance to utter a word, his father demanded to know why he had kept these delightful ladies waiting.

'I-I'm–m-most dr-dreadfully sorry.' Charles was suddenly deflated.

'It's no matter,' his mother said in her calm, reassuring voice. She knew that any reprimand from his father would set off her son's stammer even more.

'Ladies,' Charles announced with a bow and as he did so glanced down at his riding boots that bore a quantity of mud, far too much to be allowed into the drawing room. He blushed and hoped the assembled gathering would not notice.

'Charles, come and meet our new neighbours from Braziers Park,' said his mother casting an eager eye towards the four ladies sitting on the sofas.

But before introductions could be made, Charles, oblivious to his father's angry presence, and grinning from ear to ear, addressed the ladies in a melodic tone that betrayed a slight Devon accent.

'I sincerely apologise, ladies, for my lack of punctuality,' he stammered. 'I was riding by the brook and spotted the-m-most beautiful blue k-kingfisher. I c-c-could not take my eyes off her dazzling blue feathers as she skimmed and darted across the water. I was q-quite taken with the beauty of the afternoon and time slipped by and-' His dark, piercing eyes shone with excitement.

'Come, Charles,' interrupted his mother. 'Let us do the introductions before you treat us to another of your Natural History lessons.' She smiled. Once he started, he would be hard to stop.

Francis Eliza was delighted that this member of the family was so different to his brother and, like a breath of fresh air, had dispelled the stuffy atmosphere. Her face lit up with a smile. Charles caught her eye and returned her warm welcome with an unabashed grin. The other three sisters glared in amazement at this wild-haired man with the muddy boots and stammer. 'Uncouth' was a word that came to the mind of the eldest sister, Georgina.

'This is Georgina,' Mrs. Kingsley announced as the waspish, elder sister stood up and tried her best to hide her disapproval. 'And this is Charlotte'. She gave a welcoming smile and with a slight flutter of the eyelids, offered a slim gloved hand.

'And Henrietta.' As Henrietta stood up, she was so nervous of this tornado of male energy, she withdrew her hand as swiftly as was polite, carefully avoiding his penetrating gaze.

'And this is Frances Eliza.'

'But you can call me Fanny,' interrupted an eager, fresh-faced Fanny who was by far the prettiest of the Grenfell sisters. With a slightly buxom figure, her wide smile and expressive grey eyes, Fanny was unabashed at this man before her and secretly admired his honesty about the reason for his delay.

'How wonderful to spot a kingfisher,' she trilled without thinking. 'I have been there several times and not caught sight of one.'

'Then you must allow me to show you the brook where it nests,' Charles replied, gazing at her with a penetrating stare and showing an indiscreet eagerness to please this vision of beauty.

Before Fanny could say thank you there was a sharp harrumph from the Reverend Kingsley. 'Well, now we all are here shall we resume tea? Mrs. Kingsley can you ring for more hot water?'

Mrs. Kingsley was so relieved at her son's appearance, that she was unaware of any disapproving stares from the rest of the company. Charles was her most cherished son and, in her eyes, could do no wrong.

'As I was saying before you came Charles, you are in your first year at Cambridge,' she said proudly as she stood up to ring for the maid.

'You are enjoying your studies there?' chimed in a smiling Charlotte, not to be outdone by her younger attention-seeking sister.

'Oh, v-very much,' Charles replied, looking for somewhere to sit. His father directed him to a window seat with a stern nod. His muddy boots had not gone unnoticed. 'It's so w-wonderfully stimulating and I h-have made firm friendships there. We hunt, shoot and f-fish in the Fenlands.'

His eyes were fixed on Fanny who was equally intent on returning his gaze. Whilst Charles recounted tales of university life that enthralled her, but not so much her sisters, Mrs. Kingsley noted how his abundance of energy was so different from her other sons who paled in comparison.

Her husband, however, would give him a stern dressing down later.

It was disgracefully impolite to keep these society ladies waiting and all because of a kingfisher! It beggared belief. It was unforgivable and, he commented to his wife later, that all the decadent living at university was having a detrimental effect on the boy.

Georgina, Charlotte and Henrietta had already come to their own conclusions. The Kingsley brothers were not to their liking especially the eldest who, as they later remarked in their carriage on the way home was unkempt and too full of himself. Furthermore, sensing Fanny's enthusiastic reaction to meeting him, they voiced their opinion quite emphatically that no sister of theirs should ever entertain the idea of seeing him again.

Fanny however was thrilled. On their departure, Charles had repeated his invitation to show her the habitat of the blue kingfisher or 'Alcedo atthis'. He had given its Latin name with barely a stammer. And she noted he had squeezed her gloved hand a little longer than was necessary.

Love Blossoms

After a week away in Devon and on the pretext of visiting his parents at Ipsden, Charles called on the Grenfell sisters at nearby Braziers Park. Undeterred by a hard-nosed footman who answered the imposing front door to announce that the ladies were not at home, Charles did not give up. Did he see a curtain twitch in the upstairs window as he glanced over his shoulder as he left? Did he see a head bob out of sight as he glanced round?

Leaving his card with the footman and informing him he would call the next day, he found the sisters were again indisposed. In desperation, Charles wrote a note to Fanny and appealed to her to make contact on his next visit in two days time, before he returned to university. He wanted to keep his promise to show her the kingfisher. On the appointed day, the frosty reception of the footman was echoed by Georgina's who received him in the drawing room.

Fanny could hardly contain her excitement as she bustled in, wearing her best blue mantle and matching bonnet, reticule in hand and beaming from ear to ear like an excited child on her first solo outing. Georgina would reprimand her severely when she returned. This was such indecorous behaviour. It was perfectly obvious that both Fanny and Charles lacked the refinement of their family backgrounds.

With Fanny's younger sister Charlotte, as chaperone, Charles drove them in his father's modest open carriage to the stretch of water where he had seen the kingfisher. Charlotte was nonplussed at this indulgence in ornithology. With heavy clouds hanging over the countryside, they sat down in a grassy hollow and, with Fanny wrapped up in a wool shawl over her mantle, they spent an hour waiting for the kingfisher to appear.

Charles entertained the two ladies with his elaborate descriptions of other birds that lived close by. He pointed out a reedy nest of a moorhen tucked away on the bank and as he did so, at that moment a little family of dainty moorhens swam past. When Charles pointed out the Grey Wagtail, Fanny was excited as he, and both smiled admiringly as they watched the pretty bird fly along the bank, flashing its yellow breast.

Partly hidden amongst the ivy and blackberry bushes, he showed them the neat hole that was the entrance to a wren's nest. Fanny sat riveted, hanging onto Charles' every word, oblivious to the chill wind now sweeping the clouds away to the south. Wrapping her mantle around her, Charlotte yawned at frequent intervals and wished she had brought a book to read.

The cawing of the rooks high above the elms, prompted Charles to explain how intelligent these birds were. Fanny had thought these birds ugly and demon-like but he assured her they were extremely intelligent. She thought Charles' eyes were like a bird's, a very intelligent one, as they darted about looking for other wild life. When the blue and orange kingfisher finally skimmed along the bank, Fanny jumped up so excitedly, she frightened the bird and it disappeared in a flash. Charles laughed at her reaction but pointed out bird watching was a silent and patient game. Fanny promised him that in future she would be far more serious and not cause a disturbance. They shared a look of hope they would have many more happy experiences together.

On the way home, Charles halted the horse, and with Charlotte growing even more bored, he escorted Fanny alone to the edge of a meadow. He had spotted a skylark and wanted Fanny to hear its unique and beautiful call. Flying high above them, its wings fluttering and sounding its alarm call to protect its nest below, it was for Fanny a most unforgettable moment. Briefly, the sun appeared and the meadow was bathed in a golden haze of buttercups and dandelions. Alongside this charismatic man who oozed energy and kindness, Fanny felt alive and blissfully happy.

In the intimacy of their surroundings, and elated he could share all these simple pleasures with her, Charles grasped the opportunity to tell her he found her madly enticing.

Out of earshot of Charlotte he leaned his head towards her. 'Fanny, please excuse me if you think me too forward, but I have to tell you whilst we have this moment alone, I am enchanted by your company. We seem to share the same love of Nature and –'

'Oh Charles,' whispered Fanny, her eyes glistening with delight, 'I feel the same way too. It has been such a wonderful afternoon.'

'May I write to you when I return to Cambridge?'

'I would so love that,' and lifting her head, she gave Charles her most coquettish smile. His dark eyes bore into hers in a way that made him appear so wildly masculine that Fanny's heart skipped a beat. She wished the moment would last forever.

Charles was so aroused in her presence, he was shocked at his own responses. He had this overwhelming desire to take her in his arms and he knew then, without any doubt, he had met the woman he wanted to spend the rest of his life with.

'Then I shall do so the m-moment I return.' he stammered aware his breeches were growing tight. The effect Fanny was having on him was deliciously arousing but totally inappropriate. Now he had to get back into the carriage and hope Charlotte did not notice anything amiss. He heard footsteps behind and saw Charlotte approaching.

'It's time we returned,' she called in a bored voice. 'I'm sure Georgina will be concerned about us.'

She glanced at the pair. It was obvious she had interrupted a private matter between them. Charles was blushing, and Charlotte was assiduously avoiding eye contact. The return journey in the carriage was silent. Fanny and Charles were alone with their thoughts.

Later, Georgina gave Charlotte an interrogation. How did the pair react together? Was Fanny being too forward? Was Charles appearing to show too much interest? Charlotte's uneasy answers led Georgina to conclude the afternoon had been a big mistake on her part. It was now up to her to stop the floodgates from opening any further.

Fanny was taken up with constant daydreaming of Charles since the object of her distraction had returned to Cambridge. On his return to university, Charles threw himself into another term of indulgent living, and having an athleticism that was hard to match, was in demand for the university's sporting pastimes. He found the physical exertion of rowing, shooting and riding across the Fens at full gallop, an easy way to counter his sexual frustrations. Fanny had awakened a desire that was a revelation to him. In the past, his contact with women had been minimal, preferring outdoor activities with his male colleagues. Now he was fully aware of his sexual drive and it was a force to be reckoned with.

He spent time with Mansfield and confided in him the bewitching effect Fanny had made on him. On a fishing trip to the upper reaches of the River Cam they relaxed by the riverbank in the warm sunshine. Their rods had lain undisturbed in the water for an hour or more. Both men had lost interest, and had taken to idle talk. Their empty picnic basket of beer, bread, ham and cheese lay discarded and Mansfield was sprawled out on the grass alongside Charles. He sat up and leaned towards him on his elbow.

'So Kingsley, what's it to be? A banker's job- earning a substantial income to support your future wife? Or perhaps a lawyer? You have a sharp enough mind for both.' Mansfield could not disguise his look of admiration as he poked a dozing Charles.

'Oh, hush man. I'm under enough pressure with the family as it is to come through university with flying colours and take a job of prestige to uphold the Kingsley name.' He emphasized the last words and gave a loud yawn.

'If Fanny Grenfell is to be allowed to marry this wild student friend of mine, then you have to settle down to your studies and prove yourself worthy, old chap.' He was teasing Charles but he knew he had touched on a sensitive point. Charles had already spent many hours turning over the problem in his mind, so much so, his head ached with misery and he no longer found it amusing.

'I think she would have me whatever my station in life,' he reflected half dozing in the sun. 'But her family - they strongly disapprove of me, yet I have no doubt of Fanny's admiration. We write on a daily basis and her letters are full of enquiry and discussion about philosophy and poetry. She has an alert mind I find so attractive.' He sighed and turned over to face Mansfield. 'I can hardly sleep at night without fantasising about her. Is it unwholesome to have such an obsession?'

'Ha!' Mansfield exclaimed. 'You are a normal male who is in love. Lust it may be but I think it is more. And for young men such as ourselves, it is entirely natural. I would advise that if you intend to marry this Fanny Grenfell you do not go to her as a virgin.'

Charles' eyes widened. 'What do you suggest? I could never fall in love with another woman whilst I still have a chance with Fanny.'

'There are other ways – more mechanical, I confess but it would be advantageous to you both.'

Mansfield's advice was abruptly halted as they became aware of a loud splashing and tugging on one of their fishing lines. In a second, the two men were on their feet and reeling in their catch. It was Charles's line that had caught the prize of the day. They cheered, and slipping their arms around each other's shoulders, admired the fat grey chub flapping on the grass beside them.

'You see, Charles. Have a little patience and you will land your catch.'

Charles grinned but he was left with the thought that his sexual longings were growing more urgent. And yet it would appear the woman he wanted most to satisfy these with was way beyond his reach.

TEMPTATION

The following year at Cambridge was one of torment for Charles.

He wrote constantly to Fanny and although he still enjoyed a decadent lifestyle, with it came a closer examination of his beliefs in God and his religion. It was only with the freedom of university life that his enquiring mind considered the old conventional practices of the Church. He wrote to Fanny on the subject that caused him so much turmoil.

'I struggle with my faith despite my strict Christian upbringing. I find more and more, I am repelled by tepid Christianity such as we see amongst the clergy of today. The Church uses its rituals and blind belief as they have done for centuries, so that its followers do not question their principles.

If only more men could have the opportunity, like I have had, to find the true essence of religion and spirituality; to convene with God's perfect creation in nature. Some day I must tell you of the dreamy days of boyhood when I worshipped nothing but the physical and the semi-sensual delights of ear and eye, from sun and stars, from wood and wave....'

He laid bare all his inner beliefs in his letters to Fanny. But there was one confession he did not make. In a moment of recklessness he had indulged in lustful and ungodly behaviour. He had succumbed to Mansfield's advice to satisfy his sexual cravings.

The evening started out innocently enough. Charles had joined Mansfield and his colleagues in a drinking session at one of the local inns in the city. As the night wore on, the others drifted off leaving Mansfield and Charles to make their way back to their lodgings. They staggered home along the deserted streets. What followed was blurred by alcohol. Charles had a faint recollection of bawdy women smiling at him and fondling him in parts he would not have deemed at all respectable.

Devastated, Charles woke up a few hours later with a nagging hangover. Mansfield had deliberately taken a diversion past a brothel popular with the students. The memories floated in and out of Charles' mind, filling him with revulsion - the smell of cheap perfume and stale sweat, of being undressed by a woman with fat red lips and heavily made-up eyes. Using her wiles she had made him hard despite his over indulgence in brandy. He remembered the coming together of warm flesh, her ample breasts pressed against his chest. Even in his drunken state, he would not deny this intimate coupling of male and female was pleasurable in an animal-like, primitive way. Then he had lost control and, spreading her fleshy limbs wide, had thrust deeply until he unleashed a devil that, he later realised, had always lain dormant within him. With a final thrust and jarring of flesh, he had let out a primeval cry as his body released his pent-up frustration.

Even in his exhausted state he had slept little. Tossing restlessly in his bed, he was filled with self-loathing. How could he ever consider marrying the woman he loved after such an indecent act? It went against the code of his strict upbringing and everything he believed in. He spent the last hour before daylight wrestling with his conscience. His only thought was how to atone for his wrongdoing.

The next evening Mansfield called on him unexpectedly. Charles had not attended lectures that day. In the dim light of his lodging room, Mansfield entered and saw Charles hunched over the washbowl, his head resting on his naked chest. He was moaning quietly.

'What is it, Charles? Are you still suffering from a hangover?' Mansfield enquired with a bemused smile.

'Can't you knock before you enter a room?' Charles snapped as he spun round in surprise.

'In the Lord's name what is it? What has happened to you?' Even in the failing light, Mansfield could see Charles' features were rigid, his face deathly pale. As Charles turned away, Mansfield caught sight of his back. Horrified, he drew closer to see blood pouring from deep gashes.

'In the devil's name! What is this about?'

Charles still refused to look at him.

'Your back–it's a bloody mess. You look as if a bear has mauled you. Let me help you.'

Charles hung his head so that his friend could not see his shame or his eyes red with tears. Reaching for the flannel, Mansfield poured cold water from the washstand jug and ordered Charles to sit down. With no energy to resist Charles slumped down on the bed.

'I will get some antiseptic presently but first you must tell me how you came by these injuries.'

Charles flinched as Mansfield dabbed the flannel onto his open wounds. He found the gathering darkness of the room easier to confide in him.

'How can I explain? After the events of last night ....' His voice broke with anguish, 'I awoke filled with regret and mortification. I have let myself down and now I will never be worthy of Fanny. How could she consider me after my base behaviour?'

'Charles, let's be honest with each other. You are a young man of twenty-one and, like most men you have needs. Yes- sexual needs. It's only natural and it's common before they enter into marriage that men lose their virginity- one way or another. If they have any sense that is. Otherwise the marriage could be a complete disaster at the outset.'

Charles could only shake his head.

'So what are all these flesh wounds about?'

Charles winced as Mansfield extracted a thorn from his shoulder.

'It was an act of penance. I left this morning at first light and rode into the Fens. I stripped to the waist and rolled in a bank of brambles until I could bear the pain no longer. There you have it – my confession. You might think it extreme but I could think of no other way of absolving myself of guilt.'

'I'm jolly glad you didn't call me to join you on this little expedition. I can think of other ways of getting over what I thought was a gratifying experience.' Mansfield tried to make light of his friend's dilemma. He would not make things any worse for Charles by mentioning he had arranged for one of the most experienced prostitutes to initiate his friend. And Charles kept it to himself that, despite the excruciating pain, he found his self -inflicted punishment had been a joyous release that until now had been outside his experience.

Despite his mortification of his first sexual encounter, a steady courtship flourished between Charles and Fanny. Now in his final year, Charles adopted a more serious approach to his studies. The roistering, drinking and wild parties stopped as he concentrated on his final exams. He had good reason to moderate his life as he realised his future lay with Fanny and, through her influence, Charles restored his faith in God. After much soul-searching he informed her he had finally chosen to enter the Church. He confessed to her he had found life without Christ was dark, blank and hopeless.

After entering the clergy he vowed he would do all in his power to make a difference to the lassitude that currently existed in the Church and, he determined to make every effort to bring about a change to the poverty and disease that was rife throughout England, no matter how small .

Having earned a first class degree in Classics and a second class in Mathematics, three months of hard study of theology followed and Charles was ordained into the clergy of the Church of England, much to his parent's delight. Fanny couldn't wait to tell her sisters the news.

SEPARATION

At Braziers Park there was growing unease amongst the Grenfell sisters. They were well aware of the continual letter writing between Kingsley and their younger sister. Quite out of character, Fanny was spending long hours hidden away in her bedroom. Georgina was adamant their courtship be halted, and having informed Henrietta and Charlotte of her decision, she summoned Fanny to the drawing room one afternoon.

Fanny had hurriedly written yet another letter to her beloved Charles and handed it to the footman. As she entered the finely furnished drawing room she was aware of a distinctly icy atmosphere. Henrietta and Charlotte sat demurely sipping tea as if it was just another afternoon tea gathering. Georgina was pacing up and down like a restless panther.

'Fanny, we have called you here to discuss your intentions with the Kingsley fellow.' Georgina was in no mood for niceties.

Fanny guessed what was coming and hurriedly sat down. She felt like one accused and looked to her sisters for support. They appeared unusually preoccupied with drinking their tea and pointedly, avoided eye contact.

'You mean Charles,' corrected Fanny, astonished at her sister's aggressive tone. She was not about to impart her good news.

'I have given consideration to his future prospects. If he enters the Church, as you have suggested he might, he will barely earn a hundred pounds year. What sort of lifestyle will he provide for you? It will be a frugal and tedious existence! A poor clergyman's wife is not what our father would have wished for you.' Georgina's voice was growing more insistent as she continued to pace up and down the room.

'You can't even speak his name, Georgina. Do you loathe him so much?' Fanny, retorted in a rare mood of defiance.

'Yes! I cannot think of one redeeming feature. He is uncouth, outspoken...'

'Stop,' Fanny cried on the verge of tears. It was as if Georgina's vitriol was piercing her heart with a knife and she could not bear to think of Charles' character denigrated in such a way.

Charlotte replaced her teacup to its saucer with a loud clatter and saw the distress in Fanny's face. 'Georgina, I think you have said enough,' she interrupted. Her eldest sister was showing not an ounce of sympathy towards Fanny.

Georgina ignored her. 'But do you agree with my sentiments?' She turned to Henrietta sitting demurely on the sofa. Before she could reply Fanny stood up and confronted her sisters.

'Charles *has* passed his exams to become a clergyman and, whilst he may not have a living with a large income, life as a clergyman's wife with him would never be boring.' Fanny regained her composure and hoped to win over her sisters.

'His letters are inspirational.' She raised his long missive that had arrived in the post that day. 'He is so full of enthusiasm about his future and he dreams of doing so much good in the world.'

'We have heard enough, Fanny.' Georgina interrupted. 'As for letter writing this has to stop immediately. His incessant correspondence is ridiculous. The man's mind is clearly disturbed. He has an obsessive character. Further, I have decided, that as head of the family, you are to embark on a long trip abroad and I have arranged a very pleasant companion to accompany you. I think a visit to the Continent might clear your mind and bring things into perspective.

Henrietta and Charlotte are in agreement,' she added forcefully and looked to them for support. On the contrary, their expression was more of sympathy with their younger sister than agreement with the eldest.

'The break will do you good, Fanny' Henrietta volunteered. She was quite jealous of Fanny's intended visit to Europe. 'Just think of the highlights and all the history and culture in Paris and Nice.'

But Fanny could think only of Charles and their enforced time apart. He was like a pulse beating within her and without him she would feel bereft.

'You don't understand. I've been so unhappy since father died. I have been desolate and so full of grief, I feared I would never get over his death. Charles is such a wonderful man with a pure heart. We are in love.' Fanny sat down on the sofa next to her sisters, shocked at her own admission.

Georgina stood up so quickly it was as if a lightening bolt had hit her chair. Her face contorted with anger. How could Fanny let herself be taken in by this man? She clenched her fists. 'That's enough Fanny.'

Charlotte attempted to put her arms around Fanny.

'Don't touch me. You have no idea what Charles means to me.' And sobbing into her handkerchief, she mumbled. 'When do I leave?'

'At the end of this month,' Georgina announced tersely.

Clutching the letter to her breast, Fanny ran out of the room, tears streaming down her face. Later that afternoon she wrote to Charles and poured her heart out to him, giving him the bad news. She was going away for an indefinite time and her sisters were opposed to any further contact with him. Charles wrote back straight away suggesting they meet before her departure. He had come up with an idea.

* * *

With the excuse that Fanny wanted to spend some time with Aunt Agatha in Bloomsbury and that it was imperative she visit her dentist in London before leaving on her European trip, she announced her intention to her sisters one morning at breakfast.

'Oh what a good idea,' Henrietta agreed. 'After such a long winter, life has become so boring here and with spring on the way, our time in London would be far better spent.'

Charlotte also expressed an interest in joining them. Fanny was not pleased. She had wanted to go alone. It would be far easier to slip away and meet Charles without her sisters spying on her. Georgina looked up from her breakfast of smoked haddock.

'But you leave for Europe in two weeks time. Is it wise to go away so soon before your departure? Surely you have things to organise here?'

Fanny forced a demure smile. Her relationship with Georgina was barely on nodding terms since her outburst two weeks ago. 'I was thinking I might make time to choose a new dress for travelling. One can never be certain of the weather in late March.'

Georgina could find no reason to object. A week later, Fanny and her two sisters departed in their barouche for London. Charles had arranged an afternoon visit to his parent's rectory in Chelsea and Fanny had reassured her sisters that an onset of toothache made it necessary to visit her dentist for a second time. Leaving two excited sisters preparing for an eagerly awaited visit to the theatre, Fanny took a carriage to St Luke's Rectory, Chelsea.

As Fanny entered the large airy drawing room, Mrs. Kingsley greeted her warmly. Despite this, Fanny could barely breathe, she was so nervous. She had hardly slept for two nights in anticipation of meeting Charles and during the morning had changed her dress three times, arranged and re-arranged her hair carefully so that it sat neatly curled on her shoulders. Dressed in a taupe silk dress with green ribbons and bonnet to match, she took a seat whilst Mrs. Kingsley called for the footman.

'Please inform Charles that Miss Grenfell is here.'

For two long minutes Fanny fidgeted restlessly. Her eyes darted about the room and she barely heard a word Mrs. Kingsley was saying. Relief flooded over her that the stern Reverend was nowhere to be seen. She heard heavy footsteps across the hall and prayed that it was Charles and not his father. The door opened and her beloved stood in the doorway.

Dressed in a new frock coat with a smart crimson waistcoat and cravat, his hair neatly smoothed down, Fanny thought how boyish he looked. Charles walked over to her and suddenly her concerns vanished. He gazed at her with his dark eyes that shone with adoration.

'Fanny, how lovely you could visit on such a beautiful spring day. You have brought this glorious sunshine with you.' Charles bowed his head then took her gloved hand and kissed it slowly. Their eyes lingered on each other.

Mrs. Kingsley was obliged to clear her throat more than once before the spell was broken. Feeling uncomfortable in the presence of the two lovers so besotted with each other, nonetheless, she rang the bell for tea, hoping to bring the two back to the present moment. An hour passed in a haze for Fanny. She held onto Charles' every word. At every opportunity their eyes devoured each other and Mrs. Kingsley lost count of the number of times Fanny's cheeks flushed with happiness. Much to his mother's relief, Charles suggested that it might be a good time to show Fanny the garden before the sun disappeared and an evening chill set it. Gratefully, Mrs. Kingsley retired to her parlour.

Alone at last, Charles took Fanny by the arm as they ambled down the long path in amongst the beds of daffodils that were effulgent in the late afternoon sun. They found a seat in the arbour, and sitting close to each other for warmth, they discussed their future. Fanny had already broken the news in a letter to Charles that she was going abroad on a long trip. Instead of showing frustration at the plans Georgina had devised for them, he remained calm.

He took her hands in his and gazed at her intently. 'Fanny, I have thought of a way to remedy our situation. It is clear that your family strongly disapproves of me and they wish to end our relationship.'

'Yes, but Charles, I could not bear to lose you.'

'If it ever came to that and we had to separate permanently then I would not hesitate but to join a monastery and become a monk,' Charles declared seriously but his eyes lit up with a smile. Fanny did not share his attempt at humour.

'Please do not jest with me,' Fanny said her eyes welling up with tears.

'I do not jest- I am serious. I would wish for no other person than you, Fanny Grenfell to share my life with. But we have to prove our love so that we can be together.'

'How, Charles?' Fanny said wiping away a stray tear with her glove.

'I know this will be painful for both of us but,' and he hesitated unsure of her reaction, 'I propose we do not communicate with each other for a year. That way your family will know this is no passing dalliance. They will know our intentions are serious.'

Fanny was speechless and her mouth fell open in shock as Charles looked at her intently.

'You cannot mean this?' she whispered at last and turned her head away unable now to stem the flow of tears.

Swiftly, Charles reached for her and took her into his arms. He kissed her passionately, his longing for her finally realized. Regardless of the rules of her strict upbringing and unable to resist him, impulsively, she returned his embrace. It seemed the most natural thing in the world to be kissed by him. Wiping away her tears with his handkerchief, he said solemnly. 'Do not fret, dearest Fanny. I have some good news.'

She met his intense gaze with a questioning stare.

'I have received news that I am to be accepted as Curate of Eversley. It is a parish in Hampshire, a pretty place with three hamlets, a river, and heath land. It has a small church but a wide parish. I have found my calling there. Is that not a reason to be happy?' He gave her a wide satisfied grin.

Fanny nodded but her mind was elsewhere. The thought of Charles busying himself with his new church and its congregation whilst she remained at Braziers Park with no distractions mortified her. She would return from her travels in Europe but after that- what then? But Charles had made plans for her year apart. He leaned forward and stretched his arm around Fanny who was bent over and sniffing into her handkerchief.

'Fanny dearest, this is what I suggest, that you make time for study,' he said passionately. 'Study nature in all its forms so that each day you find some wonder that you can give thanks for, whether it be a storm, the trees, flowers and that you spend time drawing and painting these wonders of Nature. Do not dwell on the misery of us being apart but observe the beauty around you that God has so freely given. There is so much to learn and appreciate in our short time on Earth.... music, art, geology. Through study and intellectual pursuits you will have no time to be miserable.'

Fanny broke into a fresh bout of sobbing. 'How can you be so commonsensical about our separation? How can I study when my mind is desolate and I can find no solace, not even to receive a letter from you? A year apart is an interminable time.'

'Mm, commonsensical, I've never been described as that before.' Charles scratched his whiskers and unseen by Fanny, gave a hint of a smile. 'But I am being practical and yes, logical.' Charles was now desperate to reassure his future wife. 'We cannot let this time apart be wasted by our yearning for each other. If we do, we shall become morose and no good will come of it. Have faith in me, Fanny and have faith that we shall spend the rest of our lives together. A year will soon pass and think on it, when we are finally reunited we will never take each other for granted.'

Fanny leaned back and saw the reassurance in his eyes she so desperately sought. Charles took her in his arms once more and their parting was sealed with a long endearing kiss.

A Curate's Life

The three hamlets of Eversley Street, Eversley Cross and Bramshill were situated in the pretty valley of the River Blackwater and a few miles from the army barracks of Aldershot. With its picturesque village green, bordered by red brick cottages, Eversley was a pleasant country procurement for a young curate. St Mary's Church was nestled in a country lane and had a history dating back to the fourteenth century. Curate Kingsley newly installed in his cottage at Eversley Cross, was eager to see the whereabouts of his appointment.

Charles glimpsed the Church of St Mary's and felt he had come home. Here was the beautiful, small parish church he had dreamt of. Its red brick walls glowed in the midday sun and on first appearance, its battlements and four pinnacles on its squat tower, gave it a slightly grand impression. However, as he drew closer, he noticed tiles were missing from the church roof and the churchyard, to his surprise, was sadly neglected.

The Rector, the Reverend Toovey-Hawley was waiting for him at the entrance gate. A smallish man with a rotund figure giving the impression he indulged a healthy appetite, he was business-like in his greeting. Dressed in his long black cassock with the belt stretched to its full width, he offered a pudgy hand to Charles and reciprocated his new Curate's strong handshake with a limp one.

As they walked up the churchyard path, Charles, in his enthusiasm, bombarded him with questions but soon found his enquiries were not well received. It was apparent the Rector regarded them as quite inconsequential. Charles persevered.

'And how many do you have in regular attendance on a Sunday?' he asked, hiding his disappointment at the headstones overgrown with brambles, yellow ragwort and nettles and wondering how it could have been so overlooked. It was all beyond the help of a lawn mower and would need a scythe and a sturdy arm to bring it back to a tidy condition.

The Rector must have read his mind. 'We could, of course, do with some help with the upkeep here. A local farmer obliges and brings his sheep here to graze. It's by far the easiest option as we have so few volunteers. Regarding the congregation, numbers vary, depending on the amount of sickness in the parish. I confess it's not as many as one would hope.'

The Rector gave his new charge a disparaging look as if to say 'no more questions on the matter.' But by way of an excuse he volunteered, 'You will find most of the villagers frequent the alehouses of a Sunday. A few of the older congregation are loyal but if Evensong is held at Bramshill, many do not wish to exert themselves for the long walk. Is there anything else you wish to know?' he enquired testily, removing his pocket watch from his cassock. 'I have a luncheon appointment and I can be of assistance with any further queries before Morning Service on Sunday. Do feel free to acquaint yourself with the interior of the Church.'

Charles was aware he was being dismissed. The Rector bid him a good day and Charles entered the Church via the gabled brick porch. Hesitantly, he opened the creaking oak door. He found a pew and kneeling on a threadbare hassock, bowed his head and prayed for guidance in his new appointment. He also asked for God's help with his courtship of Fanny and finished his devotion to remember his family. When he lifted his head, he took in his surroundings with a keen but wavering heart. His nostrils were assailed with the cold smell of damp and he saw the crumbling plaster hanging precariously in patches on the walls. Despite the warmth of the July day outside, he shivered in the damp chill.

Three wooden arches painted brown separated the nave from the chancel. Beyond, a faded and frayed cloth covered the altar that was bare of the ornate gold and silverware that embellished his father's churches in Chelsea and Clovelly. The box pews were in a sad state of repair, some with their hinges missing and Charles guessed only a few of these would be occupied on a Sunday. He paused to study the imposing pulpit crowned by a wooden canopy where, at some time in the future, he would deliver his sermons. There were boards on the wall dedicated to past benefactors. Charles read these with interest but as he did so, his mood ebbed.

Not only was he missing Fanny, he envisaged the Rector would not be receptive to any changes he might wish to make. With head bowed and his footsteps echoing on the cracked flagstones of the aisle, he could only hope it would be within his power to bring this house of God back to life. Despondently, he closed the door and went out into the warm July sunshine.

The morning of his first service, Charles dressed carefully in his black cassock and white tie. He knelt at his bedside, as he had done since a child and prayed for God's help on this auspicious day. Downstairs, Mrs. Scrimshaw, his new young housekeeper, had left him a breakfast of fresh baked bread and a small basket of eggs but Charles had no appetite. Instead he waited for the kettle on the range to boil and brewed a pot of tea. This was his first day as Curate. It should have been a day of celebration and joy, yet Charles felt neither. He tried hard to steady his nerves that were fighting doubts. Would the parishioners receive him well? Would he be able to control his stammer when reading the lesson?

With long strides, he walked the one and a half miles from his cottage to the Church, breathing in the fresh morning air and admiring the trees as their leaves shimmered in the morning breeze. A blackbird on a nearby branch burst into full song and Charles took this as a sign of encouragement. With God's help all would be well.

He arrived in plenty of time and was met by a solitary bell-ringer. There was no sign of the Rector or congregation.

'You, the new curate then?' the local asked.

'Good morning to you.' Charles offered his hand but the man barely doffed his cap.

'Tis a shame we 'ave such a poor turn out. You won't see no more than a han'ful 'ere, not till Harvest. Then you might get a few more.' Pushing open the heavy door, he shuffled off to his bell-rope behind the curtained recess at the back of the church.

The Reverend Toovey-Hawley had asked Charles to read the first lesson. As he stood at the lectern he prayed that his stammer would not spoil his delivery.

'The f..f..first lesson is f…from Isaiah 43 verses 1 to…. .'

Charles looked up nervously at his congregation of nine expectant faces. Sitting in the front pew was Sir John Cope, patron of the church and owner of the vast estate of Bramshill Park. Behind him were six regular churchgoers from the rundown cottages in Eversley. Labourers, Charles assumed, judging by the worn dresses of the women and the patched shirts of the men. Next to them sat two children giving the new curate their full attention.

The small group exchanged surprised stares as the Curate faltered with his first sentence. One of the children leaned across to his father and in a loud whisper, loud enough for Charles to hear, said, 'As 'ee got some'at stuck in his throat, Dad?'

The father gave the boy a harsh glare whilst his mother stifled a giggle. She pursed her lips tightly as Charles continued with the reading.

'B-But now, O Jacob, listen to the Lord who created you.'

And when Charles had stammered through the second verse and read-

'When you go through deep waters,
I will be with you,

When you go through rivers of difficulty
You will not drown-'

Charles thought how appropriate the words were to his present situation. He felt as if he were drowning with nervous embarrassment. In spite of this, he held his head up high and continued with a strong voice, sure of his commitment to God's calling.

The musical accompaniment of a trombone player and clarinetist got off to a shaky start with the hymn *'Love divine, All Love's excelling.'* The off-key voices of the congregation joined in. It was during this hymn that Charles noticed a woman sitting at the back in the last pew. Well-dressed and wearing a flouncy bonnet and, Charles noted, a heavy amount of lipstick, she appeared overdressed for the occasion. He also noted the Rector's eyes straying more than once in her direction. The woman kept her head bowed and sang quietly.

The Rector led the rest of the service in a monotone voice, seemingly indifferent to the words he was reading. His boredom was clear for all to see. A few of the adults stifled their yawns. The two children kicked their legs against the backs of the pews, afflicted with the same condition as the Rector. When Sir John Cope stood up to read the second lesson, their attention was swiftly revived. In a clear strong voice he announced it was from Corinthians 13, Verse 2 to 13.

'Love is patient and kind. Love is not jealous or boastful or proud or rude. It does not demand its own way...'

The Rector Toovey–Hawley's eyes wandered towards the back pew and a hint of a smile crossed his lips as he regarded the solitary woman. He felt his arousal as he visualized that in a week's time he would be with her in a hotel in Italy, indulging in all the bodily passions he had been denied since his last visit to a brothel a few months ago. He had met her at a parish meeting when he had made one of his rare appearances. She had shown more than a keen interest in him and much to his surprise, asked if she could attend the Rectory to talk about the recent loss of her husband. It hadn't taken much - two glasses of wine in fact, to seduce her. He had taken her up to his bedroom and had made short work of consummating their relationship.

Now he was taking her away for a few weeks and his mind raced at the thought of her pleasuring him and he, in turn demanding more, whilst listening to her foolish and pious whimpering that he dress in his cassock for these indulgences.

'Love does not demand its own way.' The verse stuck in his head. Little did she know he would demand his own way and more times no doubt than she had envisaged. Naturally, he would take her to see the sights of Rome but not before his lust had run its course.

Forcing himself back to the present, he made a mental note to inform the curate of his impending absence. With a final hymn accompanied by the out-of-tune musicians, the Reverend Toovey-Hawley announced the blessing and the parishioners filed out. Charles was there to meet them at the door, smiling benevolently and shaking each one by the hand. The villagers were impressed that he appeared so eager to please in his appointment.

'Aye,' said one as they filed through the church gate.' Let's 'ope this one lasts.' They all nodded in agreement. The young Charles Kingsley could turn out to be the best curate they had had in a long while.

At the age of twenty-three Charles found himself with an unexpected challenge. He had not visualized a parish so bereft of support from its Rector. Nor had he imagined a congregation of so small a number. There was so much to do. He believed that with time, the village folk would accept him as one of them, and most of all with God's help, he could make their miserable lives better. Now that the Rector had left for a tour of the Continent, and it was reported, with a woman recently widowed, Charles looked forward to making improvements in the parish.

His daily routine was a walk of two miles across the heath land to visit his parishioners in their tumbledown cottages. Charles exuded a friendliness and warmth the Rector had never shown. In fact the Rector had rarely bothered to visit them. He was more concerned with entertaining the patron, Sir John Cope and the local wealthy landowners. The village folk began to look forward to the visits from the new Curate especially now he was administering to them with his well-organized medicine bag. He called on the elderly, the sick and the dying. He made sure they were as comfortable as possible and when death came, as it often did, he read the last rites and arranged a proper burial.

'Curate Kingsley is a good man,' the word went round. He was a very different type to the present incumbent who was so idle the parishioners prayed he had disappeared for good.

'He's even teachin' the little'uns to read and write in his 'ome in the evenin' time.' Word spread so quickly amongst the poor folk that within a week, the boys of the hamlets were forming a queue outside his cottage for evening classes.

'It was a right kindly offer from the good-hearted clergyman and not to be missed,' the parents had pointed out to their children, and with the promise of a bowl of soup and a warm fire to enjoy in the winter evenings, the urchins needed no further encouragement to join Curate Kingsley's home study class.

Slowly, during the Rector's absence, the Church congregation grew in numbers.

'He preaches a fiery sermon,' commented one woman to her husband. 'It would be no bad thing if you gave that alehouse a rest on a Sunday and joined me at Church.' The women folk were determined to change their husbands' Sunday drinking routine. Besides, they argued, attending church was easier on the purse than supping beer.

Reluctantly at first, the men began to join their wives. Sir John Cope was effusive in his praise for Curate Kingsley and complimented him on his fine sermons. He was also relieved for Charles' sake that, once in the pulpit, his stammer left him.

Despite his busy life, Charles was lonely. He could no longer share his news with his beloved Fanny. At night he yearned for her body and to rid himself of these carnal thoughts, he would sleep naked on the bare boards of his bedroom floor. On other occasions he would deal with his frustrated desires by escaping into the woods at night and rolling naked in the brambles until his body bled. Charles revelled both in the pain and the pleasure of his mortification. And, he reminded himself six months had already passed since their separation.

PART TWO

Misery

Wheels thud monotonously across a stone track. They creak with age. Mud splashes onto the rusted rims. Every once in a while the driver, a sad hunched figure, coughs and spits out a heavy gob of sputum with a sharp growl from the back of his throat. Apart from this, all is silent. Trees, skeleton-like with bare branches, form silhouettes against a leaden sky. In the bleak November dawn an early winter's breath hangs above the fields and heath land. The cottages dotted in amongst the trees already have their fires lit and plumes of vapid smoke rise vertically in the still air.

The boy sits on the lowered tailgate of the cart, his legs dangling. He stares at his bare numbed feet, gnarled and calloused like an old man's and chapped with cold. He has seen seven summers yet he has neither friends nor family. Wearily, he listens to the grind of rumbling wheels, the cough of the driver, and an occasional snort of protest from the grey old nag who struggles to negotiate the stony road.

Lacking the energy to raise a whistle and so lift his spirits, the boy sees nothing; neither the forlorn trees nor the cheerless barren fields waterlogged with rain. His mind is consumed with other things- hunger and tiredness and cold. They had left early, too early for his meagre bowl of porridge. The boy's emaciated body protests with hunger. His belly growls with emptiness. He pulls the old worn coat closer to his chest against the morning chill. It is overly large and has seen a life much longer than his. As his master explained, he had found it 'abandoned' in the village, so the boy could not complain.

It was and would be the only present he would receive in his short life.

The rumbling of the cart sends the boy into a fitful doze.

'Almost there,' calls the driver, his voice gravelly from many years of soot finding its insidious path into his lungs. His haggard face is beyond his thirty years. A tattered topcoat and waistcoat splattered with food stains protects him from the chill. His cap is pulled low, hiding the pockmarked face that in his youth had seen many of the inside of a chimney and left his sallow skin ingrained with soot. His boots are worn beyond repair. He pulls out a flask and swigs greedily from it.

The boy jerks awake and turns to see their destination. Having felt the smooth gravel of the drive underfoot, the nag picks up a pace. The entrance is long and lined with stately beech trees, the last of their coppery leaves still clinging to their branches. The house comes into view. It is a grand country house. Portico entrance. Columns flanked by lion's heads on pillars. But the boy notices none of this. He looks skyward towards the roof and counts the chimneys. There are twelve to climb. He feels the fear already - of being trapped -as he once had in one of those dark narrow crevices. In those crevices is the overpowering smell of soot and smut that finds refuge in his lungs, his eyes, his nose, and in the pores of his skin, now permanently blackened. Shinning up into the filthy blackness, his knees and elbows are calloused from constant use. Sometimes the flues are still hot. He has more than enough burn marks to prove it.

His small arms push the spiky brushes way beyond his strength to release the build-up of soot. Despite wearing his cap tightly over his brow, it penetrates his eyes. Higher into the blackness, he spies a glimmer of light as he reaches the top of the stack. The clamber down is just as precarious. Try as he might to remember the direction of the flues, it is easy to get lost in amongst the maze of chimneys and end up trapped or lost. In a grand house like this it could easily happen.

As he struggles to keep a steady hold in his descent, he prays that the avalanche of soot below has not left him trapped. It had happened once. By the time his master had released the bricks of the stack to free him, he was a breath away from death. They had not heard his weak cries of fear and panic for over an hour. He hadn't wanted to die this way. But the boy had a foretaste of what it was like to die of suffocation. He had come too close. It was the stuff of nightmares. His one friend in the world had not been so lucky. He had suffocated before they got him out.

If he is too slow to crawl through the tiny gaps barely the width of his small shoulders, his master lights a torch of dried twigs and thrusts it up the flue. The flames lick his feet and the smoke smarts his eyes forcing him to edge further and further up. He hears the curses of his master as they echo up through the darkness. And all this for just enough scraps of food to keep him alive and a bed at night on the soot bags. Even in sleep he cannot escape the acrid smell of his daily life.

So another day begins..........

His master jumps down from the cart, now parked at the rear of the house by the kitchen. He grins and his blackened teeth and sallow skin reveal a man in sickly health.

'Look lively lad,' he barks at the boy as he throws the bag of brushes onto the gravel. 'There is a tidy sum to be made here t'day.' The boy's face is sullen. 'What y'got a face like thunder for? You not up to it t'day, lad?' Grabbing the boy by his torn shirt, he whispers, 'Git to it, you li'l scrap of nothin', otherwise I swear t' God I'll put a burnin' taper up that chimney. That'll wake you up. You 'ear me? Now put yer cap back on yer head and git on with it.'

The boy says nothing but his eyes speak volumes - of hunger and a weariness of life that has no part in a child's world.

'Well now, you did'na make time for yer porridge before 'e left? Ain't that just the best thing? The skinnier you is, the easier the climb. We don't wan' you gittin' fat and gittin' trapped up there, do we now? It'll make a right ol' mess of the brickwork to git you out.' He lets out a mocking laugh before spitting out a mouthful of yellow sputum.

Having cleaned five of the most convoluted chimneys, the boy descends into the fireplace and sits hunched in the hearth, coughing and wiping his dust-filled eyes, now red and sore. The sweep has disappeared to the cart to load more sacks of soot.

A young maid enters the drawing room and sees the small pitiful figure.

'You look done in, poor li'l mite. Looks like you could do with somethin' t' eat. Follow me at once.'

The boy looks around for his master. He might just escape for a few minutes if he hurries. In the vast kitchen there is a bustle of cooks and maids preparing lunch. A smell of baking fills the air. There are mountainous piles of vegetables- more than on a village market stall. Two industrious kitchen maids are slicing potatoes, leeks and carrots. And the bounty of meat! Skinned rabbits and plucked pheasants are being prepared for the pot and smaller game of partridge and pigeon are ready to be trussed. The boy's eyes pop out like saucers. He has never seen such a display. The maid hands him a glass of milk and a chunk of warm bread.

'Now git that down y' belly before you pass out 'n us.'
The well-rounded head cook glances up from moulding the pastry rim of a pie large enough to feed an army of hungry boys. She is about to chide the maid for bringing filthy vermin into her kitchen. Then a second glance at the skinny mite tells her this is not godly conduct. But the portly head butler thinks otherwise. He looks up from the table that dominates the kitchen. He is on his second pot of tea and is munching on a fat buttered scone still warm from the oven.

'Git 'im outta 'ere this minute,' he bellows, crumbs spewing forth from his mouth.

Without a second warning, the boy scampers towards the kitchen door leaving a trail of sooty footprints. He stuffs the bread into his mouth and gulps down the cup of milk into his famished belly knowing the punishment if his master catches him. Skiving off the job means no supper. He also knows the speed at which he devours the food might well bring its hasty return whilst up the chimney. The boy swipes a grubby hand across his mouth to erase all traces of his unexpected nourishment.

'Boy, where y' gorn?' He hears a rasping, angry shouting from the front hall. The boy trots across the floor, following the path of sheets laid out ready for his next chimney.

'Stir yer stumps.' His master's breath is close and smells of cheap wine as he drags the boy into the library. His patience has run out along with the emptying of his flask. He wants to finish the job before nightfall and the sober grey skies forebode an early twilight.

'Git on with it.' The Sweep has another an attack of coughing just as a footman peers his head round the door. He is dressed in a gold and red uniform complete with a white wig.

'Refreshment will be served at lunchtime *outside* the kitchen. We'll see to it the boy has a glass of milk,' he announces.

The sweep straightens up and, in deference to the immaculately dressed servant, bows in gratitude. 'Thank-ee very much, kind sir,' he replies doffing his hat, any trace of his Hampshire accent lost for the moment. His mood changes instantly. He will have lunch as well as a good day's pay. No need to top up the flask tonight, he thinks. He can go straight to the alehouse and sup on some ale and eat a pie before turning in. He smiles. It's a heartwarming sensation that is alien to him. In his reverie, he misses the streak of white the milk has left around the boy's mouth.

The sky is pitch black and threatening more rain as the heavily laden cart makes its way down the drive. The boy wedges himself between the bulging sacks of soot and in seconds is asleep. Some while later he is woken by the sound of voices. He shivers as he pops his head up into the drizzle.

'Yes, Curate Kingsley, Sir. That's terrible to 'ear. I'll keep a good look out, 'n all, Sir.' The sweep addresses the stranger in his accent used for superiors as his rasping cough returns.

The boy is alerted to the man's name. He has heard of this Mr. Kingsley, the new Curate, a kind man, by all accounts. Climbing up onto the sacks, the boy sees his sharp profile lit only by a large lantern. He observes the strong, tapered chin covered by a pointed beard and the ample sideburns on his cheeks. His eyes are hidden underneath a large brimmed hat but the tall lanky figure has an agreeable voice.

'Good evening, young man,' he says, his eyes alighting on the boy.

Before the boy can respond, the master snaps at the reigns and the pony moves on at a reluctant pace for the final mile home. He is content. It has been a good day's work. Five shillings earned and a handsome tip thrown in for good measure. The staff had been pleased with his tidy workmanship, and the hardworking boy. Mind, the lunch was not up to much – a thick slice of buttered bread and some tea was less than he had expected. However, if they didn't find work tomorrow, it wouldn't matter. The money would keep him going for a week unless he succumbed to the liquor tonight.

The sweep turns to the boy who is undistinguishable in the dark. His face and clothes are as black as the night. Even his eyes are barely visible, so reddened are they by the smut the boy has tried to rub from them.

'That were Curate Kingsley o' the parish', he says, continuing with the one-sided conversation, as always. The boy rarely spoke. At first the sweep wondered if he had been born dumb. But that was none of his concern. The boy didn't need to speak, only climb a chimney. That was all he was fit for.

'He ask me if we'd be seein' any suspicious types on the road. Them sheep rustlers 'ave bin at work agin on Eversley farm. 'Nother ewe taken and 'er lamb gorn. Nothin' changes round these parts. Families 'ave to feed their young 'uns some 'ow. If starvin' don't take us, then the cold will. But 'e 's a good man that Kinglsey fellow. I 'ear he's even teachin' the young 'uns to read! 'Eaven help us all. What good will that do us? Still each to 'is own.'

For the first time that day he sings to himself before another spasm of coughing hits him and he removes more phlegm from his chest. Meeting this 'man of the cloth' has reminded him that perhaps he should attend church again.

The boy also has a plan to seek out this new Curate. Somewhere in his harsh world there has to be a glimmer of light and tonight he feels he may have met the man to help him. As the cart rumbles into the cobbled alley of the sweep's hovel, the two are of a happier frame of mind than when they had left that morning. The sweep is counting his blessings for his profitable day's work. The boy is happy for the chunk of ham pie the kitchen maid had surreptitiously thrust in his hand as he climbed up onto the cart. She had felt sympathy for the boy and he reminded her that she too had a boy of similar age working in a factory in Reading where the conditions were much better than this young boy's livelihood.

The boy dreams of swimming in black murky water. He is drowning in the swirling darkness but as he struggles, accepting death, an angel in white appears before him and, taking him by the hand, pulls him gently to the surface. His nightmares are normally of cramped holes filled with soot and blackness. This one has left him feeling calm and peaceful, an alien emotion in his young life.

* * *

A GLIMMER OF LIGHT

The sweep's boy awoke to find a muted shaft of light falling through a thin strip of window draped in cobwebs. His sleeping area was no more than a shed next to a rank smelling privy. There was one corner where the water didn't seep through the leaky roof and this was where his bed was, on a pile sacks used for carrying soot. The hour was late. He dressed quickly, crossed the small yard and peered into the sparsely furnished room where his master lived. Loud snores emanated from behind a shredded piece of cloth that was once a bed curtain. He guessed his master had spent most of yesterday's hard earned money in the alehouse and would sleep off his hangover for a while longer. The boy had never had a day off work but maybe today....

Running back to his damp rat-infested lair, he hunted under the sacks for his one and only possession–a rusty old tin he had found whilst scavenging in a pile of rubbish. Some day he would find a use for it. He could only imagine the contents it once held, chocolate, toffees or other delicacies beyond his reach. It was there he had stowed his remaining piece of pie, to keep it safe from the rats that co-existed with him in an equal state of malnourishment. He carefully tugged at the lid and paused before taking the last bite of pie. It was heavenly but the one mouthful only made him hungrier.

He returned to check again on his sleeping master and slipped out through the yard ignoring the protests of the old nag in the 'lean to' waiting for his daily ration of hay. Passing along the narrow muddy street and the two small shops of the hardware shop and butcher, he reached an expanse of open common, home to a large family of scrawny chickens scratching at the muddy grass.

Spotting the church tower and its battlements half hidden amongst the trees about a half of a mile away, he broke into a sprint. At the churchyard gate he stopped to catch his breath. He had never been into a churchyard before, let alone a church. This was foreign territory in his young life. And by the time he had walked to the main door, he was trembling like the few remaining leaves caught by the breeze on the oak tree above him.

The door gave a high pitch squeak as he turned the iron handle. The noise terrified him. His presence would be discovered. The unknown sweep's boy, whom nobody saw or knew, was announcing his arrival. He was in half a mind to flee. But the scene in front of him stopped him. He peered into the dim interior and his eyes alighted on the rows of pews and the faded green cloth behind the altar. Religion was for older folks, for those in the community who had Sundays off and for those who had riches. It had never occurred to his innocent mind that, with their hypocritical ways, they attended church to give thanks for all their blessings, whilst remaining deliberately ignorant of how the rest of the locals struggled to keep death from their doors, of their daily struggle against starvation, disease and overwork. Of this they knew nothing nor cared to.

The boy slipped into the aisle. As if by magic, a shaft of sunlight burst through the clear glass of the nave window. A beam of golden light illuminated the dim interior and reflected on the flagstones beneath his feet. Mesmerised, he was unaware of footsteps behind him.

'Can I help you?'

The boy turned and found his path blocked.

'Can I help you, young man?' The boy recognized the friendly voice from the night before. But alone in the church, it frightened him. He was in an alien place, somewhere children shouldn't be. He waited for what had become a daily routine in his life, a sharp cuff around the ears and a stern warning to be gone.

The boy tried to find his voice. He couldn't remember the last time he spoke except to cry out in pain inside the chimney. He was a voiceless being and even if he had uttered a word, no one, least of all his master, would have listened to him.

The Curate was tall in stature. His eyes were kindly but piercing. He wore a furrowed brow and a slim but prominent mouth that broke into a wide smile. His hands, one of which rested on the boy's shoulder were fine, white and delicate. The boy could smell an aroma of pipe tobacco- a familiar smell in his master's room when he could afford to buy the 'baccy'.

Charles surmised the frightened urchin to be about seven years old. He was no different to the many youngsters working in the fields and factories in the district, with his clothes worn and unwashed and his hair, unkempt and matted. But he could tell by the blackness of his malnourished body, his bare arms and legs and shrunken face, he was a sweep's boy. As jobs go, this was one of the worst. The little ones were taken from the workhouse or sold by their parents and rarely survived to adulthood. An early death of lung disease was their common fate.

The boy looked into the eyes of the stranger and his mouth opened but no speech came forth. He darted past him and fled, panic and fear overtaking his best intentions to seek out the clergyman. He ran till his heart pounded, terrified of the consequences if his master found him missing. Arriving back at the familiar mud and rubbish-strewn street, he crept through the door of the one-roomed hovel. Relief flooded over him as he saw the drunken, haggard face of his master still unconscious. He threw an armful of hay to silence the hungry nag and returned to his shed; to the only place he knew as home. There, amongst the grimy sacks and the family of rats, he drifted into sleep, a luxury he rarely encountered after daybreak.

At the end of October and, with the first frosts on their way, Charles prepared for his evening class. In anticipation of hungry mouths to feed, he had made a pan of thick soup of carrots, potatoes, and swede, seasoned with herbs from his garden. He had found a battered blackboard in the Church vestry on which to write the letters of the alphabet and had bought new chalks from a hardware shop in Yateley. But he was daunted by the fact that the numbers arriving were now outgrowing the confined space of his small parlour.

As the clock on the mantelpiece struck four, an hour before the expected rush of eager youngsters, there was a timid knock on the windowpane. Charles turned from his task of adding logs to the fire and looked towards the casement. Framed against the blackness of the night were a pair of terrified, darting eyes and the shadowy pinched face of a child, barely able to see above the sill. Charles remembered the boy from the Church the previous week and hastily jumped up to open the front door. He called to the figure sprinting down the path.

'Don't go. Come inside for a moment.'

The boy turned. He stopped at the garden gate and saw the man standing at the open door. Behind him he could see the glowing halo of a lamplight and logs burning brightly in the fire grate. Charles approached him with an outstretched hand. The boy hesitated.

'Come boy, come and warm yourself.'

Drawn to the inviting scene inside the cottage, the boy made his way hesitantly up the path, his head buried in his chest. As he hovered on the threshold, Charles took in the abject poverty of the child before him; his blackened ragged shirt, his trousers several sizes too small and covered in holes that no mother would consider worth patching. He wore a pair of decrepit, oversized boots and judging by the colour of his skin it had been a while since it had seen soap and water.

The boy stared up at the welcoming face. It reminded him of the wonderful white angel he had seen in his dream. No one smiled at him like that.

'Can't stay, mister,' he muttered, surprised at the sound of his own voice.

'We are having a reading class here tonight. Can you stay for a short while?'

'Me master– 'e thrash me if 'e knows I'm not in me bed.' The boy still avoided the man's gaze.

Then, drawn to the mouthwatering smells coming from the kitchen, he stared through the open door. The saucepan on the range held the most heavenly offering of food and it fuelled his pangs of hunger even more.

'What's your name, boy? I can't call you 'boy' now, can I?'

'Don't 'ave a name, mista.'

'Come inside and we can think of one,' Charles said cheerfully. 'My study group won't be here for another hour.'

As the boy cautiously stepped into the cosy living room, it was as if he had entered another world. Here there was homeliness- a colourful red rug covered the floor, a gleaming brass oil lamp lit up a bureau and a fraying leather chair stood by the hearth. The fire crackled and blazed, its flames licking the newly split logs. Above the mantelshelf, on walls discoloured by years of smoke from the fire, there was a framed picture of Christ- a white angelic figure surrounded by young children at his feet. Below were two photographs in tarnished silver frames, one of an elderly couple in their Sunday best. The stern looking man was dressed in clerical robes. Alongside was a photo of a boy in his late teen years, in a stiff, proud pose holding up a sizeable fish and a rod in his other hand. Between the two pictures was a plain wooden clock, its tick drowned out by the crackle of the fire.

The boy was drawn to its warmth and edged closer towards it, but his eyes turned towards the kitchen with a desperate unspoken request.

'You look as though you could do with some food, young man. Would you like to try my soup?' Charles guessed the rumbling coming from the boy's stomach meant that he hadn't eaten much that day. The boy needed no further encouragement. He was at the kitchen range, standing on tiptoe and peering inside the large pan before Charles could even reach for a bowl from the dresser. Charles served him double helpings and looked on in amazement at the speed at which the boy devoured the food. But he smiled at the change in the boy's face now flooded with relief. There was even a hint of a smile. Of all the children Charles had come into contact with in the parish, this one touched his heart the most. He wondered if he was an orphan, sold by the workhouse to a sweep, or perhaps his parents had sold him. Either way, a sweep's life would be a lonely existence with a harsh taskmaster whose only aim was for the boy to stay as stunted as possible so he could climb the narrow chimneys. The easy method was to starve his charge until he either dropped with exhaustion or illness.

Charles removed the bowl from the boy before he licked it clean for the umpteenth time. They moved to the fire as Charles relaxed in his leather chair and the boy kneeled on the rug. The boy relished the warmth of the wool fabric as he brushed his hands along it. Noticing the ingrained dirt on the boy's little hands, Charles made a mental note that, on the next occasion, he would implement his strict rules of cleanliness and hygiene. 'A clean body must mirror a clean mind' was his adage.

'Now, what shall we call you? You must have a name?' Charles asked, relieved to see the boy relaxing a little.

The boy shrugged in ignorance and lack of interest. What was the point of a name? Who would call him by his name even if he had one? Not his master, although *he* had a name he used on occasions. 'Mr. Clough' was his name. It made him feel important. *'Clough the Sweep- 'Impeccible' service and good clean work'*, was painted in faded lettering on the side of his cart. Clough didn't know what "impeccible" meant but he had heard it used to describe the cobbler's workmanship and knew it must be praise-worthy. On the rare occasion he allowed his charge to speak, the boy had to address him as

'Mr. Clough'. It made him sound proper and showed some respect, or so he reminded the boy. Generally though, he was content not to converse with him at all unless it was to issue an order or reprimand him for not doing as he was told. But as often as not the stick he kept in the cart worked to far better effect.

'Let's keep your name short and simple so when you come to my class you can learn how to write it without difficulty,' Charles said enthusiastically.

The boy fumbled with his hands and avoided the gaze of this good-hearted man. In his young mind he knew the reason why he had come to see him. He would love to learn how to write and read books. With the same determination that steeled his exhausted body to get up and work another burdensome day, he held onto this hope. Hope - that one day his life would change. In brighter moments he thought of earning money by another living.

Taken as an infant with his mother to the local workhouse, he had no recollection of family life. His mother was bereft on learning of her husband's death by drowning, in one of the nearby heath bogs between the hamlets of Eversley Street and Eversley Cross. He had lost his way in a heavy rainstorm as he had taken a short cut back to their woodland cottage. It was rumoured he had been up to no good with the local sheep rustlers. But it mattered little to his wife who was now destitute and unable to provide a home for her son. Within a year she had succumbed to rheumatic fever and the infant was left to the mercy of an austere life in the workhouse.

With no response from the boy, Charles thought for a moment.

'How about *'Tom?'* His eyes lit up at the idea. 'That's a good name. It suits you and besides it would be easy for you to spell.'

The boy gave a cautious nod. He was in awe of this man who wanted to give him a name. If he had ever known a father, this was the man he would have wished for.

'Excellent. Then it's decided. *'Tom'* it shall be from now on. And if you attend my classes on a Tuesday evening you will learn how to write it in no time at all.'

He reached over to his desk and removed one of his pipes lined up in a wooden rack. He took the 'baccy' jar sitting in its rightful place next to the pipe rack and, with obvious relish, he inhaled the strong smell of its contents. Then, taking a small pinch between his thumb and forefinger, he pushed the coarse tobacco into the bowl of the pipe and repeated this several times. The boy had seen his master light his pipe many times but not in the zealous, concentrated way the Curate set about his. His eyes never left him for a moment. Charles bent forward and with a spill lit from the fire he held it above the pipe bowl until the flame caught the tobacco. Charles drew on the pipe and blew out smoke with a satisfied grin.

'There now, life seems infinitely better, wouldn't you agree, Tom?'

Tom gave a timid smile and secretly he agreed. He felt much happier now he had a name. But his escape from everyday life was broken by the urgent sound of knocking on the front door. Charles glanced up at the clock on the mantelpiece as it chimed five high-pitched rings.

'My goodness, is it time for class already?' Charles made a long stride towards the front door and was greeted by a crowd of eager boys of all ages, joshing and pushing forward and beaming in anticipation of their class. They welcomed it as a relief from the dull routine of their lives. Inside the warm cottage there would be laughter, fun and learning and, as a reward, there would be food as well.

'Now, Tom let me introduce you to the class,' Charles said after he had reprimanded the boys for making a disorderly line. But Tom had darted past the waiting group and was away down the path.

Tom repeated his name all the way back across the dark common. He passed the alehouse that was quiet on the weekday night, its candles showing the silhouettes of two figures. One stride was followed by a repeat of his name out loud, so that by the time Tom reached the dimly lit street leading to his hovel, he had said his name a hundred times or more. He was now called '*Tom*' and somehow he would attend Curate Kingsley's class on a Tuesday night. He would become like the other children, not the anonymous, nameless orphan he had been for as long as he could remember.

But as day follows night, Tom's excitement at what lay ahead was about to change. The glimmer of light at the end of his dark wretched tunnel was not to last.

WINTER

A bleak November made way for a bitterly cold December. In the first week the temperatures dropped to below freezing. Small lakes around the heath land froze and were to remain so for a month. Heavy frosts covered the trees that sparkled and glistened in the brief periods of sunshine. The fields were covered in a mantle of white and the countryside looked as typical a Christmas scene as it could be. Chimneys puffed out blue smoke from the cottages huddled together around Eversley Green. Sheep struggled to graze in the frozen fields. Ewes, heavy with unborn lambs, were taken into roughly made shelters and fed hay from the summer harvest.

It was the time of the year when sheep rustlers would be out searching for easy food to put on their Christmas table. The poachers, who braved snaring wild game from the estate of local squire, Sir John Cope, risked imprisonment if caught. A second offence meant seven years deportation. It was not an activity to be taken lightly. Many of the villagers depended on the generosity of their neighbours who possessed wily means to put meat on their plates. The rabbits had all gone to ground and there was nothing to be had in the traps on the heath, save for a few unfortunate game venturing out. Those caught suffered a slow death as they waited for their trappers to finish them off.

There was no let up in the weather. The leaden skies threatened snow. Wood and kindling gathered from the forest floor was piled high outside the doors of the village folk who kept their fires permanently lit. Some of those too idle or too poor to have their chimneys swept suffered unfortunate consequences. A chimney fire made short work of a thatched roof. There had been a disaster in Eversley Street the previous week. A chimney had caught light in a thatched cottage and there was a huge panic. Neighbours, joined by other village folk fought the flames with buckets of water in a brave attempt to stop the fire spreading to the shop of Elliot's and Sons, the butcher's next door.

As the sweep and Tom passed by in the cart the next day they stopped and surveyed the smoking ruins. Clough shook his head.

'If they're too mean to employ me, what d' they expect?' he said with a shrug and a satisfied smirk as he urged his nag forwards.

But it was a salutary lesson for others and "Clough the Sweep's" cart with his "Impeccible' Service" sign could be seen in various locations around the hamlets and the outlying districts. As the cold weather persisted the chimneys were working without respite. His services were in high demand. And so Tom was working harder than ever. The cart left before dawn, and the fires remained unlit the previous night, allowing the chimneys to cool before sending the sweep's boy to do his work.

After the long hours, Clough was drinking more alcohol. The profits of his frugal work were gone at the end of most days. The alehouse keeper welcomed his business as his other customers struggled to put food on the table and, out of necessity, had curtailed their drinking. Their vegetable crops of mangold, swede and turnip not already picked and stored, were well and truly frozen in the ground. Much to the annoyance of the villagers, the baker put up the prices of his bread. He blamed this on the increased price of coal. It was out of necessity, he argued. If he didn't he would be out of business.

Despite his heavy coat and oversized boots, Tom struggled to generate any warmth on his bed of sacks. He would rise in darkness, broken only by the glinting of stars above and the covering of frost on the frozen ground. If Clough had recovered enough from his drinking, he gave Tom the remains of his porridge. Even though he was a harsh employer, it had not escaped his notice that his boy was losing weight and was developing the "sweep's cough" that grew more persistent in the wintry mornings. It was in his own selfish interest to keep the boy alive. If he lost him then he would have to buy another one; not difficult in this cold winter when the workhouse was full to capacity with the homeless. But his boy was proving to be good at his work. He was quick and nimble. A new apprentice might not be so agile.

They had finished a long day's work and travelled as far as Aldershot. Clough had received word that there was so much demand for the one sweep in the area, his customers were looking elsewhere. The trip had paid handsomely. As the old cart rattled its way home over the heath, the lights of the outlying cottages glowed faintly in the murky darkness. A light snow was falling and the flurries, picked up by a sharp wind, tore into Tom's sore lungs. The long hours and the bitter cold were taking their toll. By the time Clough unsaddled the weary nag in the yard and unloaded the empty sacks, Tom had collapsed on the stone slabs of the hovel.

Clough lit the remnants of two candles in the windowsill. The fire grate was empty.

'T'is cold enough to kill an elephant,' he mumbled. He was about to step over the boy then thought the better of it. As a sweep's boy for many a year, he reminded himself that it was about a tough a life as you could get for a child. He had always defended his treatment of the boy saying 'if I got through it so can yoursel'. This time it was different. The boy had never collapsed before. His breathing was laboured and his face had a bluish tinge. 'You must give him a bit o'sympathy,' he said as he reached for a bottle of cheap whiskey.

He picked up the boy and laid him on the stinking blankets of his own bed. The boy curled himself in a ball and winced in pain as the spasm of coughing took hold and exhausted his weak lungs.

Clough lit the stove in the corner of the bare room that smelt pungently of coal dust, unwashed bed linen and a full bedpan. He warmed some of his own cough medicine, a brew of thyme leaves and onion juice. His precious laudanum he kept for emergencies could wait for another day. He took a swig of whiskey and as a further gesture of generosity added a drop to the boy's beverage.

Tom gripped the chipped mug with both hands as he tried to control his shivering and drank the warming liquid, soothing his parched throat. Meanwhile Clough produced a pan of left-over mutton and potato he had covered securely from the rats. He removed the lid and sniffed it. Between them they shared the frugal supper and Tom quickly fell asleep with the sweep snoring beside him. Outside the wind howled and made its way under the battered door. For the first time both man and boy appreciated each other's company and the warmth they shared.

* * *

December was a month that kept the Curate of St Mary's Church busy. There was the Parish Council meeting to attend, an audience with Sir John Cope in a bid to obtain more money for the poor folk, confirmation classes to arrange and all this before Christmas. There were more hungry mouths to feed, homes to visit and the sick and elderly to attend to, and now that the children weren't employed in the fields, the village schoolroom was his responsibility. A small low-ceilinged room crammed with boisterous children was not how Charles imagined a suitable environment for education.

But his 'hands on' approach with his parishioners made him popular. As a lover of the outdoor life, Charles thought nothing of striding out in the early morning across the fields to visit his parishioners. So taken up was he with his duties, it was only after a week he noticed Tom had not made an appearance at his weekly class. He had given him his promise he would attend. Charles decided to go and to find him. Striding across the common he stopped an elderly woman to ask directions to the sweep's cottage. His question was met with a surly reply.

'What you be doin' with that good for nothin', Sir? 'E got no friends, no family. He's more as like to be found in the alehouse as in his own filthy hovel. And as for that poor little'un that's near to death - he should be ashamed. You'll find the beggar livin' down past the ale 'ouse 'bout quarte' mile,' she added before starting on her way again muttering under her breath.

As Charles walked towards Eversley Street, his boots covered in thick mud from the sleet that had turned to slush, he barely noticed the stiffened, forlorn carcasses of rabbits and pheasants that hung in the window of Elliot's and Sons, the butcher's. Next door all that remained of the burnt out cottage were the charred remains of roof beams standing stark and desolate against the night sky. Further on, Taylor's Hardware shop showed the dim light inside of a single oil lamp. Shopkeeper, Herbert Taylor had to keep a sharp eye out for light fingers that chanced their luck when the twilight came. It was easy for those with no money in their pockets to come in and try their luck at stealing something off the counter. Even a box of candles was worth the risk of being caught.

A woman passed by Charles, her bonnet pulled down low, her worn dress and cloak covered in mud several inches above the hem. So preoccupied was she with coughing, she didn't see him and almost collided with him. The village had gone down with a bout of coughing and consumption that in the current weather worsened to pneumonia amongst the young and old. Charles was concerned at how it was spreading so quickly. His time was in demand more than ever.

At first he walked past the wood shack, dismissing it as uninhabitable. It was no more than a tumbledown shed. Then he saw the horse, head down and tied to a post in the yard.

In the corner stood the cart with its signage. Fearing this was where the sweep and Tom lived he called out to them. He walked towards the door hanging precariously on its rusty hinges, and pushed it open. Charles blinked to adjust his eyes to the darkness. The room stank of urine and filth. Withdrawing a handkerchief from the top pocket of his coat, he hurriedly covered his nose. A small grate in the corner of the room glowed with a few embers providing the only light and heat in the dismal surroundings. He saw a torn curtain torn hanging in shreds.

Instinctively Charles pulled it aside. His body stiffened with shock. Curled up in a ball was a child. Was this Tom? He bent over and seeing the bony arm protruding from a blanket he whispered his name. The arm stirred and a grimy little hand moved a finger. A weak sound emanated from the heap of rags, a rasp of a cough Charles deemed would be his last. He uncovered the boy.

'Tom,' he whispered again. But Tom gave no sign of recognition. Charles gently pulled away the blankets and even in the semi-darkness he knew that this emaciated body ravaged by illness and starvation was close to death. Charles had seen it many times before. The smell of death was in his nostrils now. Charles held his hand and felt his cold arm. It was as light as a twig. There was no strength left.

He made a quick decision. Either the boy died where he was, in filth and alone, or Charles carried him back to the comfort of his cottage. He pulled off his topcoat and lifting the boy, wrapped it around him. As he did so, he almost knocked over a cup of water that had been left beside the bed. Next to it was a bottle of laudanum. So the sweep had shown some kindness and given him a dose of the drug to lessen the boy's pain.

Tom was so light it was an easy task to carry him back up the street and across the common to his cottage. The only sound Tom uttered was a small moan as his head lolled from one side to the other, like a rag doll. Charles pushed open the front door with his foot and was relieved to see that Mrs.

Scrimshaw, his housekeeper was there. She was stoking up the fire. Her hand went to her mouth as she saw the bundle of rags in Charles' arms.

'The Lord have Mercy upon us,' she uttered and crossed herself as Charles lowered the lifeless body into the chair by the fire.

'Fetch a blanket, Mrs. Scrimshaw,' he ordered, breaking her out of her trance.

She scuttled off up the stairs as Charles carefully removed his coat from the boy. Tom flopped into his curled position. Charles could see by his dry parched lips he was in need of some liquid.

'Heat up the broth as quickly as you can, Mrs Scrimshaw. He needs some warmth inside him,' Charles called. In the glow of the lamplight, Charles saw Tom's legs were covered in scabs and sores, his knees chaffed and bloodied and his feet blacker than the crows in the churchyard. He wondered how close he was to dying. As the glow of a roaring fire and the soft blanket Mrs. Scrimshaw had wrapped tenderly around him warmed his body, Tom showed a glimmer of life. His eyes opened briefly as Charles put some water to his lips. In the hollowness of his eyes, Charles saw fear and despair.

'Come Tom, you are safe now. I will look after you.'

Tom couldn't swallow the water. It dribbled from his lips onto the side of his soot-stained face that had seen the inside of too many chimneys. He made a small choking sound. It was shallow and one Charles was familiar with. In laymen's terms they called it the 'death rattle' in the moments before death when the lungs struggle in their weak state to breathe their last.

Charles fought back his tears, staying by Tom's side for the rest of the night, determined that this unloved sweep's boy would not die alone. He cleaned his forehead with a flannel and soothed his lips with water. He was past drinking the broth Mrs. Scrimshaw had prepared. Kneeling beside him, Charles prayed. He prayed like he had never prayed before.

He promised God if he spared this young person's life he would do more than ever with his life to repay this one request.

In the hours before dawn Tom stirred and Charles, who had fallen asleep in his leather chair, was at his side.

'Water,' mumbled the small voice.

Holding his head, Charles put the cup to the boy's lips and Tom slowly opened his eyes. A suggestion of a smile passed his lips.

'Thankee....' came the smallest of whispers.

Taking this as a positive sign, and eager to put some sustenance into him, Charles darted into the kitchen where the soup pan was still warm. He returned to the living room with a cupful of broth. Tom was unconscious, his eyes closed and his head crooked in an odd way to one side. Charles knew then the Lord had spared his pain and taken him.

Charles closed his eyes and the tears welled up. He sobbed from his very inner being. He had implored his Maker to spare Tom's life. His prayers had gone unanswered. How could fate be so cruel to this little soul who known nothing of kindness or love in his short life and whose life had ended so pitifully? His faith in God was severely tested that night. He held the boy to his chest and prayed for his soul as his tears flowed onto his limp body.

A Dark Time

The Reverend Toovey-Hawley had returned to the parish after an overdue absence in Europe. Charles was summoned to see him and received into the warm parlour of the Rectory. He envied the Rector ensconced in his extravagantly furnished home. The house had a character about it that was warm and friendly. Charles brought himself up sharply as he was reminded of the tenth commandment. '*Thou shalt not covet*'. But then an idea crept into his mind that perhaps one day, with promotion, it would be his home.

The Rector addressed him brusquely, staring at him somewhat disdainfully, Charles thought. He was anxious to have an update on the Church's business, in particular the amount of money taken by the Sunday alms.

The look of disdain faded. Pleasantly surprised his curate had doubled the monies, he congratulated him with a punctilious smile that made his jowly face even more bloated. His interlude away with his new woman whose sexual appetite had matched his own had left him an even more debauched appearance.

Charles methodically went through the names of the parishioners who had succumbed to illness and died in the harsh weather and those still suffering from consumption. The rector waved a hand in dismissal.

'That's usual at this time of year,' he responded dryly. 'And how many are there for the pauper's graves and how many for burial within the Church?'

It only mattered to him in so much as those who had sufficient money for a churchyard burial would add to the income of Church funds. And with Christmas only a short time away, he needed money, and lots of it, for the lavish entertaining of Sir John Cope, who, as the Church's patron rightfully expected it. The Reverend's empty wine cellar also needed replenishing.

'You appear to be upset Curate Kingsley? You are troubled by something?' he asked and for the first time took a closer glance at Charles and saw his eyes shadowed with dark circles and the whites stained red.

'It is of no consequence to you, Sir, but a young sweep by the name of Tom died last night. '

'Nothing infectious, I hope?' came the indifferent reply.

'No Reverend, but he is laid out in my housekeeper's cottage and will have to be buried shortly.'

'With the paupers naturally.' The rector's attention was now distracted to a pile of post sat by his chair. He reached over and opened the first envelope and threw down the bill demanding eight pounds for a new frock coat.

'Absolute robbery,' he muttered.

'No, I beg to disagree,' Charles said ignoring the Rector's last comment. 'He will have a proper burial in the churchyard. On that I insist.'

The Rector's eyebrows shot up at this seeming insolence. 'Come now, man. Don't let's dwell on the death of one child, an orphan, no doubt from the workhouse.'

Then he saw the anger mounting in Charles' face. His mouth hardened and his jaw line grew taut.

'Does this boy mean anything to you?' the Rector asked somewhat surprised.

'As a man of the Church committed to God's work, every child, whatever their birthright matters to me.' Charles could barely disguise his disgust at his callous manner. Isolated from his sick parishioners, his superior knew little about their everyday lives. He was the perfect example of the 'tepid Christianity' Charles had rebelled against at university. Now he had become party to it.

'I assume the monies for this burial will naturally be met by you.' The Rector stretched out his legs before the fire and picked up another envelope with a flip of the hand. 'And as this is highly irregular, it may be necessary to go to the Bishop of Reading to seek his approval.'

He peered over his glasses to the tall figure seated before him whose suit appeared overly large on his gaunt frame. He was a dogged and determined young man, new to his profession and possessed all the vim and vigour the new recruits had in their first year. Of that the Rector was in no doubt. But this new curate had proved his worth. He would not upset him unnecessarily. As long as the Church alms were paying for his extravagances there was no further need to cause the young curate displeasure. Besides, he had already planned another holiday in the New Year that would take him away for a month. If he could persuade Sir John Cope this Curate was worthy of the job, then another leave of absence would cause no further inconvenience to the parish or its patron.

On the day of Tom's funeral, Charles accompanied by his housekeeper, Mrs. Scrimshaw, escorted the roughly made coffin through the churchyard. The young carpenter apprentice shouldered the lightweight box by himself to the hastily dug grave. A blustery wind brought ominous rain clouds. The bare trees bordering the churchyard swayed rhythmically against a gun metal sky. At the entrance, two of Charles' pupils who had come out of curiosity, peered through the wooden bars of the gate to watch the young boy's burial. It was reported that the Curate was deeply upset at the death of this orphan and, as a man with a big heart, had seen to it that he had a proper burial.

Charles' black cassock whipped against his legs as he read from his prayer book, the pages twirling as a gust blew across the churchyard. Charles made the sign of the cross as he finished the short service. His attention was drawn to a cart in the lane outside the entrance gate. A lone figure of a man sat hunched against the wind as 'Clough the Sweep's' cart moved slowly off.

That night Charles had a vivid dream he was fishing by a river. A young boy was flailing in the swift flowing stream. He caught sight of the anguished face crying out to him and knew instantly it was Tom. Charles waded urgently into the river to rescue him. But the boy's cries for help were lost as the current swept him past and he disappeared beneath the surface. Charles woke up abruptly. His feelings of guilt and angst lay across his chest like a stone block. He struggled to breathe. It had been in his power to save Tom's life and he had failed.

In his darkest moments, his only consolation was the memory of the wonderful woman he had lost his heart to. Fanny Grenfell's smile was never far from his mind.

Good News

The following year, a bitterly cold January gave way to a mild February. Charles immersed himself in work for the parish and reading volumes of political and theological works. Spring blossomed early and was a busy time for the village folk. The annual sowing of crops had begun. The children were sent to work in the fields, the youngest assigned to act as scarecrows.

After a winter of smoky fires and stifling stale air, the cottages had their windows thrown open. Bedding was draped over the casements, and billowed in the fresh breeze. Doors were left ajar to let in the warm sunshine. Easter arrived and was a time to rejoice in new beginnings. Those who had survived the winter illnesses looked ahead to a more prosperous time when, after the seed sowing, the crops would produce good returns.

Fanny, however, was not faring so well. After her return from abroad, she was living in her aunt's house in London and was spending more and more time in bed complaining of agonizing pains in her chest. Her sisters, growing concerned for her wellbeing, increased her dose of opiates.

'I think we should summon a doctor,' Charlotte implored over breakfast one morning. 'Fanny has not moved from the bedroom for two weeks and this is the fourth day she has refused to eat. She is getting weaker by the hour.'

Even Georgina, who was nibbling at her aunt's lavish breakfast of coddled eggs and kidneys in the ornate dining room, could not deny that Fanny's health was deteriorating.

'It is a worry. I was hoping by now she would be over that Kingsley character and started a new chapter in her life. Her time away seems to have done her no good at all.' Thinking ahead to the evening concert at the Chesterton's grand house near Regent's Park, she reflected, 'And she certainly won't be able to return to the London social circuit looking like a half-starved sparrow. The younger Chesterton, George, is keen to meet her and has been more than patient. He will lose interest if she doesn't appear at one of their gatherings soon.'

'I'm sure she has no intention of doing that.' Charlotte remarked, her eyebrows arched in surprise at her sister's flippant remark. Not only had Fanny returned from Europe looking frail, she had become withdrawn.

'She has hardly uttered more than a few words since her return. She couldn't possibly be expected to go back to her old way of life as she is now,' continued Charlotte who had returned from Fanny's bedroom with her breakfast tray untouched.

'What are we going to say to the Chesterton's tonight? It's becoming quite an embarrassment,' Henrietta wined as she helped herself to another cup of Indian tea. 'They are so looking forward to seeing her.'

Charlotte put down her knife and fork and, thrusting her serviette to one side, stood up hastily. She smoothed her skirts and glared at Henrietta.

'It's not a question of whether she's well enough to attend parties. It's about how much longer we are going to just sit and watch our youngest sister grow more malnourished by the day. Georgina, I think we have no choice but to call the doctor straight away,'.

Both sisters stared in amazement at their usually calm sibling appearing to berate them.

Dr Cracknell arrived promptly just before two in the afternoon. Charlotte waited impatiently in the front parlour for the arrival of his hackney cab. Alerting her sisters to the knock on the front door, she dismissed the maid and showed him in. The doctor removed his hat onto the hall table. Georgina, dressed severely in black, affected her most serious voice, informing him of Fanny's symptoms. Leading the way through the hall, and now joined by her two sisters, she escorted the doctor up the stairs and into Fanny's darkened bedroom.

Fanny was dozing but was aware of the company standing before her. The doctor leant over her and his cold hand reached for her pulse. He placed a stethoscope on to her chest. The doctor removed it after a minute and solemnly shook his the head.

'Miss Grenfell, can you hear me?' he asked.

Fanny opened her eyes that were now shrunk into her sockets and ringed with shadows the colour of dark plums. She nodded.

'I really think you must force yourself to eat some soup, my dear. You are not in a strong condition.' He turned to Georgina. 'I will prescribe a tonic for her.'

Downstairs in the front parlour, the sisters were most anxious to hear the doctor's assessment of Fanny. But it was he who asked the questions.

'How long has she been like this?' he enquired taking a seat by a large Maidenhair fern sitting on a mahogany desk.

'It's been two weeks since she returned from France. You don't think she has picked up an illness do you? She's so terribly weak,' Georgina asked.

'She has no obvious sign of illness. Her temperature is normal but she has a very weak pulse. I've seen this condition before. It's typical of a woman who…' he hesitated 'has been spurned in love. Would this be the case?'

'Err not exactly,' Georgina began. She was suddenly lost for words.

'There was a gentleman friend,' chipped in Charlotte. 'She was very sweet on him before she went away. And yes, Fanny has taken it very hard that they are apart.' Charlotte was looking daggers at Georgina.

'Well, whoever the scoundrel is, he deserves to be brought to task. Her body is shutting down and if she continues to deteriorate like this she will waste away.'

Georgina's normally pale complexion turned a deep shade of puce as she felt the eyes of her two sisters boring into her.

'Doctor Cracknell,' Charlotte said, now taking the lead. 'If I may inform you of the circumstances.'

'What my sister is trying to say,' interrupted Georgina, having found her voice again, 'is that she has *not* been spurned in love, but with her interests at heart, we have prevented her from seeing a wild young curate whom she foolishly grew fond of.'

'He's been banished.' It was Henrietta's turn now to give her version of events. 'And Fanny obviously cannot live without him.' Her words were delivered emphatically, her eyes never leaving her older sister's.

'That is enough, Henrietta. She will recover in time,' Georgina snapped.

'Listen to the doctor,' Henrietta pleaded.

With a shake of his head at the wrangling between the women, the doctor wrote out his bill, removed a small brown bottle from his bag and stood up. 'I suggest you do not leave the situation as it is for much longer. Otherwise, if I may put it bluntly, you will have a corpse on your hands.'

The three girls gasped in unison.

'I'm sorry to speak so plainly but what is so terribly wrong with this young man that they have been forbidden to see each other?'

'Nothing I can think of,' Henrietta said spitefully. She was in no doubt that Georgina was to blame for her younger sister's condition.

'Well ladies, I suggest most adamantly you let the courtship resume and I guarantee you will see a marked improvement. And please make sure she has three drops of this in water – three times a day,' he said, handing the bottle to Georgina.

'Thank you Doctor.'

"This wild young curate', as you describe him, must be a decent chap. I'm sure your sister has discerning taste. I wish her well,' he remarked to Georgina as she followed him into the hall. The doctor took his hat from the maid and bid Georgina farewell.

Charlotte and Henrietta remained in the front parlour. They heard the bustle of Georgina's dress and urgent steps ascending the stairs followed by a slam of a door. Georgina had retired to her bedroom.

'We have no choice then. Mr. Kingsley and Fanny must be reunited,' Charlotte said with a bemused smile.

It was Henrietta who broke the news to Fanny.

'Please, please take some sips of soup, Fanny,' she pleaded as she lifted a spoon to her lips.

Fanny looked blankly at Henrietta. 'I'm tired, please leave me alone.'

'Ah, but I have good news from the doctor. He insists that you resume correspondence with Mr. Kingsley straightaway and that the said gentleman pays you a visit. That is his recommendation and we are all in agreement,' she lied.

Fanny opened her eyes wide as if for the first time she was fully conscious.

'I can write to Charles?' she asked unable to believe the words.

'Absolutely, my dear. Now this soup is growing colder by the second. Dear sister, you must regain your strength if you are to meet with him again.'

REUNION

But it was several weeks before Fanny was strong enough to resume a normal life. When she was able to get out of bed and dress, her sisters decided she should return to Braziers Park, away from the stench of London and all its airborne illnesses. In the meantime, she had dictated a letter to Charles informing him of the new developments. She received a reply posthaste. Three letters in one day were delivered to Fanny's bedroom. The curtains were thrown open and for the first time in weeks, sunshine flooded into the cheerless room. Within minutes, Fanny was smiling as she read Charles' eight-page suggesting that as soon as she was well enough to meet, they become engaged.

Their reunion was held in a country house on the Dorset Downs. A friend of the family had invited Fanny to stay there with her sisters. On the day of their meeting, Fanny could hardly draw breath as she dressed in her bedroom

Charlotte came running up the stairs. 'Mr. Kingsley has arrived, half an hour early, would you believe? Are you ready Fanny?' she asked breathlessly.

Fanny was seated on a stool by her dressing table. She had chosen to wear a dress of pale blue silk, one of her best, and her hair was arranged in fashionable ringlets and tied with blue ribbons. Despite her cheeks having filled out again, she thought she still had the appearance of an emaciated sparrow. The paleness of her dress seemed to drain the colour from her face even further. But there was no time to change. In an effort to disguise her pallor, she pinched her cheeks so hard she flinched.

She smiled at Charlotte. 'I've waited so long for this moment. This year of separation from Charles has been the longest of my life. And now I am so nervous.'

'Come, and take care as you descend the stairs.' Charlotte offered her arm to Fanny.

'I can manage. I don't want Charles to see me as an invalid,' Fanny replied as she took a final look in the mirror.

She paused at the top of the stairs. Charles stood at the bottom clutching a bouquet of wild flowers. They beamed at each other. Fanny wanted to fly into his arms, so eager was she to be with him. However, it was a slow descent and just before reaching the last few steps, she stumbled. Dropping the flowers, Charles bounded up to meet her and caught her in his arms.

'My darling Fanny,' he whispered and kissed her gently on her cheek.

Carrying her into the drawing room, he laid her on a chaise longue, his gaze never leaving hers for a second. Georgina and Charlotte followed. Henrietta was in the kitchen organising coffee and nettle tea for Fanny.

Charles was shocked at Fanny's decline. He stroked her limp hand as he gave her the flowers. In her eyes he saw the suffering she had shared with him. Their separation had been an ordeal he would not have wished on any other couple in love.

'Forget-me-nots, primroses and cowslips.' Fanny said, smelling the flowers in delight. 'How beautiful. Thank you Charles. When I was taken poorly in London, I thought I would never see a wild flower again.'

Forget-me-nots for affection and love that never dies, how wonderful he choose those, she pondered affectionately. Georgina was unimpressed at the inconsequential bunch of flowers as she left for the kitchen to put them into a vase.

'Will you be well enough to take a walk shortly? I have so much to tell you. I need to be alone with you,' Charles whispered urgently.

Fanny could feel his hot breath on her ear. His hands eagerly sought hers. It was as if he were connecting his life force directly into her. His lingering gaze was full of desire or, as the sisters later commented, 'indecorous lust'. He desperately wanted to express his declaration of love to Fanny but for now he could only show it through his eyes.

When Georgina returned to the drawing room, Fanny was a changed woman. She was smiling from ear to ear, her cheeks rosy and her ringlets shook as Charles recounted a joke about how he had cooked a pheasant for a friend and it had come out of the oven as charcoal. Even she had to admit, it was a pleasant change from the sad, wan sister they had grown used to. Fanny appeared to be her old self again.

With Charlotte as chaperone, it was decided Fanny was well enough to take a walk with Charles in the gardens. Wrapped up in a thick wool shawl over her mantle in the mild April weather, she strolled along an avenue of yew trees with the man of her dreams. Despite the overcast day, they had eyes only for each other. Charlotte, tailing behind could only listen to their laughter and sheer joy at their reunion. She hoped one day it would be the same for her.

The following day, Charles and Fanny ventured up the gentle slope of Cranbourne Chase. When she grew tired, Charles carried her until she was strong enough to continue and, as the weather had turned even warmer and the sun shone in a heavenly blue sky, they lay on the grass and planned their future together.

Charlotte, bored by her constant chaperoning, had brought a book with her and was sitting on a seat under a cedar tree some distance away, heavily engrossed in the novel 'Sense and Sensibility' by Jane Austen. She did not observe Charles and Fanny's blissful embrace. Charles took the opportunity to kiss his loved one so passionately that she had to sit up to take a breath. Their thoughts returned to their time of separation.

'Darling Fanny, I will tell you every day for the rest of our lives, how much I love you. Your sisters may have thought they were acting in your best interests. But....'

'I realize that now. And I told them I could only marry a man who made my heart stop every time I looked at him. In truth, I think they are quite jealous of our deep love for each other.' Fanny stroked his lips with a gloved finger.

They were so relaxed together she felt she could tell him anything. 'Isn't it strange that when love is denied, the heart suffers so? I felt I was dying. I had no reason to live. I was dying of a broken heart. It was punishment enough. But now.....'

'Now I have a pleasant livelihood in the Church at Eversley, surely they cannot object to me?' Charles reasoned.

Fanny saw the seriousness in his dark eyes and the deep furrow on his brow and laughed. 'Oh but they do!' she teased. 'They object to your hair.'

'And what is wrong with my hair?'

Fanny stroked his curly locks that straddled his collar. 'They think it's indecently too long.'

'Fanny, I will have it all cut off tomorrow if it means...'

'Yes?'

'If it means we can be married.'

'Oh my darling Charles, I can think of nothing better in the whole world.'

He kissed her more slowly this time. 'Nothing and no one will ever, ever separate us again,' he whispered.

He stroked the line of her breasts beneath her shawl and felt their firmness. His hand travelled down to her waist, to her thighs and reached under her skirts. All the while Fanny held onto his strong body as he lay on top of he. He found her stocking tops and stroked the soft limbs underneath that he had dreamt of a hundred times before.

'Oh heaven! Dear Fanny, I have just reached the gates of heaven. I love you so utterly, so completely.'

Fanny gave a heartfelt sigh as she stroked his hair. 'This is our new beginning. We both have suffered enough, my dearest. Our time apart has proved beyond doubt we are meant to be together.'

'And we will have a lifetime together. Every night as we lie in bed and entwine our limbs we will share such passion.'

'I hope I have the strength and fortitude to satisfy you.' Fanny looked up at him with her wide flirtatious eyes that promised so much. 'You may well make an old woman of me prematurely.' She laughed.

'I will always take care of you and you will bear my children but only if you are strong enough. If they are as beautiful as you, the Kingsley name will start a generation of angels.'

From a distance Charlotte could see the couple entwined and dared not risk the wrath of her sisters if they found out. She stood up and coughed loudly. The happy couple quickly rearranged their clothes and Charles helped Fanny up.

'After all we've been through, I know I can wait for you, my darling,' he said to her.

'And I, Charles, have waited long enough. We will set the date of our betrothal as soon as it is decent –despite any objection from my family.'

As Fanny kissed him touchingly on the cheek, she realised she could never have imagined such happiness that pulsated through her at that moment.

Her reunion with Charles brought a sudden change in her energy, especially when they announced their engagement. Charles wrote a letter to his future bride marked not only with passion and delirious joy but also a suggestion of abstinence. He suggested that once married she remain a virgin bride for a month 'to show I have gained purity and self control' and after they would consummate their love. So in tune was Fanny with his views on marriage, she agreed to go along with his wishes. Their wedding date was set for January.

* * *

Bath, Somerset. January 10th 1844. The wedding ceremony between Fanny and Charles took place in Trinity Church followed by a wedding breakfast at the imposing eighteenth-century house in Queen Square where Fanny's sisters now lived. Much to the chagrin of Charles, it was a subdued affair, devoid of any sense of jollity of the occasion. Fanny's sisters had witnessed the marriage with strong misgivings, and Georgina was forced to accept that her plan for ending the relationship had failed spectacularly.

The ten guests stood on the front steps to wave farewell to the bride and groom. Charles' parents beamed happily as they showered the couple with rice and flower petals. As the brightly polished barouche pulled up outside the house, Charles was impatient to be away before dusk fell and the threat of snow worsened. Kisses were exchanged and jokes shared about Fanny now being 'Mrs. Kingsley'. Charles' sister, Charlotte, a pretty sixteen year old and one of the bridesmaids, broke down in tears as Charles hugged her goodbye.

Once in the carriage, the first few moments alone together were magical. Charles and Fanny didn't notice the first snow of the year dusting the streets, nor did they turn to watch the wedding guests waving until the carriage disappeared out of sight. They only had eyes for each other. Charles removed Fanny's fur muff and kissed her hand. Fanny threw back her head and laughed as she felt her tensions disappear. She removed her bonnet richly adorned with white ostrich plumes so Charles could kiss her more easily. Wrapped in fur rugs against the cold, they revelled in their new status as a married couple. Their life together was just beginning and now nobody could stand in their way.

'Mrs. Kingsley,' Charles said loosening his cravat, 'May I kiss my newly betrothed?'

Fanny, dressed in her travelling clothes, had changed from her cream bridal dress into a matching oyster-grey cloak and dress, trimmed with white ermine. She sighed, as she held her husband's arm. Charles leant over and kissed her gently at first, then more intensely. He moved away briefly to gaze into her lustrous eyes that shone with happiness. Her lips, red and ripe were so tempting, he only now realised the enormity of the pledge of sexual abstinence they had agreed on. It would, he decided, be the most difficult of challenges.

'Fanny dearest, you looked so beautiful in your wedding dress. A pure vision of beauty,' he whispered and reverently picked up her hand and kissed the shiny, gold band on her ring finger.

'And the wedding went splendidly, did you not think?' Fanny trilled excitedly. 'After the family had toasted us with glasses of champagne they appeared quite inebriated and mellow.'

'It was the best day of my life.' But Charles hid his disappointment at her sisters' muted response to the celebrations. His parents, thankfully, had been overjoyed. 'So to Cheddar, my love, and four blissful weeks of honeymooning,' he said leaning back on the leather squabs and feeling as if his life had finally started a new chapter.

Honeymoon

Choosing to stay at an isolated farmhouse in the Cheddar countryside, in Somerset, Fanny and Charles luxuriated in spending time alone and going for brisk walks in the winter sunshine. In the evening after dinner, prepared by a cook, they would sit by a log fire and read books and discuss literature and theology. Despite huge temptation, they remained true to their promise and the marriage remained unconsummated in their first four weeks together.

After their self-imposed abstinence, they eagerly anticipated their sexual union. In Charles's eyes, mortification went hand in hand with the physical expression of their love and, earlier in the evening and, unbeknown to Fanny, Charles had stripped naked in a nearby wood and beaten himself with thorny branches until his skin was punctured. He had endured the pain, stifled his cries and wept with guilt and sadness he was not coming to Fanny as a virgin. He had rolled on icy wet grass, crying out for forgiveness in the silence of the trees around him. But with his penitence came absolution. He had washed away his sins and was ready to indulge in the wild passions of sexual bliss. He dressed quickly and as one possessed, hurried back to the farmhouse, and to his waiting wife.

Solemnly, in their bedroom lit by one candle, and dressed only in a canvas shirt for humility, Fanny knelt before her husband. Charles read the Holy Sacrament to her, absolving her of all guilt. He lifted her from her kneeling position and removed her shirt. His eyes glistened as he took in the beauteous form before him. Instantly he was aroused and guiding her gently to the bed, he removed his shirt and lay on top of her.

Fanny moaned with pleasure. That they had waited so long for this consummation of their love, it only served to make it more spiritual and heavenly. Charles kissed her urgently as he entered her, slowly at first, then ecstatically they both moved as one. Charles cried out so loudly that he startled Fanny as he came inside her. Their sexual union was complete.

Day after day they satiated each other's desires. Charles marvelled they were so compatible together and Fanny consumed with such a long held desire, often initiated the intimacies between them. On the last day of their honeymoon, Charles was relaxing in his nightshirt, unshaven and his hair uncombed. Fanny smiled at him across the breakfast table. He was still attractive, despite his dishevelled appearance. In fact, in her eyes he was even more desirable. Charles was distracted, opening his post, unaware of the adoring look in Fanny's eyes.

'There is news from Eversley, my dear wife. I have a letter from Sir John Cope. *'The Reverend Toovey-Hawley has been dismissed on the grounds of misdemeanors with another lady in the parish and has subsequently fled abroad,'* he read with surprise. 'What a scandal that must have caused.' He looked serious for a moment. 'But I'm sure there will be many in the parish who welcome his departure. And Sir John,' he continued, his face now beaming, 'goes on to say that on my return I will be offered the permanent appointment as Rector of St Mary's!'

'Oh that is such good news!' Fanny clapped her hands. 'You will have sole charge of your own parish at last and you will be able to do so much more now in your new promotion.'

'And we will be able to move into the Rectory. It will make a wonderful home for us.'

Charles and Fanny celebrated their news in the best way they knew how.

On the day that Charles took over his new post, a cart piled high with furniture came to a halt outside the Rectory. With the help of two village carters, Charles moved his scant belongings from his cottage into the seventeenth century house nestled next to the Church. He darted from room to room hardly able to believe the house was finally his, with its beautiful gardens and stunning views across to a tree-lined hill and a forest beyond. He was overjoyed. This would be home to their long and happy marriage.

It was only when Fanny arrived in her smart barouche and, accompanied by another carriage with her contribution of furniture and her immense wardrobe of clothes, did Charles see the house in its real light. Fanny set about writing a list headed 'Remedial Works.' She inspected the rooms that, although light with large casement windows, smelled of damp and were in need of repair.

'Charles dear, why are there buckets in these downstairs rooms?' she asked.

'The odd heavy downpour seeps through but do not concern yourself, dearest, we can get it fixed,' he replied with boyish enthusiasm.

'The walls in the parlour are black with dirt and mould.' Fanny wiped a finger across the wall above the fireplace. 'And we shall need a new fireplace in here.'

'And this range!' she fretted as she surveyed the poorly maintained kitchen. 'I wouldn't ask cook to boil an egg on this. Did Noah deliver this from his Ark?'

On inspection of the garden she observed, 'Are the ponds not a further source of damp? I will worry that our children will get too close to them.'

'Everything will be done to insure our children are not in any danger. If necessary, we will have the ponds filled in,' Charles assured her whilst scratching his head and calculating the cost of the two pages of repairs that Fanny was busy adding to.

Coming from a family of considerable wealth, Fanny was disappointed to see her new humble surroundings. As rectories went, this one was far inferior to the many that she had visited. Bravely, she hid her feelings and tried to share her husband's delight.

Although Charles had warned her about his classes for youngsters, she was taken aback when a group of scrappily dressed urchins filed through the kitchen door and into the adjoining room for their weekly lessons. Nor did she realise she would have to share her home three nights a week with the adult evening class. Life at the Rectory was anything but dull. And there was always some poor unfortunate who, often in the middle of supper, would knock at the door asking for food for their 'young 'uns'. Charles never refused their requests for bread and soup.

Night after night of satisfying their long-denied passion, Fanny conceived almost immediately. In those early days they would wake up and lie in bed listening to the soft soughing of the wind in the trees outside. Charles never failed to delight in the view across the lane to the hill he now called the Mount. He watched the early morning mist dissolve in the trees and, with the sheep grazing in the field below, it leant an eerie mood to the scene. The rooks wheeled around their scraggy nests now exposed on the bare branches of the elms. It would absorb him and thrill him at the same time. Then he would turn his attention to Fanny, who because of her pregnancy was still having bouts of tiredness. But as he stroked her thighs, she was aroused so quickly, her malaise was soon forgotten and they would once more christen their marriage bed.

Meanwhile, Charles had employed a full time maid, Emily. Mrs. Scrimshaw, his housekeeper and cook, continued to work for him as did the gardener, Old Eric, who had worked at the Rectory for twenty years. Under Charles' supervision, within a few weeks the house sparkled and shone, smelling of beeswax and pine-resin soap. Proudly Mrs. Scrimshaw declared it was as clean as a new pin. Unlike the Rectory's previous owner, one of Charles' strong beliefs was that a man should be clean in body and mind. And he applied this rule to his home as well.

His world was now complete. He had an adoring wife, a beautiful home for his new family, a Church he loved and a life-long mission to improve the lot of his parishioners. Fanny tried to share her husband's enthusiasm when he showed her the poorly maintained Church. She was deeply touched as they stood before the simple grave of 'Young Tom'. Charles recounted again the harrowing story of his life and tragic end. In deference to this sad life, Fanny would regularly pick a bunch of flowers from the Rectory garden and place them on his grave.

She attended the church services, and despite the disappointing numbers, she grew even more aware of how committed her husband was to his faith. Once up in the pulpit to deliver his sermon, his stuttering left him. His speech was engaging and passionate. His congregation sat spell–bound, for most of them, having neither the ability to read or write, this was the one way they could learn the truths from the Bible.

Fanny thought his sermon was equal to any delivery in Westminster Abbey, so inspiring and eloquent were his words. His eagle glance penetrated every corner of the church and, on this particular Sunday, it didn't take long for him to spot the huddled figure in the back pew. It was Clough, the chimney sweep who quickly averted his eyes from the rector. Charles was shocked at his ashen, gaunt face but his sermon on this day was particularly appropriate. It was the subject of goodliness.

He stood before his congregation trying hard not to use his arms in wild gesturing poses, a habit he was well aware of.

'*My friends,*' he began, '*whosoever of you have ever felt angry with yourselves, discontented with yourselves, ashamed of yourselves? He that has not, knows no more about himself than a dumb animal does. If you have felt so, listen to St. Paul's glorious news and take comfort. Do you wish to be what God intended you to be before all worlds? "And God saw all that he had made, and behold it was very good?'* He stole a glance at the sweep whose mouth hardened. '*For at times we shall need that faith not only for our neighbours, but for ourselves. We shall find it hard to believe there is goodness in some of our neighbours or ourselves-.'* There was a shuffle amongst a few of those in the pews. At the front of the church, the trombonist, Mr. Henry Scrimshaw, married to the Kingsley's cook Mrs. Scrimshaw looked across to the clarinetist. They had exchanged sharp words earlier when he had complained to his fellow musician that he was out of tune more times than he cared to name. It had ended abruptly when Charles came along to thank them for turning up.

Charles continued-

'God saw everything that he made and behold it was very good. And God made you and me. Are we therefore not very good? Here is a great mystery. It would seem we must have been very good if God made us. For God can make nothing bad. For he who makes bad houses is a bad builder: and he who makes bad men is a bad maker of men. Yet God is perfect and without fault in all his works. Yet men are bad.'

There was a scraping of boots on the stone flags from Walter Watson, the innkeeper. His wife gave him a hard nudge in the ribs as their seven-year old son next to him looked on in surprise. She had caught her husband watering down the beer in one of the kegs and had threatened to spill the beans to the brewery if it happened again. Walter gasped in pain and with a stern glance at his wife, stifled his cry with a pronounced cough. Charles witnessed this and repressed a smile. As he had expected, there was a reaction to his words - there were frowns on some of the faces of his congregation, a few were smiling angelically, but he continued with the seriousness of his sermon.

'Then believe this. All that is good in you, God has made; he will take care of what he has made, for he loves it. All that

is bad in you, God has NOT made, and therefore he will destroy it. If you are wishing and trying to conquer the bad, then you are on the side of God himself. Take courage, then,' he declared earnestly and raising up his arms *'If you dislike your sins, so does God. If you are fighting against your worse feelings, so is God. Believe, and endure to the end and you shall be found in Christ at the last day.'* Here Charles directed his gaze at the sweep who was trying hard to stifle his coughing and had buried his face under his coat.

'In the name of the Father, the son and the Holy Ghost, Amen.'

Charles bowed his head and gave thanks that he had delivered God's message to the best of his ability.

Several of the older men in the congregation were so enthralled by his words, the wives had to slap down their hands as they attempted to clap. Old Mr. Elliot, the butcher even called a 'Here, here' from the rear before heads turned at his unseemly conduct. Compared to the previous rector's delivery that had been so dull and repetitive, these words had stirred their hearts. Henry Scrimshaw shook hands with the clarinetist afterwards.

'No 'ard feelin's then?'

'Na,' said the clarinetist, slipping his instrument under his arm. 'I doubt if we'll make the Regent Centre in Reading but we'll do right enough 'ere for the Reveren' Kingsley.'

After the service, Charles shared convivial conversation with his parishioners outside the church. Fanny, who now dressed demurely as a rector's wife in navy muslin, joined the wives and they exchanged stilted pleasantries. Old Mr. Elliot had news for Charles.

'That sweep, Clough –'ow that man dare show his face in this church I'll never know Reveren', but I think 'ee should know he's in a bad way. Sick as a dog, he is. I'm surprised 'e made it 'ere. '

'He did appear to be unwell,' Charles agreed.

'He's not had a boy to 'elp him for many a month. He sits in that 'ovel most days. His horse is near t'death through starvin.' I dunnow 'ow the man has 'nough money to feed 'is'elf. I 'ear 'e tried to buy laudanum on account but they was havin' none of it.'

'Thank you, Mr. Elliot. I will call on him tomorrow.'

Elliot gave a look of undisguised surprise. That the Reverend should take time to visit such varmint was beyond him.

A Visit from an Old Friend

In the newly decorated dining room of olive green, Charles was in a distant mood at breakfast the next morning. After two cups of tea, he abandoned his toast, and rose abruptly from his chair.

'You are in a hurry this morning my dear,' Fanny remarked. 'Have you letters to write?'

'Later. First, I have to pay a visit to one of my sick parishioners.' Charles bent over and kissed Fanny tenderly on the nape of her neck.

'And who would that be? '

'I am away to visit Mr. Clough, the sweep. His illness is serious. The man could hardly stand in Church yesterday.'

'Oh Charles, you can't go to him. He is sick with consumption or worse. You never know what disease you might pick up from him. And the man deserves no sympathy after what you have told me about his treatment of his boy who now lies in the graveyard.' Fanny pushed away her plate of poached eggs. Her nausea that had been slight in early pregnancy was now returning.

'He is one of my flock. Would you have me ignore the man and his illness because he's done wrong in the past?' Charles said briskly, raising his voice more than normal.

'Yes,' Fanny replied emphatically. 'If I had to choose between you catching an illness from him or him lying in his own filth – and guilt, I would choose the latter.' She looked up him and knew from the dark glare in his eyes she had spoken out of turn.

'I have a duty here to look after these poor wretches. They have little money to buy bread nor to heat their homes, such as they are. Have you visited one of these '*homes*?'

He didn't wait for Fanny to reply. With her privileged upbringing she had no understanding of the poverty and living conditions in the surrounding community.

'When you are well again and recovered from childbirth, I shall take you into one of these '*homes*'. You will see for yourself how bad things are amongst the poor around here.'

Charles strode into hallway and picking up his topcoat and medicine bag, strode out into the clear morning air.

Despite the worry of her husband having contact with the sweep's contagion, Fanny had deep respect for his compassionate concern that was so much a part of his nature. The poverty Charles witnessed every day made him even more determined to help those whose daily life was one long grind to keep them away from the workhouse. He had little time for the likes of the local gentry, who accepted that their wealth was theirs, and theirs alone and not to be shared. Charles would do whatever he could to help those unfortunates, however bad their reputation. And Clough the Sweep was one of them.

He arrived back at the Rectory two hours later in a desolate mood. Fanny was there to meet him in the hallway.

'How is he?' she asked tentatively, hoping her concern would improve her husband's mood. Charles put down his medicine bag, removed his coat and laid it across the hall seat.

'He is close to death. There's not much that can be done for him now. I have made him comfortable, lit the fire and given him some laudanum to ease the pain. A neighbour is tending to him. I will return in a while and, I fear, to read the last rites. He is a sad, pathetic character now and full of remorse.'

Seeing the angst in Fanny's eyes, he kissed her on her forehead.

'There is a horse outside. Whose is it?' he enquired.

'You have a visitor. He's in the parlour.' Fanny smiled, well aware the visitor would restore his spirits.

'Who has called on us? Is it good news?' Charles smiled at the prospect of a friend calling. Sometimes he felt isolated after all the male camaraderie he had enjoyed at university.

'Charles Mansfield! What a glorious surprise,' Charles exclaimed. The tall, immaculately dressed visitor stood up and the two embraced earnestly. 'My word, you are still the handsome rogue you ever were!'

'And married life is suiting you well, I see,' his friend replied, his eyes gleaming with delight. They shook hands and embraced each other.

Fanny had entered the room and witnessed the strong bond between the two men. The energy between them was tangible.

'How pleased I am to see you, Mansfield.' Charles' face lit up with love and joy at seeing his old friend.

'Would you care for some refreshment?' Fanny ventured.

'Thank you, Fanny. You are most kind. I will take some coffee.' Mansfield turned to see her hesitantly looking at her husband.

'Why, we must have something stronger. This is an occasion to celebrate. Fanny let us have a bottle of our finest wine. Sometimes we feel quite removed from our old friends,' said Charles, his eyes never leaving Mansfield's for a second.

'I have given up alcohol and I shall not be tempted!' Mansfield smiled, the old devilment in his eyes returning.

'Ha! Next you will be telling me you've converted to Christianity. Fanny, let us have coffee then, the next best thing to wine.'

Charles and Mansfield retired to the study and, Charles lighting a pipe of tobacco, settled down to catch up on the news of his good friend. He had often regaled stories to Fanny of their raucous student life.

If she were honest, she envied the intimacy of the two men, together with the fact that Charles Mansfield was exceptionally handsome and had the charm and dress of a gentry cad. His expressive grey eyes and lithe stature were most attractive to the opposite sex and Fanny was at a loss to understand why he was not in a relationship with a beautiful woman.

When Emily, the maid, entered with a tray bearing cups and a pot of coffee, Charles was sat in his leather armchair puffing avidly on his pipe. With his long legs crossed, he was laughing with gay abandon at a tale his friend was telling. Fanny followed Emily carrying a plate of scones fresh from the oven.

'I hope you will stay with us for a while?' Fanny enquired.

'Of course,' said Charles. 'Our visitor will be staying with us for as long he wishes! Fanny, have Emily make up the bed in the guest room and light the fire there.' Charles stretched out of his chair to reach his cup of coffee.

'I wouldn't want to impose on my newly-married friends.' Mansfield stood up and met Fanny's eyes with a steady gaze. Fanny was mentally and physically ruffled by this man's charismatic presence.

'Nonsense, how long is it since we've seen each other? A year?' insisted Charles 'And I would like you to have the opportunity to get to know my adorable wife,' he added mindful of Fanny's subdued manner.

'I believe according to your last letter, I am to congratulate you both on the forthcoming event of a child.'

Fanny blushed and Charles smiled proudly.

'How fine life is when you are wed,' he declared looking across to his wife. 'I cannot recommend it highly enough, dear friend.'

'If you chose the right bride, I may mention. Which obviously you have,' added Mansfield.

Sparing any further blushes, Fanny announced lunch would at one o'clock, and left the men deep in conversation.

She envisaged the next forty-eight hours would be one entirely devoted to catching up with latest news and reminiscing about their university days. But she was wrong.

As soon as Charles finished his coffee, he excused himself telling Mansfield he had an urgent appointment but would return before lunch.

'And please make yourself at home. Fanny will be delighted to show you to your room. And we will see to it that your horse is stabled and fed.'

Charles returned late, his mood changed completely. He was melancholic and out of sorts. Mansfield sensed it immediately.

'Is there anything I can help you with?' he asked.

They had retired to his study and studiously Charles lit a pipe of tobacco.

'I apologise for my low mood,' he said 'I have just witnessed the death of one of the village folk. He was not the kindest of men but in his dying breaths - and he struggled hard to talk- he begged for remission of his sins. It is never easy to accept death and, in his case, he was barely a score and ten, I would guess. A sweep's life is not an easy one.'

Over a late luncheon of poached cod in a white sauce with pickled runner beans and potatoes, Fanny informed Charles there had been two visitors to the Rectory in his absence. Charles listened attentively. She recounted the washerwoman, Mrs. Wicks had pleaded for some broth and bread for her ailing husband who was off work again with painful limbs after his riding accident some while ago. The head stable lad from Bramshill Park, Sir John Cope's estate, had called and asked if he could he confirmed – 'again,' added Fanny cheerfully. 'He feels it would be right, if the Reverend Kingsley agreed, that he and all the stable lads attend confirmation study classes.' She giggled. 'Charles is so popular now that they all wish to re-take their confirmation classes.'

Watching Fanny's face light up, Charles was reminded why he had married this warm-hearted woman.

'I see you are a popular figure,' Mansfield said. 'It must make a lot of demands on your time.'

Charles nodded. 'Tomorrow we have Bible Study class for adults. This evening there are reading lessons for the children and so it goes on. Never a dull moment in the Kingsley household!' Turning to Fanny he enquired 'Is there a pudding for us, my sweet wife?'

'I have never known a man with such an appetite,' Fanny said, relaxing in the company of these two men. Catching sight of a suggestive raised eyebrow from her husband, she blushed. 'I....mean cook has produced a treacle tart,' she stammered. Mansfield dabbed his mouth with his napkin attempting to hide his broad grin.

After lunch Fanny retired to her bedroom for a rest and later, Charles suggested that he and Mansfield go for a walk

'I cannot sit in when the weather is so pleasant. Let us exercise the lungs.'

'An excellent idea,' Mansfield agreed.

Mansfield and Charles fell into step in the mild April air. The wind had picked up and the light was fading as they made their way across the fields and to the Mount opposite the Rectory. They reached the line of fir trees and elms that stood atop the hill. The plaintiff cry of rooks circling their nests was the only sound to break the silence. Charles turned to look back at his home, its red brick walls and welcoming windows, its red tiled roof and chimney pots looking so handsome and surrounded by freshly mowed lawns and borders of daffodils. In the hollow, the trees showed the first buds of green in the late spring. It was a view he never tired of. They followed a grassy track through young firs, their trunks and branches now glowing a deep mahogany as the shafts of the setting sun made a brief appearance into the forest. Charles drank in their fine aromatic smell.

They were soon reminiscing about university life. They had formed a bond that few could emulate. It was as if they had never been apart. They laughed about their wild drinking days and Mansfield recalled Charles' prank of climbing the oak tree at midnight, duck shooting out on the Fens and fishing on the Cam.

'Life seems very quiet here after our misspent youth,' Charles admitted as they came out into a clearing.

'Our misspent youth made you what you are today,' Mansfield chuckled. 'When you arrived at Magdalene, you were such a shy young man, we hardly ever saw you. You were so devoted to your studies.'

'I had a stammer I couldn't control. Ha! That didn't make for me being social. The other students you may recall used to mock me.'

'It didn't affect your public speaking though, did it? You gave many a fine lecture that students still remember. You developed into a fine orator.'

'And that was all thanks to you- you were so popular and I confess, I hung on to your coat tails. You gave me the confidence to mix with the other students. Were you aware of how we all envied you? With your charm and social graces you made us appear like peasant folk!'

Mansfield gave a hollow laugh and grew serious. 'Sad as it may seem, I wish those days back.'

Charles halted and looked at the fine featured but desolate man before him. 'Indeed. We were as close as kin. We were – we are like brothers.'

The trees seemed to cloak themselves around their intimacy and silence. Charles wrapped an arm around his shoulder.

'We were... that is the sad gist of it my friend,' said Mansfield. He sighed. '*My melancholy haunts me and not one kindly gleam pierces the gloom of my dark thoughts, to give a glimpse of comfort.*' That is a quote from Thomas Southerne. I have been reading his plays of late.' He gazed at Charles with lost spaniel eyes.

'My dear Mansfield, it grieves me to see you this way. What has brought this on?'

'What I omitted to tell you in my letters was that a while back, I married in haste. It lasted only weeks, days even, before she left me. I am ashamed of my failure. She- Catherine- refuses to divorce me so I cannot re-marry even if I found the right woman. My romantic life is a disaster. I am lost without religion or career. I confess I am lonely.'

'What an unholy mess.' Charles was visibly shocked. This was not the carefree bachelor he had known at university. And Charles had been enthusing about the delights of wedlock and his beloved Fanny and had no idea about his friend's disastrous marriage. It was Charles who had been the awkward shy one, the student with the stutter, unsure of the opposite sex. He had been very naïve with women.

During the next two days, Mansfield's low mood improved as he and Charles spent time together discussing a range of subjects in the study. Mansfield was amused at the disarray. Not much had changed since his university days. This was a man's room lined with bookshelves overflowing with tomes on religion, fishing, natural history and geography. Fishing rods and landing nets were propped against the wall. Strung from one wall to the opposite side was a hammock that Charles loved to sit in whilst writing his sermons. Under a window overlooking the garden was a table on which rested clay pipes in amongst fishing flies, reels, feathers and half-written manuscripts, letters and papers. It took Mansfield back to their days together at Cambridge.

That evening the Rectory echoed with the voices of excited children who had come for their reading class. Charles taught his pupils with such enthusiasm, it was infectious. There were whoops of delight and joy as they revelled in the learning of letters and their names. The atmosphere in the house was one of lively chatter. For a while, the children forgot the harsh realities of life outside the Kingsley home.

Fanny continued to be the polite hostess yet Mansfield's sensitive nature alerted him to her unease in his company. Did he imagine she felt him to be a threat to her stable marriage with Charles or that the two men shared a secret she could never party to?

PART THREE

Unrest in the City

Summer in Eversley was about as perfect as it could be. It was neither too hot as to scorch the fields of wheat and barley, neither was it too wet as to flatten the crops, rot the potatoes or spoil the haymaking. Sun followed rain and by the time September came the farmers had harvested bumper crops. The good harvest had meant there was barely an empty stomach in the parish and this did much to lighten Charles' load of caring for the poor.

He helped with the haymaking, eager work off his energy in the fields. Sharing his lunches of cold ham pie and cheese with the children, he joined in with the impromptu singing of the men and wives as they worked in the fields. Charles was completely at ease amongst the camaraderie of country folk. Not only did he make a good impression with those who had left the Church after the previous rector's apathy, but word had spread and it was not long before the congregation at St Mary's had swelled in number.

Meanwhile, Fanny being of a delicate disposition, struggled in the latter months of her pregnancy and it was with immense relief that their firstborn, a daughter, Rose Georgina was born in November. Baby Rose was the pride and joy of her parents. Charles nicknamed her 'Cocky' and idled away time, admiring their little wonder in the cradle. He described to her in hushed whispers the birdsong he had heard that day, the 'churr' of the Mistle Thrush, the low warbling of a Redwing and the startled cry of pheasants as he disturbed their feeding. He made a promise to 'Cocky' that one day he would share all these wonders of nature with her.

The year passed and although Charles was ecstatically happy with his new daughter and domestic life, he was suffering from financial problems. Despite a modest income from Fanny's inheritance, his living as a clergyman did not pay handsomely. He needed to find another source of income. He decided to finish a play he had worked on during his courtship with Fanny. Based on the life of St. Elizabeth of Hungary, '*The Saint's Tragedy*' had been intended as a wedding present for his new wife. It was risqué in content with the main character, St Elizabeth, suffering penance with self-inflicted lashes to her naked body. Charles described the joy that came with this as he reflected on his own experiences.

But both Fanny and his mother advised that the play would undoubtedly cause offence to the strict Victorian reader, and with this in mind, Charles deleted some of the more explicit passages. The illustrations he had drawn himself were also somewhat lewd. He was left wondering how easy it would be to find a publisher.

Charles was also preoccupied with the deteriorating situation in England. There was great unrest amongst the workers and he made it his mission to meet with groups of like-minded thinkers who wanted to bring about change. On this occasion he looked forward to meeting one of his heroes whose book had given him so much inspiration.

As he made his way in a Hackney cab through the busy London streets in amongst all the madness of rush and bustle, he was struck by the contrast of his quiet country parish. The green fields and village common with its duck pond were another world away from all the dirt and smells of the city. Here there were no green spaces. There was no fresh air. Already Charles was wishing he were back in his peaceful home environment. The multitude of chimneys cluttering the London skyline pumped out swathes of grey and yellow smoke that Charles could feel invading his lungs.

The noise of the carts, carriages and people were an assault on his senses. The foul smell of horse dung on the streets filled his nostrils. And there was a great tide of humanity, the city folk, who fought and struggled their way along the overcrowded streets. It was an easy and often lethal mistake to step off the pavement and into the path of the horses and carriages that bowled along the thoroughfare. Charles watched the beggars, flower sellers, the gingerbread and orange sellers all jostling and plying their trade hoping to earn a pittance for their families. His heart went out to them.

But all this was a diversion from the meeting that lay ahead. Charles was to meet a well-known theologian and author, a Mr. Frederick Denison Maurice. Maurice had already written several books on his ideologies and held the post of Professor of English and History at Kings College London. He was a man who was revered and feared; feared by the Church for his radical views yet revered by men such as Charles and Mansfield for his social beliefs.

In the early days of their relationship Fanny had sent Charles a copy of Maurice's book *'The Kingdom of Christ'*. Charles was so impressed with its content that it proved to be a turning point in his life and influenced him considerably with his decision to become a clergyman. It was with huge trepidation and anticipation that he now found himself on his way to meet him.

The cab dropped him off outside a Georgian house in Bloomsbury where the pace of traffic had slowed. Here was a more genteel way of life with its smart landau carriages and barouches of the wealthy.

A young maid bobbed him a curtsey as she opened the front door to him. Taking his topcoat, she escorted him to a heavily wood panelled room. Here, large sash windows opened onto a manicured garden of box hedges and rose bushes and provided light into an otherwise gloomy room. It had a distinctly masculine feel. Turkish rugs of deep red and magenta covered the floors on which stood heavy mahogany furniture of a large desk, table and chairs. The walls were elegantly decorated with portraits from a bygone era. It was aptly appropriate for the assembly of these men. This was no casual meeting of friends.

Mansfield was seated in a leather chair and jumped up as soon as he saw Charles, vigorously shaking his hand before Charles had time to look around at the assembled guests.

'Charles, it's good to see you. I hope your journey was tolerable.'

'It was, thank you, bearing in mind the traffic,' Charles said returning his wide grin.

Behind an imposing round table stood Fredrick Denison Maurice.

'Welcome,' he greeted in a soft kindly voice, stretching out his hand to Charles. Charles saw in the distinguished handsome face, a peace and calm he wished for himself. There was an air of humility about him that intrigued Charles. He knew him to be one of the greatest theologians of the day as well as having a profound knowledge of literature and philosophy and Charles was only too aware he stood in the presence of a very learned and respected man.

Charles was eager to converse. 'I have read your book, *'The Kingdom of Christ'* with great interest and studied its contents avidly. We have much in common on our views of the Church today.' The words tumbled out with barely a stammer.

'I, too am an admirer of yours, Reverend Kingsley. I have also heard reports of your standing in the parish at Eversley. The good works you are doing within your parish are reaching us through the officers at nearby Sandhurst. It is rare occurrence that a clergyman takes such interest in the welfare of his parishioners.'

'Thank you.' Charles felt humbled by the unexpected praise.

Maurice then introduced him to a young man by the name of John Ludlow, a barrister and a small man with arresting eyes that Charles later recounted to Fanny 'ambushed you with their brilliance.' After they had they seated themselves around the table, Maurice addressed his friends.

'One thing we have in common, gentlemen, is that we are not popular with the Anglican clergy for our reformist views. We are, it is whispered, awakening a sleeping lion. Would you not agree? Indeed, they describe my book *'The Kingdom of Christ'* as revolutionary. So be it. But I digress. As you are aware through newspaper reports, there is growing unrest. The working classes, particularly in the North, are now facing the worst depression for many years. They cannot feed themselves or their families. Their only option is the workhouse if they fail. I fear this will result in violence.'

His beautiful, expressive eyes filled with sadness and Charles, hypnotized as he was by this man, thought he had never seen such an angelic face. 'Our parents will remember the massacre of Peterloo in Manchester in 1819. Yet almost thirty years on, still there is no progress and the plight of the working classes continues to be ignored. The message of the working class is the same now as it was then.'

The men nodded their heads.

'Which is where you and the Reverend Kingsley as churchmen fit in?' suggested Ludlow.

Maurice nodded. 'Our aim is to persuade the Church to finally wake up and accept social responsibility for its people. The clergy cannot remove themselves from the inhuman conditions these workers have to live in. For too long they have turned a blind eye. It is time for change, my friends, but by peaceful means and our Reverend here is already setting an example. I hear your preaching is attracting a following from many areas outside your parish. You have a rare gift.'

'It is a small matter,' Charles replied shaking his head.

'I believe from the many letters we have exchanged, we are in agreement, the Church must now become democratic in its outlook, that it must work *with* the government on improving the social conditions of the working classes. The Government must heed the call and listen to its workers, - workers that are growing more vociferous in their demands for voting rights. The Chartists are demanding universal male suffrage, annual parliaments, voting by ballot and the end to property qualifications for Members of Parliament. And the time is overdue for reform. The small measure of reform in 1832 has done little to appease the militant working class.'

'And look at the unrest in Paris. It could well be a foretaste of what will happen here. There could be violence on the streets,' Ludlow added earnestly. A few months previously in February there had been a revolution in France and King Louis Phillipe had abdicated.

'It is true,' continued Maurice. 'It is time we took action. And as a man of the Church, Reverend Kingsley, you will undoubtedly be named as the most outspoken when we do. The Church will undoubtedly disapprove of our views but I feel it imperative that we publish them in the form of pamphlets. Do you not agree?'

'We have the backing of such luminaries as Dickens, Disraeli and Gaskell do we not?' Mansfield asked. 'Charles Dickens, through his novels, has vividly depicted the appalling life of the unfortunates in London. His books are one of the best selling yet nothing is done to remedy these vile living conditions he describes.' Mansfield was thinking of the harrowing accounts in Oliver Twist.

After much discussion they agreed they would give their name and backing to the Chartists, but by peaceful means. They were of the same mind that written protests should be expressed in a new periodical called '*Politics for the People.*' Ludlow was happy be its editor. Charles, wildly euphoric to be in such eminent company, agreed along with Mansfield, to contribute and Ludlow appointed him as his assistant.

Now that the transport system was much improved with the introduction of railways, these publications were able to reach large areas of the country. Their voices would be a wake up call for the Church, government and the aristocrats who remained isolated from the lower class poverty. Not only was Charles delighted to be asked to write for the magazine, but it would also help his finances that were, with all the domestic outgoings, falling short of expectation.

Charles dined with Mansfield that evening, and much to his relief, found his friend in much better spirits than when they had last met. He asked if there were changes in his life to account for this.

'I have finally converted to Christianity,' Mansfield ventured as they dined in a Chop House in Bloomsbury.

Charles sat back and abandoned his hearty meal of pork and potatoes.

'Well my friend! I am more than pleased that you have found faith in God. And not before time! If you were not an abstainer, I would order a bottle of the best house wine to celebrate!'

'And,' Mansfield continued hurriedly, 'that is not all. I have been asked by the Royal College to experiment with a new idea that will revolutionize the world. It is the extraction of benzol from coal tar. The possibilities of what can be done with this are endless.'

'Congratulations – you have an excellent scientific mind and a rare talent which is finally being recognized. I shall await to hear your results with keen interest.'

Charles took a sip of wine and leaned forward, keen to inform his good friend of his news. 'And I also have some to share with you. Fanny is with child again. She has taken to motherhood so naturally and Rosy is the most adorable baby. You must come and stay with us again. Enjoy the country air. London is shocking for its poisonous fumes. Indeed, I cannot wait to leave, but I would not have missed our meeting today.'

They discussed at length the ideas for their articles for the journal. But Mansfield was distracted as he thought of the enviable family life Charles had and knew he would never experience it himself. He left in a pensive mood.

As soon as he returned home to Eversley, Charles set about writing for *Politics of the People*. The name alone was enough to cause panic amongst the clergy and upper classes. Charles worked hard on his contributions that he signed *'Parson Lot.'* He hoped they would help the working man escape from his monotonous life. In his letters he called for a public enquiry into the working conditions in the sweatshops where workers were denied a decent wage and lived in dire conditions. In his second letter he laid emphasis on the Bible that was the 'Reformers Guide,' its scriptures demanding more help for the poor than they demanded themselves. In another letter he extolled the virtues of the museums and art galleries. These were all free to the working man and he declared them a paradise compared to the dull bricks and mortar and ugly factories of the city.

Whilst Charles filled his spare time writing these articles, his second child, Maurice was born and, to add to the good news, his book, *'The Saint's Tragedy'*, was finally published. It was well received by Coleridge, Tennyson and even the Prince Consort himself. Nor did it escape the notice of university students who were taking an interest in this eloquent and rebellious writer.

The press, however, were disclaiming the contributors to the new *'Politics for The People' as* firebrands. Fanny was adamant his articles would damage his chances of further procurement within the Church. But Charles was not a man to be swayed and, aware that Chartist protests led by Feargus O'Connor, had reached boiling point, he set off for London with his friend, Ludlow, to witness events.

He had learnt that five million people had signed a petition on articles of reform for voting rights and there was to be a march from Kennington Common to the House of Commons to present this. It reawakened memories of his schooldays in Bristol and the riots he had witnessed there first-hand. The pent up anger of the working classes had turned to murderous violence and these images remained embedded in his mind.

When Charles arrived in London, he found it a deserted city and in a state of high excitement, he wrote to Fanny of the events.

'Dearest,

I write to tell you of the extraordinary scenes in London. The Duke of Wellington has planned the barricade of the city like a military operation. The streets are deserted and most of the shops are closed. The Bank of England and Somerset House have put up defences. How everyone is frightened of this revolution by the people! 200,00 are expected. Special constables have been recruited of which Mansfield is one and it is believed they number 85,000! Even the Queen has left the capital for Osborne House. Regiments of soldiers from all over the country have been brought in and I hear the Duke of Wellington has closed the bridges in attempt to stem the flow of rioters who will deliver a petition to the House of Commons.'

Yet imagine our disbelief as we approached Kennington Common and found the meeting disbanding. And I hear a mere 20,000 turned up. It was a poor spectacle but the mob was in good humour despite the rain. And how it rained. It was not the show of strength that had been expected. I, for one however believe that the Chartists must not give up on their striving for more equality. Not that I'm in favour of complete voting reform but I hope and believe the government will now listen to the populace and there be a better representation of them in Parliament.'

Disappointed in the poor turnout for this demonstration, Charles was even more determined to get his voice across to the people. On his return to Eversley, he worked at demonic speed writing his first full-length novel *'Yeast'*, desperate to bring public awareness to the conditions of the working class. In a letter to a Chartist author, Thomas Cooper he wrote, *'I would shed the last drop of my life blood for the social and political emancipation of the people of England as God is my witness.'*

And shed blood he did.

A First Novel

Fanny sat at the dining room table admiring Mrs. Scrimshaw's supper. A roast leg of mutton lay on a serving plate surrounded by spring vegetables from the garden. Mint sauce and gravy sat side by side in silver sauceboats. The delicious smell of the meat was dissipating as it cooled. Despite the early hour Fanny was exhausted and ready to retire. It had been a tiresome day with the children. Rose had been unwilling to go to sleep and, protesting vociferously, had woken baby Maurice who was now being soothed to sleep by Emily, the maid.

Agitated, Fanny tapped her fingers on the table. Finally, in frustration she stood up, and wrapping her shawl around her, she knocked at the study door.

'Charles, dearest, our supper is getting cold. Can you not leave your work for just half an hour?'

'Leave me be,' came the abrupt reply.

Fanny stiffened. Her husband was being unreasonable. He had barely surfaced from his room for five hours. Lunch had been a rushed plate of bread, ham and pickles. Charles had abandoned his food and jumped up from the table and disappeared back into his study. At three o'clock he had hastily thrown on his coat and disappeared out to visit some of the ailing folk in the parish.

'Charles, evening classes start in twenty minutes. You must eat before then.'

'I shall, God willing'.

A disappointed Mrs. Scrimshaw cleared away the supper plates, muttering under her breath that her afternoon's work had gone unappreciated and the Reveren' would make himself 'right poorly' if he carried on the way he was and not making time to eat.

No sooner had she cleared the table, there was the familiar rap at the door and fifteen labourers from the hamlets filed into the house. Each one deferentially doffed his cap to Mrs. Kingsley as she ushered them in. By now they knew the routine. The eldest, by the name of Gabriel, had arranged the Bibles on the table in the room set aside for teaching. They sat and waited patiently, having been warned by Emily that as the babies upstairs had only just got off to sleep, they must be especially quiet. There were hushed mutterings around the table. It had been a long day for most of the men, a rushed supper at home and then on to the Reverend Kingsley's whose enthusiasm had inspired the men to turn out on a cold wet night. Enviously, they breathed in the last of the fading smells of roast mutton, and could only imagine what delights had been served up earlier. The door opened and the group saw before them a weary and shadowy-eyed Charles. A small dog followed him in.

'Good evening, gentlemen. Let me introduce you to our newest member of the family. This is Dandy.'

The sandy-haired dog, a newly acquired Dandy Dimont, wagged its tail as it sat obediently, his large brown eyes never leaving his master's.

'Cor. Ain't she comely?' one of the men said. 'but 'e won't be no good for catchin' vermin around 'ere though will 'e?', refraining from further comment about the dog's short legs.

'We shall see,' Charles said doubtfully. 'Besides, I wouldn't want to put the vermin catcher out of business, now would I?'

The men gave a smirk. They liked their teacher's sense of humour. He was always ready with a quick, witty response. Tonight though, he didn't seem himself. His passion and vitality was missing but no one ventured to pass comment.

Wearily, Charles continued with his teaching of the Bible scriptures but aware he was not giving his pupils a hundred per cent of his concentration, he cut short the lesson. His pupils were not about to complain. There was more time to devour Mrs. Scrimshaw's Victoria sponge before they left for home and an early night.

Fanny found Charles tidying up the Bibles. His manner was unusually out of sorts.

'Charles, I insist you eat something before you go back to your writing.'

Without looking up at her, he said matter-of-factly. 'I will eat shortly,' and as he passed her on his way out through the door, he absently patted her on the shoulder, already absorbed in the next chapter of his book. Fanny heard the study door close. He had returned to his sanctuary and she knew it was useless to try to persuade him to do anything until he had finished his work.

A while later, as Fanny was about to retire he rushed to the parlour to find her. He was in the middle of writing his first novel *'Yeast'* that was to be published in serial form in Fraser's magazine, a literary periodical.

'I'm almost done,' he said, his mood now lighter. 'The first chapters are ready for publication. *'Yeast'* is well under way.' He smiled at her, hoping for praise.

'My dear husband, I am pleased for you, but look at you, half-starved and exhausted.' She stood up from her chair by the fire and kissed him gently on the lips and stroked his stubbly face. 'Tell me about it in the morning, at breakfast, when we are both refreshed.'

Charles went back into his study, ostensibly to sort out the order of the papers he had written. Frustrated, that he couldn't share his storyline with Fanny, he lit a fresh pipe and glanced outside. The garden was bathed in moonlight. Excitedly, he opened the French windows that led onto the terrace or 'deck' as he had named it.

'Ah,' he sighed. 'What a perfectly heavenly night, Dandy.' His four-legged companion was more than happy to join his master outside and sniff around the flower border.

'Look how the moon traces the outlines of the clouds. How beautifully the large billowing Cumuli are backlit.' His eyes followed the shadows across the lawn to the view across the fields and to the Mount. The firs and elms were silhouetted in the moonlight and between the clouds Charles could see a sprinkling of stars. Somewhere in the adjoining field an owl hooted.

As he surveyed the universe above him, his heart was filled with emotion and humility. In spite of his weariness, Charles felt extraordinarily exhilarated. It was as if he was seeing the night sky for the first time. No man could better God's natural beauty, he declared to Dandy. He breathed in the pure still air, relishing the silence, and mulled over the latest chapter of his book. Another few hours of work and he would be half way to its conclusion. This alone was enough to add to his elation. Before he closed the doors to the French windows and blew out the candles, he picked up his well-worn pen from its stained inkpot and hurriedly wrote a paragraph.

Tomorrow, he thought I will include this piece in one of my articles for '*Politics for the People.*' That night he slept the sleep of the gods. His last waking moment was filled with thankfulness for his beautiful wife who lay by his side, his two wonderful babies in the nursery, a home he loved and, next door the Church that he held so dear.

The words he had written were published in the next edition.

'Never lose an opportunity of seeing anything beautiful. Beauty is God's handwriting- a wayside sacrament: welcome it in every fair face, every flower and thank him for it, and drink it in simply and earnestly with all your eyes: it is a charmed cup, a cup of blessing.'

A Chance Meeting from the Past

Fanny looked a picture of contentment. Baby Maurice was cradled in her lap and beside her, Rose, now a 'grown up' three year old was gently washing the face of her doll with a clean piece of rag. Her father had advised her that even dolls and toys must be kept clean to avoid the spread of germs.

Fanny closed the folder of papers on which Charles had scribbled the title, '*Yeast*'.

'You look most becoming today, my dearest,' Charles announced in engaging mood. 'The cornflower blue of your dress suits you well.'

Fanny had been exhausted the night before when Charles finally retired to the bedroom, but it didn't take much persuasion for her to respond to his advances. Their lovemaking had been brief yet deeply satisfying.

Not only was Fanny contented with married life and all the physical rewards that accompanied it, she also maintained it was important to keep her dress to an acceptable standard, for the sake of her ardent husband. In a moment of recklessness, and with the excuse that she was jaded following the birth of Maurice, Fanny had ordered a new blue silk dress from her London dressmaker. It was less corseted than her previous ones, since her figure had 'relaxed a little' as she described it to her sisters. But with a frilled collar of lace and smocking at the waist, it was, she decided, a well-earned gift to herself despite the fact that it had eaten into her allowance from the family trust.

Charles picked up Maurice from her arms and held him high above his chest.

'Now my little Maurice, how about we have a stroll in the garden and see if we can find some frogs in the pond?'

'Oh yes please, please, Papa.' Rose tugged at her father's shirtsleeves. 'You promised us. Em'ly won't take me out into the garden.' Her chubby face creased into a frown.

Fanny smiled. Even baby Maurice would break into the most disarming smile when he saw his father, and Rose so idolized him that she had to be reminded not to be so possessive of her father now she had a baby brother. A half-hour spent with her father meandering in the garden looking at nature was heavenly to her. And now that Dandy was a part of the family, their time together was even more fun.

'Well, dear wife, what is your opinion of the content of my novel? Will I be ostracized by society for my views?' Charles asked exuberantly after he had told Rose to have Emily put on her boots.

Fanny gave her husband a whimsical smile as she pointed to the chapters of the book on the table next to her.

'Dear husband, I admire the way you write. '*Yeast*' will stir up the social conscience and yes, I do think your book will be met with resistance. You describe the wretched lives and mean drudgery of the labourers admirably, and no doubt this will cause ripples of protest and guilt amongst the gentry. It is a strong message. Your middle class character, Lancelot Smith is a very likeable hero though.'

'You are in agreement with its content then?' Charles was coddling Maurice in his arms who gurgled contentedly.

'It is beautifully written but I am also aware that it is taking a toll on your health. We have much to do here in the house, to keep it dry and free from damp. We continually suffer from colds. When you have submitted the next chapter we have do something about this. It is long overdue.'

'You have my word. The damp is not good for any of us, least of all for our children but first I have to attend to them.

Come, Cocky,' he called Rose by her nickname. She was at his side in the blink of an eye. 'Let us investigate the garden and see what we can find.'

'Damp?' repeated Fanny testily as Charles led the children to the front door. 'It is a veritable stream of water that comes through this house on a wet day!'

Charles was mortified when an anonymous review of '*Yeast*' in the Guardian accused him of heresy and conveying 'most pernicious doctrines'. Charles' response was free of malice.

'Life is too short and too full of hard work to give one time to hate and argue with people,' he commented to Fanny.

But Charles was well aware of their financial problems. His articles published in '*Politics for the People*' and now the serialisation of '*Yeast*' would not provide sufficient income to make repairs to the Rectory. His patron, Sir John Cope, despite living in luxury in his vast mansion at Bramshill Park, a short distance away, made it clear that he had no intention of spending money either on the church or the Rectory. It was soon apparent Charles had to find other ways to support his family. He was taking little respite from his work apart from a few hours of his favourite pastime of fishing. Fanny could see the gradual decline in her husband's health. His energy was torn in all directions. From conducting Sunday church services, to sitting with the ill and infirmed until late at night, to holding cottage meetings for those who were not able to walk to church, he devoted every spare hour to pursue his calling to improve the lot of his people. And like his hero in '*Yeast*', he was able to converse with everyone.

One afternoon, Henry Scrimshaw came to collect his wife for shopping in Aldershot. A neighbour, sympathetic to his arthritic condition had lent him a pony and trap. Henry Scrimshaw, late of the employment of Sir John Cope as a ledger clerk, was now unemployable. He had arthritis in both hips and could no longer make the long walk up to the large mansion of Bramshill Park. Sir John, in a small gesture of munificence, had allowed work to be sent down to his cottage but that was running out as Sir John had employed a bright lad from Aldershot. At forty, Henry Scrimshaw was out of work. Fortunately there were no little Scrimshaws' to provide for, so it was down to Ellen, his wife to keep money coming in to pay the rent.

As Henry sat in the cart waiting for his wife, he spotted the Reverend Kingsley outside the church, seated on a bench and deep in conversation with a young man. Henry noted he was better dressed than most round those parts but his coat and his leather breeches were heavily worn. His face was unfamiliar, and since Henry prided himself in knowing most of the local folk, he wondered where the stranger was from.

Catching Charles' eye, Henry called out, 'Afternoon Reveren' Kingsley,' and doffed his cap.

Charles stood up and invited his companion to do the same. The two men were still chatting animatedly as they walked over to Henry.

'Let me introduce you to Jim Hatchett, a wheel-wright from York Town.'

Henry raised his cap again as the young man nodded in return. He was slight in stature and his pinched face had a gravity about it that belied his years.

'This is a young man I met in unfortunate circumstances, when I was a child in Clovelly. Jim was a sweep's boy who came to my father's rectory and I had the indelicate task of removing him from the chimney, isn't that right, Jim?'

Jim nodded as a smile crossed his face. 'But that were a while back – twen'y years now. I was lucky-I got away from that work and now,' he said proudly, his stern features softening, 'I be makin' a good livin' not too far from 'ere. I heard about Reveren' Kingsley – word spread round these parts about his preachin' so I came to thank 'im for the good deed he did all those years past.' He stopped to draw breath.

'And p'haps I may come to join in with your service one Sunday morn?'

'You would be most welcome, Jim. I will look out for you.'

'Thank 'ee Sir. Well, I best be off. I have business in the area and I have a wife and family waitin' for me at home. Good day to you Reveren' and...?'

'Henry Scrimshaw.' Henry bent over and shook the man's hand. 'We are goin' in the direction of York Town if you would like a ride.'

Like many children of labouring folk, life was hard enough but for this man to have started life as a sweep's boy – that was one of the toughest. Henry was full of admiration for this young man who had moved on and made a successful living.

'Thank'ee, but I have to visit a farmer not far from 'ere. I shall be seeing you soon, Reveren'- at one of your services.'

'I hope so,' Charles said, 'and bring the family with you and join us for some refreshment at the Rectory after.' He waved goodbye as the man set off along the lane.

'Can I offer you a lift somewhere, Reveren?' Henry asked. It had not escaped his notice that of late the Reveren' appeared out of sorts.

Charles looked up at the sky. 'It looks like rain shortly -a lift to Eversley Cross might not go amiss.' As much as he loved striding out over the heath land, today he felt a four mile round trip would tire him unnecessarily and he also he had his novel to finish. Financial cut backs meant he had no horse and, as he had joked to Mr. Scrimshaw, his transport was now 'a horse with ten toes.'

Ellen Scrimshaw came bustling out of the Rectory gate and, clutching a wicker basket, clambered aboard the trap. Apologizing for keeping them waiting, she took her place on the seat behind. She adjusted her cloak and bonnet, all the while muttering about the nuisance of the pigeons eating the new bean shoots. Henry tapped the reigns, and the pony impatient to be off, struck out in a smart trot along the country lane. Charles and Henry passed an amiable twenty minutes discussing the music in the church. Henry agreed with the Reverend's idea of holding singing classes to improve the quality of music in the congregation.

'I think that'll go down well.' Henry voiced his opinion with an authoritative air. 'It'll make life easier for us all. We've a congregation with a keen spirit and numbers are up, thanks to you Reveren' but sometimes they get a bit lost with their timing in the hymns and that don't help me with keeping up, when they slow down.'

Charles smiled, bemused by Henry's problems as 'head musician' of the Church.

At the Eversley Common, Charles bid his companions 'good afternoon' and Ellen moved to sit next to her husband.

'Now there's a man with a good heart,' she said wistfully as Henry snapped the reigns of the pony.

'Ay, you're right, my love.'

'I could 'na wish for anywhere better to work, but I have to say, 'ees not 'imself. 'E looks worn out. 'E does more for the village folk in a week than that previous one did in two years-and more-but mark my words 'e can't carry on at that pace.'

Collapse

Mrs. Scrimshaw's predictions proved to be right. Three months later, Charles suffered a mental and physical collapse and his doctor advised complete rest. It was decided that he and the family should go to Ilfracombe in Devon for a period of recuperation. In his absence, the Reverend Kingsley senior offered to take the church services.

Fanny made sure he ate regular meals and Charles needed no encouragement to sleep for eighteen hours a day. Mansfield, who had heard about his setback quickly arranged to visit. He sat across from Fanny in the drawing room, drinking tea as he recovered from his long, tiresome journey from London. Mansfield had been shocked to learn of the illness of his closest friend and, seeing Fanny's close to tears on his arrival, was even further alarmed.

'Charles has done too much and now he is paying the price,' Fanny lamented, her face etched in concern. 'He will kill himself if this continues. Writing '*Yeast*' has taken its toll. He has been working long into the night with little sleep. Now he is so exhausted he cannot write, nor read and even talking tires him. We can only hope that rest and the sea air will aid his recovery.' She smiled at him fondly, grateful for his support. 'But I'm sure your company will do much to restore his spirits.'

Mansfield nodded. 'Charles wants to achieve so much in his life, yet gives so little thought to his own well-being. He is made of strong stuff, Fanny. He has an iron will. Rest assured, I will help you in any way I can. I don't need to tell you how much he means to me.'

He leant back in his chair and swept a hand though his dark wavy hair. Fanny couldn't help but admire his dashing looks. Absently, she refilled his cup with tea.

Opening the door to Charles' bedroom, Mansfield saw the prostrate figure lying on the bed. His vibrant and vociferous friend was quiet and unresponsive. Charles slowly turned his head and gave his friend a blank stare. His eyes showed a helplessness and despair Mansfield had never seen in him before.

After a week of rest and regular meals, and craving the sea air, Charles, accompanied by Mansfield, felt strong enough to take short walks along the coast. Slowly he regained his energy, particularly when his friend introduced him to mesmerism or healing by touch. When Fanny enquired what this was about, Mansfield enthused that this form of healing was popular in London circles. He seen it practiced and had studied it himself. He had learnt that the transfer of fluid energy from one to another could heal a patient. Fanny remained unconvinced.

After Mansfield's departure, Charles found solace and peace by the sea. The desolate beaches, the sound of the gulls crying and waves breaking, proved to be the perfect therapy for his return to health. So pleased was Fanny with his progress that, after a few weeks, she decided to leave Charles to recuperate, and return to Eversley with the children.

Ilfracombe was only forty miles away from Clovelly, the village of his childhood. Charles had so many happy memories there he resolved to revisit his old haunts. He was moved to tears of gratitude at the privileged and idyllic childhood he had shared with his younger brothers, Herbert, Gerald, Henry and his sister Charlotte. He reflected on the happy times he had spent with Herbert, and their mutual love of scavenging the seashore together.

That night he dreamt vividly of the storm that had taken so many lives of the fishermen when he was a young boy. He awoke the next morning in the small cottage he had rented and, filled with the emotion of his dream, he sat down and wrote *The Three Fishers* -

'Three fishers went sailing to the West
Away to the West as the sun went down:
Each thought on the woman who loved him best,
And the children stood watching them out of town:
For men must work, and women must weep,
And there's little to earn, and many to keep,
Though the harbour bar be moaning.

Three wives sat up in the lighthouse tower,
And they trimmed their lamps as the sun went down
They looked at the squall, and they looked at the shower,
And the night-rack came rolling up ragged and brown.
But men must work, and women must weep,
And the harbour bar be moaning.

Three corpses lay out on the shining sands
In the morning gleam as the tide went down,
And the women are weeping and wringing their hands
For those who will never come home to town;
For men must work, and women must weep,
And the sooner it's over, the sooner to sleep;
And goodbye to the bar and its moaning.'

Despite the comforting familiarity of Clovelly, his conscience reminded of more pressing matters to attend to. There was work to be done in his parish and he must return to take up the reigns of stewardship. To his dismay, Fanny had written to inform him a fever had broken out in the villages around Eversley. Cholera was rife in London and there was a fear this could spread to the counties. Charles returned posthaste to Eversley.

On his arrival, he received a letter from Mansfield, who was living in London, describing the cholera stricken area of Jacob's Island. Charles was incensed and determined to do something to help. By return of post, he arranged to meet Mansfield to see the conditions for himself. As he prepared to go up to London by train, Fanny was in a state of panic and despair.

'But Charles,' she implored, 'it is dangerous enough that you visit the hovels in this district with all the fever pervading the air. Please God you be spared from cholera. Your health is still fragile and you could be susceptible to such an illness.'

'Fanny my dear, do not fret. I will take the utmost caution.' Despite his assurances, he was nonetheless concerned. He had heard the cause of the disease was airborne and the fetid smells and air, especially around the River Thames, were the root of the problem. He recalled reading in '*The Times*', the dreadful outbreak in 1831 when seven thousand London souls had died and this current one, the medical people predicted, was going to double that number.

Fanny remained unconvinced about her husband's safety, and fixed Charles with one of her reprimanding stares, 'I shall have the clothes straight off your back when you return. And do not take anything of value with you. Leave your pocket watch behind. God forbid that you are robbed or set upon by vagrants.'

Charles accepted Fanny meant well in spite of her scolding him. He kissed her goodbye and reassured her that as he was doing God's work, he would be protected from any contagion.

Charles met up with Mansfield on Jacob's Island, a part of Bermondsey on the south bank of the Thames surrounded by filthy ditches. He had read the descriptions of the area in Charles Dickens, '*Oliver Twist* 'but even this did not prepare him for the sight and smells that ordinary citizens had to endure.

As they walked passed the slum dwellings, commonly known as rookeries, they were horrified at the state of the living conditions. Filth pervaded everywhere and the stench was as much as a man could bear. Mansfield remarked that it had the smell of a graveyard. The inhabitants, dependent on the River Thames for their water, were most at risk of cholera.

Charles saw with his own eyes that this was one giant sewer. Decomposing animals and rubbish floated in amongst the black raw sewage. To his horror, he watched as children scooped up pails of water from this stinking water.

He saw the destitution of hundreds of families living side by side in cramped hovels. Most of these were beyond repair with damp, leaking walls and roofs, broken windows and collapsing foundations. He had read that inside these rookeries, hard-up landlords would let out their rooms at night for a few pence a time and many who sought refuge there, slept side by side on dirty palliasses that had their own overcrowding problem of bed bugs and fleas. Charles and Mansfield made their way through back alleys where privies overran with human filth, and passageways also served as lavatories. In amongst this desperate environment, children and adults were dying of cholera.

The children and adults suffered continual diarrhoea and vomiting. It was a slow and painful death. Charles was grief-stricken as he heard their cries. In a gesture of desperation, he and Mansfield organized a water cart of casks of fresh drinking water from which the locals could draw water. At least those who were still free from the disease would not have to rely on fetid water from the Thames. But both men were well aware this was only a small gesture compared to the enormity of the problem.

* * *

Charles was in a dark place of despair. Back in Eversley he had mounted a campaign to source the problem of the polluted Thames. He found out who was responsible for ownership of the sewers in Bermondsey and, armed with information requested an interview with the Prime Minister of the day, Lord John Russell. He became heavily involved with sanitary reform believing that it was more important than fighting for the voting rights of the working classes. However it grieved him to learn that fourteen thousand had died of the cholera epidemic.

In order to highlight the conditions of the working classes in the city, he thrust himself into writing pamphlets and articles. Having visited the tailoring sweatshops in London, he was inspired to start a new novel, *'Alton Locke'*. The tailoring profession was similar to many of the conditions that the workers were subjected to. Some no more than children were shut away in airless attics, their wages were so poor, they had little option but to work all hours to pay their employers rent and a meagre ration of food. They were locked into a slavery system and '*Alton Locke*' vividly describes the horrors of a tailor's life.

At the same time '*Alton Locke*' was published, his novel '*Yeast*' was also re – published. To Charles's disappointment, both received many hostile reviews from a reading public who were angered by his honest portrayal of life in the 1840's. He had none of the thick skin of politicians about him and by nature was extremely sensitive to criticism. This together with money worries, his health declined and again he suffered another nervous collapse.

It was agreed that he should go away for a rest, and this time he went abroad for the first time to Germany with his brother, Henry and his parents. He missed Fanny so desperately he wrote to her constantly and wished for a second honeymoon on his return. Whilst there he was inspired to start another novel, *'Hypatia'* after visiting the Roman ruins at Trier.

Like his first novel, *'A Saint's Tragedy,'* this book had liberal amounts of impropriety. His depiction of life in the fifth century was at times brutal and in the preface to the book he recommended that 'the young and innocent would do well to leave it unread.' Nevertheless, it found favour in royal circles including Queen Victoria and Prince Albert, and despite his critics, his reading public grew. The voice of Charles Kingsley was becoming known as a candid and outspoken writer.

After an absence of three weeks, Charles returned to Eversley fully recovered. His congregation gave him a heartfelt welcome. The stand-in curate had been no match for the eloquence and firm conviction of their Reverend Kingsley. During his first service back, the musicians with the addition of another clarinetist, were so aroused by his sermon, spontaneously they played the tune, *'A good time a coming'*.

Later in the alehouse, Henry Scrimshaw struck up a conversation with the new clarinetist, Matthew Parker.

You should 'ave seen the look on the faces of those Brams'ill Park toffs in the front pew, when we struck up that tune! Did you see 'em? They were mightily put out.'

'I did, 'enry, but the look on Reverend Kingsley's face said it all. 'E was beamin' from ear to ear.'

They both chuckled as they supped their ale. Then remembering their Sunday duty was over they simultaneously loosened their collar studs. Sunday best was bearable for the service but after that the tight collar of the freshly starched shirt scratched their necks. They ran a finger along the inside of their collar and breathed a sigh of relief.

'Mrs. Scrimshaw says,' Henry continued now taking a somewhat superior attitude since his wife had first hand knowledge of all the comings and goings in the Rectory, 'she says that that there's an indecent amount of laughter in that 'ouse. Even on a Sunday, the Reveren' horseplays with those chil'ren and has them in shrieks of laughter. If he's not out in the garden with 'em showing 'em somethin' of nature, bird's nest or the like, 'e's indoors with 'em with the babby on his knee and readin' him an' Rose a fairy story. Those chil'ren have a magical time considerin' Mrs. Kingsley is poorly. She's taken to 'er bed agin with a heavy cold and don't care too much for noise. An' I 'ear, ' said Henry tapping his nose, 'they could be addin' to the family soon. Aye,' he said smiling and thinking of his own austere childhood, 'they're lovely littl' uns - always so polite and they 'ave no fear of chattin to us old uns.'

Henry took a sup of beer and looked up as the door of the alehouse opened.

'There's postman Jack -no doubt in 'ere for a quick livener after a hard week.' The two men exchanged nods with Jack.

He was not a church-going man and both Henry and John noted was not dressed in Sunday best but in a collarless shirt open at the neck and trousers tied at the waist with heavy string. His boots appeared well worn no doubt as a result of the many miles he walked a day.

'I 'ear he's not well pleased with the Reveren'.

'Why's that then?'

'He says his post bag 'tis now so full of letters 'e as to make two journeys to the Post Office just to deliver the Reveren's post. Letters comin' from all over the place- abroad too, he says judgin' by the stamps. He's certainly getting famous and not just in these parts.'

Having bought a pot of ale at the counter, Jack settled back on a trestle, seemingly content with his own company.

Henry started off again with his news. 'Mrs. Scrimshaw was sayin' that they have famous personages to stay at the Rectory now. There was this poet Tennyson who came last week and she 'ad to cook a special dinner of venison. Then there were a Mr. Ludlow and Mr. Maurice from Lunnon- them Christian Socialists. Poor Ellen, she gits all in a tither her cookin' ain't good enough for all these rich folk and she says the numbers of guests goes up all the time. Run off 'er feet she is at the weekends with all the visitors that pass through. Mind you, Charles eats less than his dawg, Dandy. Too busy writin' all those books of 'is. 'E tells me 'is pipe and 'is fishin are what keep 'im calm. He needs 'em from what I hear of his wife.' Henry chuckled. 'E gits 'is ead bitten off by 'er– he's always forgettin' somethin' or other.'

'Well don't you go decryin' that marriage. I see 'em act like two lovebirds. He's well soppy over her,' countered Matthew.

'No I weren't thinking 'bout say anythin' to anyone'. Henry was slightly peeved at his friend's rebuke.

Henry Scrimshaw was right about his news of Fanny's pregnancy. The following month she delivered their third child, daughter, Mary, St Leger was born.

TORQUAY WITH THE FAMILY

The following year was one of unusual activity in Eversley. Charles had watched with great enthusiasm, as the foundations of a school were laid not far from the Church. Through the summer its construction progressed. For Charles it was the realisation of a dream - that the children of his parish should receive a proper education. No longer would they have to suffer the small cramped room where lessons had been taught on a harsh basis of punishment by the strap with a disgruntled teacher.

By November, the school was open for business. Charles' elation at its complction howcvcr, was dampened by the heartbreak of Fanny suffering a miscarriage. Dreading another cold winter in the rectory, Fanny arranged to rent a house outside Torquay, along with the children, a governess for Rose and Maurice, and a nurse for baby Mary.

Charles stayed behind in Eversley. In his constant letter writing to her, he poured out his heart describing how much he missed her. He dreaded the days alone and without his family, the Rectory was 'quite ghastly and dead'. So concerned was he about Fanny's health and her current bout of bronchitis that his mind was constantly distracted as he waited for news from her. Fanny, depressed at their separation suffered equally.

Desperate to be re-united with her, he travelled by train to Torquay having left the business of Church services in the capable hands of a good curate friend. To his surprise, he arrived to find the family enjoying a lavish lifestyle in a grand eighteenth century mansion that was way beyond his budget.

He was now running two homes. Anxious not to exacerbate Fanny's delicate health, he declined to mention that their expenditure now far exceeded his income.

After a blissful reunion, he persuaded Fanny to take a breath fresh air and a walk on the beach with the children. It was a still, sunny day with a deep turquoise sky. Even for February the sun was warm.

'I must not be out for long,' Fanny said as she looped her arm through Charles' and hugged him closer. 'This cough still plagues me at night.'

Charles patted her gloved hand. 'I will not put you in any danger of a relapse, dear wife. The sun is surprisingly warm today and the sea air will do you no harm.' He breathed in its refreshing saltiness. 'I cannot tell you how much I have missed the sea air, and most of all you and the children. I now feel a complete human being again.' Charles smiled contentedly.

Maurice and Rose ran on ahead, stopping now and then to pick up shells. It reminded Charles of his childhood when he had spent time exploring the beach at Clovelly with his siblings. As they strolled along the seashore, Charles updated Fanny on the news from Eversley. The school was running without any hitches and had a full attendance. Fanny paused and looked into her husband's eyes that never failed to excite her with their piercing twinkle.

'My dearest, I'm afraid to tell you I have disappointing news,' she said guardedly.

Charles stopped walking and looked at her. 'What is it?' He was dreading the news that there were large outstanding bills he would be unable to pay.

'I have it on good authority that, despite your enthusiasm to preach whilst you are here, it is not to be. Word has got round of your reputation as the author of '*Alton Locke*' and '*Yeast*'. The clergy,' and here Fanny diluted the truth, 'they are a little hesitant.' She had heard from friends in Torquay that Charles was regarded as a dangerous thinker, a revolutionary. It was not only his books that gave cause for concern. His association with Frederick Maurice and the Chartists had also blackened his name. The pulpit doors were closed to him.

For several minutes, as they ambled along the shore in silence Charles remained deep in thought.

'Well,' he said finally. 'I have everything I could possibly wish for here with me now. I am content. If they chose to think of me in that regard, then I have no choice but to stay out of the pulpit for a few weeks and concentrate on my Natural History collection'.

But Charles was deeply hurt at this slight and any reassurance from Fanny remained unspoken as Rose and Maurice rushed up to their father with handfuls of shells. Deprived of his parish duties, Charles became engrossed in collecting marine life. He kept a daily journal and once more renewed his passion for the wonderful offerings to be found on the coastline. Later in the following year, he recorded all his findings in a book titled *'Glaucus'* documenting all the species of seashore life. Charles took great satisfaction in illustrating it himself.

* * *

Mrs. Scrimshaw was sitting at the kitchen table admiring her handiwork. With the Kingsley's departure it had given her ample opportunity to scrub every piece of furniture and saucepan in the kitchen as well as giving the range a good clean inside and out. It had taken days of elbow grease but it had been worth it. It was well overdue. With all the visitors she had fed over the past months the deep cleaning side of things had been overlooked. As she had said to her husband 'she hadn't had the time to turn around'.

Emily had taken a holiday to visit her parents in Essex so it was left Mrs. Scrimshaw to hold the fort. She picked up the letter delivered that morning from the Reverend Kingsley and read the four pages of neat handwriting. The family, having enjoyed the delights of Torquay had now moved to Bideford where the Reverend was starting on a new book. Sadly though, Mrs. Kingsley still had not returned to good health.

She was alerted to the sound of familiar footsteps trudging up the path and Mr. Scrimshaw put his head round the door.

'Your carriage awaits my love. Are you ready?'

'Don't you give me none of that fancy talk, 'enry. You jus' take a look at these hands,' Mrs. Scrimshaw said stretching her arms out and turning her red roughened hands one way then another. 'They 'ave just spent the last two hours blacking the range and done more work than most, I can say,' And more than her husband's had done in a month she wanted to add but thought the better of it.

'It all looks like a new pin, my love,' commented Henry, anxious to please. 'Have you news from the Kingsleys'?' he asked seeing an opened letter on the table.

'Yes, they'll be away for a while yet. But the Reveren' will be coming back for a visit to Lunnon. He always say how he misses his home 'ere. 'E's fair fond of this house. But 'e also has a duty to be with his family. If you could write back to him this evenin' that would be only right. Your handwritin' is much better than mine ever was.'

'It'll be a pleasure.' It was the reason he had got the job at Bramshill Park as a ledger clerk. His employer had always commented on the excellence of his handwriting. 'You might be busy this evenin' anyhow,' he added.

'Ow come?'

'The 'ens 'ave just laid four eggs. You might wanta' make a rice puddin' for us supper.'

'Go on with you, I'll be puttin' m' feet up for a rest afore I get m' pinny back on agin, Henry Scrimshaw.'

Henry picked up the letter and tucked it into his jacket pocket. 'Lets lock up then and be away,' he said now wondering if he was going to enjoy a rice pudding he had been hankering for.

On the doctor's advice for Fanny's further recuperation, it was decided that the Kingsley family should extend their stay in Devon. Summer had arrived and home was now in Bideford where Fanny had rented an eighteenth century house with a large garden. Bideford had been an important base for the Elizabethan escapades with the Spanish fleet. Famous sea captains such as Drake, Raleigh, Hawkins, Grenville, Oxenham were all Devon men and it was here that Charles, close to their home waters, found the inspiration to start his new book- *'Westward Ho!'*

He wrote to Mansfield who was engaged in conducting experiments on benzol in a London laboratory, imploring him to come and stay, stating how much he missed his friend's company. Mansfield duly arrived from London and after a celebration supper they sat and talked until the hall long case clock chimed midnight.

Fanny came up with the idea of a picnic for the children, an outdoor activity that was becoming popular with the visitors to the seaside. She organized it meticulously, and the July day, as it turned out was as perfect as it could be. A warm summer breeze wafted across the River Torridge and the seabirds, wheeling in an azure blue sky, were in full cry. It was the quintessential summer's day.

The cook, hired to cater for the growing family and visitors, had produced what Charles could only describe as a feast fit for her Majesty the Queen. There were small chicken pies, raised beef pies, cooked ham and tongue and homemade bread, with local cheeses and tomatoes from the greenhouse. For the children she had made egg and cress sandwiches and cheese straws. A strawberry tart and Devonshire cream for dessert was packed in the hamper, along with bottles of homemade lemonade. This was all loaded onto a pony and trap alongside chairs for the grown-ups, fishing rods, shrimp nets and specimen bottles for any new discoveries they might find in the rock pools. The children were as excited about this as the promise of an outdoor feast.

Mansfield entered into the spirit of the outing, and much to the children's amusement, presented himself casually dressed in an open shirt and his trousers rolled up to his knees and an oversized sun hat perched at a jaunty angle. The two eldest children, Rose and Maurice clutched sketch books under their arms, and Rose made sure the pencil case and India rubbers were also included. Competition was growing between Rose, now ten and her brother, seven, who could impress their father the most with their drawings of shells and seaweeds. Charles mounted the front of the trap and held the reins of the pony.

'All aboard,' he cried. 'Now have we forgotten anything?' he asked with wry amusement as he turned to see the anticipation in the children's faces.

'No,' they announced loudly in unison.

'Well, I disagree,' Charles said relaxing the reins. 'I think we have forgotten one very important little person.'

Fanny looked around her. With young Mary nestled in her arms, Maurice and Rose, wriggling impatiently behind, and Mansfield sitting between the two, there appeared to be no-one missing.

Charles jumped down from the trap and bounded up the steps to the house. In a minute he was out again carrying Dandy, his beloved dog, in his arms.

'Oh Dandy,' exclaimed the children. Charles leant over the cart and handed him to Rose. Dandy wagged his tail excitedly and licked her cheeks, relieved that he hadn't been left behind.

Winding through the country lanes, the journey to the beach from Bideford took over an hour, bumping and lurching over the potholes. Lusty singing led by Charles presented a merry picture to passers-by as the pony carried its happy company along. Even Fanny felt her spirits revive at the prospect of a day with her family. So often, Charles was absorbed in his work she was left to her own devices.

As soon as they arrived, the children were eager to cool down in the sea. It was still an hour before noon but the long sandy beach had few visitors. Mansfield, following instructions from Fanny, was quick to make camp for the day. The children wasted no time in racing down to the water and paddling cautiously in the cold waves. Charles set about tethering the pony under a shady tree, some distance away, whilst Fanny having settled two-year-old Mary, who had dozed off on the journey, poured glasses of refreshing lemonade for everyone.

It was a typical family day out. The children played in the sand and splashed in the shallows, with Dandy barking nervously at the waves. The grown-ups sat in chairs and exchanged idle talk. Fanny was now growing more relaxed in the company of the two men. Despite their closeness, she realized how much Mansfield revered her husband. She and Mansfield were both of the same minds.

Having rallied the children, Charles led the seashore party, along with Mansfield, to the nearest rock pools where a whole fascinating world revealed itself. Even though they had made many such explorations with their father, it never failed to excite Rose and Maurice, especially if they made a new discovery. Whether it was a fossil, a sea-worm or a sea anemone, they would catalogue them all for future reference.

Over lunch, six healthy appetites soon demolished most of the food that cook had wrapped so beautifully in brown paper with string. Now replete and, relieved to have a respite from the sun under a large umbrella, Fanny and Charles rested whilst Mansfield energetically built turreted sandcastles with the children.

He was so thankful to be part of such a close family and he treasured the day and the memories it held. Life was so different in London, with the stifling heat of summer and, despite the prospect of new discoveries with his experiments, he still longed for a family life of his own. He had no shortage of admirers, and as Charles assured him, he would be wed by this time next year and it would be his greatest honour to marry him and his new bride.

Mansfield was thinking these thoughts as he packed away the remaining picnic items for the journey home. He would double his efforts to obtain a divorce from his young wife who had deserted him. A family was now what he wanted more than anything.

'Uncle Charles, could you pass those bottles?' asked Maurice pointing to the basket of sample bottles that had been filled with sea water and now housed their finds of the day.

By the time the pony and trap pulled up outside their front door, all three children were asleep and later, Charles declared it had been a magical day shared with the people he loved most in the world.

WESTWARD HO!

After Mansfield's departure, Charles set about writing '*Westward Ho!*' with renewed vitality. In his study overlooking the lush gardens he was at his most inspired, knowing that at the port a short distance away, three galleons had set sail to defend their country and sovereign, Queen Elizabeth 1, from Spanish and Catholic rule. Charles' imagination was further set alight with the plundering of the Spanish colonies in the Caribbean.

The hero of his new novel was a high-spirited fifteen-year-old, Amyas Leigh who followed Francis Drake on a gold-seeking expedition to Venezuela. The ship then sailed to Barbados and although Charles had never travelled to the birth country of his mother, he was not short on imagination to describe the island and the tropics. He eagerly shared these passages with Fanny.

Fanny was relaxing in the garden, aware that Charles, despite the holiday atmosphere, was hard at work and not to be disturbed. In the late afternoon, she was relieved to see Charles appear. Fondly she watched him as he strode across the lawn, manuscript in one hand and pipe in the other and Dandy following a few feet behind. Hopefully he would tell her his business of the day was finished. Fanny put down the book she was reading and at once saw the fire and enthusiasm in his eyes. She knew only too well this meant the book was going well.

Charles leant over to kiss her and sat down on an old rattan chair.

'So husband, what have you brought to show me?' Her eyes lit up with interest.

He held up the inky scrawl of his manuscript still drying on the page. He spoke quickly, the surge of creativity still in his mind.

'It's not such an easy task to describe a country one has never visited.' He fixed Fanny with one of his engaging stares. 'One day, I hope we will travel to the West Indies. But as you know, Mother has often spoken of her childhood there.' He turned to his pages. 'The ship is approaching Barbados,' he explains, then reads from his manuscript – *'It is a long blue bar between the crimson sea and golden sky. The crew who were sick, crawled out of their stifling hammocks; strong men fell on their knees and gave thanks to God and all eyes stretched towards the far blue cloud, fading as the sun went down.'* As the ship sailed on, they approached the southern shore of Barbados and manoeuvred into the bay.'

He continued, '*All eyes were eagerly fixed on the low wooded hills which slept in the moonlight, spangled by fireflies with a million dancing stars; all nostrils drank greedily the fragrant air which swept from the land, laden with the scent of a thousand flowers, all ears welcomed, as a grateful change for the monotonous whisper and lap of the water, the hum of insects, the snore of tree toads, the plaintive notes of sea fowl which fill a tropic air with noisy life.*' Charles looked up at Fanny expectantly, his eyes questioning hers.

'You have described it beautifully, Charles. I can imagine the island perfectly. This book will be such a change from those about life with all its depressing poverty and unrest. I'm sure it will be well received by the public for its daring adventures.'

'Thank you dearest, your comments mean so much to me.' Charles gave her one of his wide smiles. 'Now I must return to start the next chapter whilst it is still fresh in my mind.'

'Please stay and have tea with me in the garden. The children haven't seen you since breakfast.'

But Charles jumped out of his chair, and, calling to Dandy, marched across the lawn, the pages of his manuscript fluttering in his hand and leaving a trail of pipe smoke behind him. 'There is more to be done yet.' He called.

Towards the end of the book he recounts the battle off the Isle of Wight where the English pursue the enemy down the English Channel. The Spanish have no choice but to retreat.

"And so, with variable fortune, the fight thunders on the livelong afternoon, beneath the virgin cliffs of Freshwater; while myriad sea-fowl rise screaming up from every ledge and spot with their black wings, the snow white wall of chalk; and the lone shepherd hurries down the slopes and gazes trembling upon glimpses of tall masts and gorgeous flags piercing at times the league broad veil of sulphur smoke which welters far below.'

* * *

To Charles and Fanny's delight, '*Westward Ho!*' was published to great acclaim and much to Charles relief, his financial problems were eased considerably. From then on every publisher was keen to get their hands on his work and it was this novel that established him as one of the great Victorian novelists. He was now socializing in London with famous names such as Charles Dickens who he dined with in Belgravia. Life had finally turned around for him. However he was to learn that with the good times invariably comes the bad.

After his visit to Bideford, Charles received a letter from Mansfield.

My dear Charles,

I thank you for your congratulations on the success of my work with benzol.

I can proudly report that the results of my work will be on display at the Paris Exhibition next year. We are continuing in earnest with the experiments and are on the point of a breakthrough, which is exciting not only for me but the world!

As a close friend I have to confess to you, I still long for the home life, that I was a part of for a brief time with you this summer. As for all the memories we have shared together-the wild times at university, the long hikes over moorland and coast, the fly-fishing –all these remain such important chapters in my life.

I still recognize that I am young enough to find fulfillment in a relationship and marriage. It is the loneliness that affects a bachelor such as myself. In the meantime, let us see more of each other. Come and visit me in London.

I congratulate you on the publication of 'Westward Ho!' No doubt it will bring you the financial considerations you richly deserve and will be most welcome with your young family to support.

Yours affectionately –

But Charles did not find the time to visit his friend in London that summer, an oversight he would always regret. Now back at Eversley, and facing another long cold winter, Fanny was restless and looking for a warmer residence. With these thoughts in mind she was occupied with her tapestry in the parlour when she was aware of Charles was standing at door, his face ashen white, and a letter in his hands. Hurriedly, she put her sewing aside.

'Charles, what has happened? You look as if you've had the most awful shock.'

Charles went to her and wrapped his arms around her. He broke into heavy sobbing on her shoulder.

Mansfield is dying.' His voice was fraught with grief.

Fanny stroked his hair as they held on to each other. She was in disbelief. Charles Mansfield was too young to die. He was thirty – five. He had a brilliant mind and a groundbreaking career ahead. He had so much to live for. After several minutes Charles regained his composure and sat down clasping his shaking hands in Fanny's.

'W...we cannot imagine the pain he is going through,' Charles stammered.

'What has happened?' Fanny squeezed his cold hands.

'He was working on his benzol experiments in a laboratory in London with a naptha still.'

* * *

As soon as Mansfield saw the naptha still in flames he knew he had to extinguish it immediately before it exploded and the room caught fire. But how? Instinctively he ran towards the window and he threw it open. He grabbed the still from his young assistant who was now fighting off the flames and had collapsed on the floor. Another second and he would have thrown the burning container out into the deserted snowy street below. The explosion of the liquid benzol caught Mansfield in the face, blinding him temporarily. Then he felt the burning on his chest and arms. Red hot, devouring his clothes and his flesh. It was too late.

He was aware of his hair alight and its scorching smell as the flames rapidly ate into his scalp. Slapping his arms, he tried to extinguish the flames. Blinded, he ran out of the room. Mansfield felt his way down the stairs until he was out onto the street. An old woman hobbling past looked on in disbelief at the figure engulfed in flames. She reckoned it had to be a figment of her imagination. Her over-indulgence of gin was getting the better of her.

Mansfield fell onto the thick slushy snow and rolled over and over until he extinguished the last of the flames. He lay there gasping. How had he come to this? In horror, he surveyed his body. His clothing was burnt off. He was looking at raw flesh on his arms, his stomach and legs. Through blurred vision he tried to make out anyone who was close by. He could just make out the disappearing figure of the old woman. 'Someone help me,' he screamed in agony to a deserted street.

Choking back the pain, he struggled to stand. Lurching from one side of the street to the other, his instinct took him towards Maida Avenue, close to the Regents Canal. There he could find help in the busy streets of people and traffic. It was the longest and loneliest journey Mansfield had ever made. After what seemed an age, he reached the street junction. He heard people's voices. Through a blur, he saw carriages and heard the sound of their wheels ploughing through the deep slush. Passers by looked on in disbelief as they saw the blackened and charred body staggering towards them.

'It's a ghost – it's the walking dead!' someone screeched and terrified ran off down the street. Mansfield collapsed onto the pavement. Women shrunk back, too shocked to help. Two men knelt over him.

'Get a carriage. This man needs the hospital now!' one of them cried out in desperation.

Within minutes they had gently lifted the blackened body into a passing carriage. Mansfield cried out and moaned out with every small jolt as it made its way to the nearest hospital.

Wrapped in bandages and heavily dosed on morphine, Mansfield lay in hospital for ten long agonizing days. Charles received a letter from John Ludlow on the ninth day.

'I must see him,' Charles informed Fanny having come to terms with the dire circumstances of the accident.

'But if he's unconscious, Charles, there is nothing you can do,' Fanny said gently.

'I have to say goodbye to my friend. The doctors are not expecting him to survive.'

Charles took a train to Waterloo and a hackney cab to the Middlesex Hospital. His face was grave, his walk that of a defeated man. As he sat at Mansfield's bedside, only then did he realize the true extent of his injuries. He failed to recognize his friend. His normally vibrant, blue eyes were closed, swollen and black, his eyebrows and eyelashes gone. The rest of his head and body were covered in bandages.

'Oh dear God. To see you suffer so my dearest friend, it is more than my heart can bear. You have been and always will be a true brother to me,' Charles stammered, failing to keep a steady voice. He was no stranger to death. He had seen it many times but he had never seen suffering like this. Mansfield's eyelids flickered. His lips, or what remained of them, moved imperceptibly. Like the suffering he witnessed in his parish, there seemed no justification for this. And for Mansfield to die in such agony was beyond his comprehension.

Charles prayed aloud convinced that Mansfield could hear him. The bandaged hand gave a small movement. Charles bid his friend farewell and promised they would meet again in the next life. Mansfield succumbed to his injuries that night. For weeks after, Charles could not reconcile himself to his death. It was the passing of a brilliant mind and the cruellest way to die.

A CHILDREN'S BOOK

To Fanny's relief, following the publication of '*Westward Ho!*' the continual worry of household finances was lifted and she wasted little time in finding a new residence for the family. Having enjoyed the summer in Devon and now restored to good health, she suggested to Charles they move out of the Rectory for the winter months. Besides, she reasoned, her husband had become an influential member of English society and his residence should reflect that. Charles succumbed to her pleas. He could not disagree with her argument that a further bout of bronchitis would deplete her health yet again.

Charles had tried in vain to persuade Sir William Cope, successor to Sir John Cope, patron of the Church, to build a new rectory on higher ground and away from the streams and ponds of the existing one. It was a losing battle. Sir William was of the opinion it had served the clergymen well in the past and besides, it would need a considerable amount of funds to replace it.

Fanny chose a house a few miles away from Eversley in Swallowfield. Farley Court was a considerable jump in their living standards. It was a handsome Georgian house standing in its own grounds with an impressive drive that could accommodate a vast number of visiting carriages. Its grandeur was surpassed only by the views from the house and Charles was thankful that despite Fanny's lavish choice, it was only a short distance away from his Church.

The house was alive with the buzz of workmen coming and going with baskets of household items and furniture being moved in through the grand entrance hall. The children were running around exploring their new house and bedrooms of which they were plenty to choose from. Mrs. Scrimshaw and her husband were working like pack horses, labouring with the children's trunks filled with toys, and suitcases full of linen and clothes. Emily was busy stoking up the fires ready for the Kingsley's arrival.

Despite all the hard work of moving into Farley Court, Mrs. Scrimshaw was elated. She couldn't wait to get into the vast kitchen and try out the new range that, she informed her husband, was large enough to cater for a royal banquet–not that she wished for such an event to be put upon her.

Charles carried his boxes of manuscripts up to his new study and tried hard to share the enthusiasm and excitement of those around him. Although he was pleased for his family, he would miss the intimacy of his study at Eversley, his hammock that provided such a pleasant resting place, the cry of foxes at night, and the familiar call of the barn owl during his nocturnal bouts of writing. The Rectory was his true home and not even this grand house could surpass it.

The family settled soon into Farley Court and apart from a few disastrous burnt meals from Mrs. Scrimshaw, who had underestimated the cooking temperatures of the new range, all was well. Fanny was in her element in the spacious and elegant house and wasted no time inviting her sisters to stay. They could not deny that life had worked out exceedingly well for Fanny and finally, they gave their approval to the marriage.

One evening after the constant comings of goings of visitors, Charles and Fanny were enjoying a quiet Sunday evening with the children in the drawing room. Dandy was stretched out full length in front of the fire, one eye on his master. Charles, with his usual exuberance, read a bedtime story to the children. He chose *Tanglewood Tales*' by Nathaniel Hawthorne. As he finished the book he waited for the children's reaction. Maurice had fallen asleep on his mother's lap and Rose professed it was not to her liking.

'In that case, I think another book is in order,' Charles declared.

'Shall I go and find a more interesting one, Papa? Rose asked. She had inherited her father's passion for learning.

'No my dear Cocky, I intend to write one. There seems to be a dearth of children's literature and a jolly good fairy tale would not go amiss. What do you think Fanny?'

'I think it an excellent idea. You have such a vivid imagination, and I'm sure the children would love that,' said Fanny stroking Maurice's forehead.

Rose clapped her hands. 'Oh please father, you're *almost* famous now and a children's book will be so exciting. You tell stories so well. *And* we can have our very own storybook written by our Papa.'

'Hmm *'almost'* might be a good description,' Charles replied. And both he and Fanny burst out laughing.

'I shall waste no time then. Almost is not good enough. I'm sure my family would want a *famous* husband and father.' Charles got up from his battered leather armchair that he had insisted come with him from the rectory.

'I have an idea already. I shall re-tell the Greek fairy tales and it shall be a Christmas present to the children. In fact, time is of the essence I shall make a start this evening. Come on Dandy. It's time for work.'

Dandy leapt up from his warm spot by the fire and stood to attention. Charles kissed 'Cocky' and Maurice goodnight and strode out of the drawing room to his new study.

The result of his efforts was a book called *'The Heroes.'* This was his first children's book and although written at great speed, it was met with huge success when published at Christmas. Charles divided it into three sections and dedicated each one to his children, Rose, Maurice and Mary. Charles illustrated the book with sketches he had made previously. It quickly became a classic and was reprinted many times.

Spurred on by this and the success of '*Westward Ho*', Charles set about writing another novel. *'Two Years Ago'* was a modern classic, its subject, the Crimean War, that two years previously had torn Europe apart and had left a lasting impression on Charles. This time Macmillans, his publisher, paid him a thousand pound advance. Finally Charles could enjoy the rare luxury of financial freedom.

The entire Kingsley household, apart from Fanny were pleased to be back at the Rectory in Eversley for the winter months. It had been three years since they had spent or in Fanny's words 'endured' a winter there. Now back in his familiar study and garden, Charles was for the most part content and his Sunday services were proving to be even more popular.

On this particular Sunday, there was a larger than normal bustle outside the church at Eversley. Horses and carriages were lined up outside the Church gate and the locals were left wondering what important event was taking place. Charles was equally curious. As he prepared for the service in the vestry he heard the clatter of swords and the marching of boots on the stone tiles of the aisle. Glancing up from his sermon notes, he was taken aback to see the smart uniformed officers from Aldershot taking their places in the pews behind the regular parishioners. Charles was thrilled at the sudden influx of newcomers. For the first time the Church was full to capacity.

He walked up the aisle and was about to start the service when his eye caught the head of a young boy peering around the porch door. Poorly clothed and from his appearance, ill fed and unwashed, Charles halted at the transept steps and turned towards him.

Without a second glance at the packed pews now awaiting the service, he walked towards the boy and invited him in. Behind him were four smaller children. They followed the eldest boy into the Church. Charles took him by the hand and led the group to a pew at the front. Wide–eyed with fright, the other youngsters followed as they felt the icy stares of the congregation upon them. The adults in the pew shuffled up to make room for the new arrivals. Charles gave them his widest smile.

'Welcome to our Church. Young or old, all are welcome here.'

Charles opened his Prayer Book and read the opening of the Matins service.

'This is the day the Lord has made. Let us rejoice and be glad of it. Our opening hymn is number 342, '*Praise the Lord The King of Heaven.*'

During the hymn, Charles marvelled at the size of his congregation and how different it was to world-weary few who had come to his first service as a curate. Inwardly he gave a prayer of thanks. Sir William Cope, owner of Bramshill Park, sang proudly in his superior manner, despite his eyes wandering disapprovingly towards the youngsters. The officers from Aldershot sang so earnestly their voices filled the church with rejoicing.

Those who had arrived from outlying districts in their smart carriages were eager to hear the preacher that so much had been written about. The regular churchgoers shifted in their seats at the unexpected arrival of the red uniforms and the well-to-do visitors. The women self-consciously adjusted the ribbons on their bonnets and the men buttoned up their jackets and stretched themselves to their full height. The three musicians, including Mr. Scrimshaw played their hearts out, as Mrs. Scrimshaw looked on, immensely proud her husband was playing for such a respected congregation. And, as she later remarked to Henry, she had never seen so much finery 'what with the all those fancy feathers on the ladies bonnets and the silk dresses and all that m'larkey, it looked like they were dressed for the Palace not our simple church.'

After the service and much handshaking from the officers and an invitation to dine with them at Aldershot, Charles' attention was drawn to the little family of children. They loitered in the churchyard looking lost in amongst all the grown-ups.

'Well, little ones, it is good to see you so keen to join in with the adults,' Charles remarked as he bent down to talk with them.

'Please Sir, we weren't meant to be 'ere for that,' said the eldest, scraping his worn boots on top of one another and examining them with a seriousness that belied his years. 'Me ma sent me to ask you to come. And then you took us into the Church and thur were nuffin we could do,' he faltered in tears.

'Ah then', Charles said straightening up. 'You poor little mites sat through one of my long sermons all so that you could ask me to see your ma.'

'Yessir'.

'And what does your Ma want?'

'She's right poorly and coughin' and can't feed us, nor the babby.' Charles felt his heart melt as he saw the helplessness in the children's eyes.

'I will come immediately, Let me change into my boots – in the Rectory over here and I shall come straight away. Follow me.'

As Charles strode through the side-gate to the house, he noted a few of the wealthy visitors stayed behind chatting to each other before alighting their carriages. The ladies waved silk-gloved hands and the gentlemen removed their top hats and bowed at Charles.

'I see I have made a good impression on the newest members of our congregation,' he commented as he led the children into the Rectory. 'Have you breakfasted today?' he asked.

The four little ones shook their heads and their eyes looked expectantly at Charles. 'No, I thought not. You look hungry enough to devour a lion.'

Fanny came to meet them in the hall. She had stayed at home as young Mary had developed a cold that she blamed on their return to Eversley. All three children had enjoyed good health during their time at Farley Court. Now it was back to the usual childhood illnesses.

'Charles,' she called. Then she saw the little brood surrounding him. 'Who have we here?"

'Fanny, would you give these hungry little people a glass of milk and some bread whilst I change into my boots? And as it's Sunday, a large scraping of beef dripping would not go amiss.'

The children gawped at the smart lady wearing a cream, shiny dress and a pearl necklace around her long smooth neck. To their naive minds she was like a princess.

'Come with me, children,' she said smiling. 'Cook is back from Church and preparing lunch but I'm sure she will find something tasty for you to eat.'

A short while later, the four children were beaming contentedly. They had a full belly and were relishing the last remnants of a strawberry sponge that had followed the bread and dripping.

Charles set off with the children. In his hand he clutched his sturdy medicine bag that was part of his daily accessory when he visited his 'patients'. He had also scooped up some eggs that were freshly laid by his hens. They walked up past the Mount and the children directed him towards the heath land now covered in yellow spring furze. They were 'heathers' children and newly arrived. A party of working folk and neighbours were helping them build a cottage of sorts. Roughly hewn timbers and walls of wattle and daub supported a scantily made thatch roof. A newly made door lay on the ground beside the entrance where a man was busily hammering nails into it. He stopped as he saw the group arrive.

'Where you bin laddie?' he demanded of the eldest.' Your ma's been right worried about thee.' Seeing the Reverend in his Church vestments, he speedily removed his cap and stuffed into his pocket.

'Mornin' Sir, sorry to bring you out 'ere but we can't afford no doctor and word got round you're as good as one. And my missus is right poorly'.

From the inside of the dwelling Charles could hear a hacking cough, and the weak crying of a baby.

'Let me see her.' Charles stepped towards the open entrance of the cottage.

In the dark interior he could make out a woman lying on a bed with a pillow and blanket that had seen better days. Although damp, the one room was not cold since the sun streamed through the open door. A young woman lay shivering with a baby wrapped up in her arms. Her voice was hoarse and weak.

'You've come.' She gave a huge sigh of relief. 'I hope you can 'elp us. Me babby is in a worse state than me'self.

Charles touched the forehead of the baby that had a worryingly bluish skin. It was burning up with fever. The woman had the same tinge to her complexion and was hot despite her shivering.

'How old is your infant?'

'Six month is our Ben.' She whispered as another attack of coughing hit her and she struggled for breath.

'What do you think is makin' 'em so bad?' asked the father standing a distance behind him.

'How long have they been like this?' Charles turned towards him.

'Just a few days. I thought with this warmer weather they would be gettin' better but they just worsen.'

Charles opened his bag and reached for his well-used bottle of medicine that contained garlic, onion juice and amber oil.

'This will soothe your cough but I strongly recommend a doctor for the infant. In the meantime, I would suggest a warm damp cloth around his neck to loosen the cough.' Charles had seen this with his own children and croup was a common illness with young infants.

'But we can afford no doctor,' pleaded the father. 'that's why we sent for thee.'

'Never mind that. I will make sure the bill is settled. You will need to go into Eversley first thing in the morning and ask for Doctor Samuels. He will attend straightaway. A cool poultice will also assist your wife's fever and make her some tea with wild thyme and comfrey, if you can find some.

'Ay,' said the father. 'We'll go and hunt for some o' that.'

Charles reminded himself to use his bottle of gargle and scrub his hands with soap and hot water as soon as he returned home. It wouldn't do to pass anything on to his children.

Later the following afternoon, he received a visit from Doctor Samuels. On reflection, it was fortunate that as Mary had sufficiently recovered from her cold, Fanny had taken the family out to a children's birthday party.

'Come in,' welcomed Charles as he showed the doctor into his study.

'I will get straight to the point of my call. I'm sorry to be the bearer of bad news, Reverend Kingsley.' The doctor, an older man of fifty and heavily whiskered like Charles, bore a serious countenance. 'The family you visited yesterday-the mother and child have diphtheria. This is the first case I have seen of it in these parts but I have it on good authority, there is an outbreak of it spreading through the counties.'

Charles sat down hurriedly in his leather armchair. His bushy eyebrows furrowed so deeply they almost met in the middle. His dark eyes spoke of the gravity he felt. Wild thoughts raced through his head. Not only were the mother and baby in danger of dying from this disease, it was also infectious. Had he put his own family at risk?

'I assumed, wrongly so, that it might be a case of croup with the infant and a bronchial illness for the mother,' Charles conceded.

'I have treated them as best as I can. A day or so will tell if they get through this but I don't hold out much hope for the young one. He is getting weaker by the hour. And then of course there are the rest of the children. If they catch it, there could be a very sad outcome. As a precaution, I have arranged for them to stay at a relative's nearby.

Charles drummed his fingers on the armrest of the chair. 'How infectious is it?'

The doctor could see the worry written across Charles' face.

'With regard to yourself- you are fit and healthy. You should escape Reverend. But it is a risk we all take when dealing with the sick. One is always at risk.'

'It's my children I think about,'

'Of course and naturally we have to be very vigilant at times like this. The outbreak of cholera was serious enough. Now we have diphtheria which is worse by the very fact that it is contagious.'

Having settled the bill for the treatment of the family and given the doctor extra money to attend to them the next day, Charles went straight to his beloved Church. As he knelt before the altar, he prayed to God for mercy that the children be spared and, that he and his family did not fall prey to this new disease. He decided it would be fruitless to inform Fanny of this latest outbreak of illness.

A few days later, mother and baby were buried together in a pauper's grave. Events such as these affected Charles deeply. With his innate sensitivity, he thought himself inadequate in helping the sufferings of the sick. Too often, he would bury a labourer who had barely reached a score and five.

But by devoting his spare time to lecturing and writing letters on sanitary reform, he believed this was a way he could help the working classes improve their hygiene standards and avoid the diseases prevalent at the time. By cleaning up the streets and back yards of human filth and improving the basic sewage system, only then, could the worst parts of the cities and towns hope to improve.

These problems weighed heavily on his mind and, as always, demanding too much of himself, and plagued by the dissatisfaction of his work, he fell into another depression. Further criticism was voiced at his book *'Westward Ho!'* despite it selling well. His critics were quick to point out that he moralised too much. Nor did he fit into the stereotype of an Anglican churchman, his sympathies being with the working classes and the Chartist movement. Charles had reached another low ebb in his life and it was at times like this he missed the support of his friend, Charles Mansfield more than ever.

A New Addition

Fanny was only too aware of her husband's melancholy and tried hard to ease him through these episodes. Despite finishing a book of poetry, Charles was struggling to start another novel. She hoped her news would cheer his low spirits

She went to his study one morning where he had spent many hours of late. 'Attending to his post and starting another new book' was his excuse but his remoteness worried her. He was hunched over his desk with his back to her.

'Dearest, are you sleeping?' she asked as she rested her hands on his shoulders. 'You haven't been fishing in a while. Why don't you give yourself some time to enjoy the river like you usually do when....'

'When I'm like this, wrapped in despair?' His voice was barely a whisper and he was lost in thought. 'What am I to do, Fanny?'

Slowly Charles turned to her and Fanny could see the anguish in his face that accompanied one of his depressions. He had visibly aged in the last few weeks. His eyelids were heavy and the dark shadows under his eyes emphasized his pallid complexion. He looked past her to the view of his beloved garden. Even that failed to lift his mood. The morning was dark for April and a heavy mist hung over the fields. The gloomy sky threatening rain only served to enhance his heaviness of heart. Imitating his master's low mood, Dandy was slumped on the arm of a chair. Both Fanny and Charles were aware that Macmillan, his publisher, had offered Charles two thousand pounds for his next novel but the year had passed without a result.

'I try so hard- yet fail so miserably. We now have six deaths in the parish. Diphtheria has taken four more infants and two adults with possibly the same disease. The schoolmaster is even thinking of closing the school until it is under control.' Fanny rubbed his shoulders in the endearing way he enjoyed.

'You cannot do any more than you already do. You risk your own health by visiting these sick people. You attend to them on their deathbeds and look after those who are left without family. What more can you ask of yourself?'

Charles pointed to a stack of papers before him. 'Heavens knows what will become of me. I have made three attempts to start a new novel and each time I look into an abyss of nothing. I feel as if I have spun my silk, Fanny. How will we manage if I can't write? I have already made the decision to cut back on our finances and let the curate go.' He stroked Fanny's hand that lay on his shoulder.

'Charles, may I remind you that you have now a packed church full on a Sunday? Remember the drab soulless Church you inherited? You receive letters from admirers all over the globe. You have this innate gift. You can relate to all your fellow men, no matter they are common labourers or aristocracy. And,' she added 'your books are selling well.'

'They are not achieving what I hoped for. I want them to stand out as beacons of change and hope and to help reform the piteous state of our working classes.'

Fanny sighed and wondered how he would receive the news she was about to impart.

'Above everything else we have each other. You have a beautiful family. Maurice is doing well at school. Rose shows great intelligence and she has your sensitivity that becomes her. Little Mary is doing well with her studies. You should be so proud of yourself and your family besides all the work you do outside.'

'And my beautiful wife.' Charles took her hands and squeezed them tightly. He gave her a wan smile. 'Whom I declare has grown a little buxom of late,' and his hands went to her stomach. 'It becomes you - but then I have always found your body irresistible.'

'Dearest husband, there is a reason for it and it is not Mrs. Scrimshaw's new-found passion for baking fruitcakes.' Charles looked up and saw her flirtatious smile.

'Why are you looking so pleased with yourself?' he asked. 'Have you some news to cheer your weary husband?'

'That depends. It means you will have to work harder to provide more...'

'Provide for what?'

Charles jumped up out of his chair and clutched her waist. 'You've put on weight and I have to work harder, can only mean one thing!'

Fanny enveloped him with her arms and whispered in his ear. 'Darling Charles, the impossible has happened. I'm with child again.'

He drew back. 'But is it not dangerous for your health at your age?'

Fanny laughed. 'It's not impossible for a woman of forty to give birth, you know.'

'Yes but ... you have a delicate constitution...we must make sure everything is done for you to keep you strong. A new addition to our family! God has blessed us again.'

His dark mood forgotten, he kissed her and stroked her flushed cheeks. Even Dandy stirred from his sleep and yapped vociferously.

Mrs. Scrimshaw tapped at the study door. She had over heard the merriment coming from the study and couldn't wait to join in with the good news.

'Mrs. Kingsley, Excuse me ma'am. I've a batch of ginger biscuits just baked and as you couldn't face breakfast this mornin', I wondered if you and the Reveren' would like some with your morning refreshment?'

It was an excuse to be a part of the news she had suspected for a while now. Both she and Emily had noticed subtle changes in Fanny that were reminiscent of her previous childbearing time. Fanny had lost her taste for coffee and the sight of breakfast made her queasy. She was also sleeping more than usual. Mrs. Scrimshaw was desperate for confirmation.

'Mrs. Scrimshaw-we have good news.' Fanny said.

'I know' ma'am.' she said, unable to contain herself, 'You're gonna hev another babby.'

Charles and Fanny broke into laughter. 'God bless us all,' exclaimed Charles, slipping his arm around his wife's waist. 'Mrs. Scrimshaw, I do believe you know my wife better than I do.'

* * *

It was six years since the birth of Mary, and despite her age, Fanny came through her pregnancy successfully to give birth to a son, Grenville Arthur later that year. Life at the Rectory centred on the new baby. Mrs. Scrimshaw having had another one of her premonitions that the new arrival was to be a boy had knitted a little blue suit for him. Emily had bought him a rattle and a small stuffed bear. Most of the parishioners, even those living some distance away, sent gifts. Bunches of wild flowers and sachets of dried lavender (to help 'babby' sleep) arrived on the doorstep. Sir John Cope sent over a filigree silver christening mug. The neighbourhood was thrilled at the Rector's news. It was a feat in itself that the Reverend's wife should give birth at such a 'mature age and to have a healthy 'little 'un' into the bargain,' the women commented.

Mary and Rose who were receiving their education at home, spoiled and fussed over Grenville. Maurice, now a student at Wellington College couldn't wait for the holidays to return home and spend time with his new brother. To add to all the celebrations, a letter arrived with a prominent Buckingham Palace insignia on the envelope. Curiosity got the better of Charles as he opened it at the breakfast table. Fanny who had now returned to full health was eager to learn of its contents.

'Well? 'she asked. 'What does it say?'

Charles put the letter down and beamed at her. 'It's from Albert, the Prince Consort,' he announced, scarcely able to believe his words.

'And?'

'He has read my book,' *The Saint's Tragedy.*' He has also enjoyed '*Glaucus*' and '*Two Years Ago.*'

'So what does he say?' Fanny was growing impatient with her husband as he deliberately toyed with its contents.

Charles jumped up from the table, letter in hand and was at Fanny's side before she could ask another question.

'See here. He very much enjoyed the books and furthermore, he *-and* the Queen- and have invited me to preach before them at Buckingham Palace.'

Fanny read and re-read the letter several times before she could believe the news.

'To preach before the highest in the country – our own Queen Victoria and her husband,' mused Fanny placing the letter carefully on the table away from clutter of breakfast things. 'What greater honour could anyone ask for? Your devotion and hard work have found recognition at last, Charles. I'm so proud of you.'

Charles bent over and kissed her fondly on the cheek. 'Maybe now my work with God is beginning to take a new turn.'

And it couldn't have come at a better time Fanny thought. Charles was still lost in his creative wilderness.

Palm Sunday 1859 was a memorable date in the Kingsley diary and much planning and preparation was afoot as Fanny was to accompany her husband to the Palace. She wasted no time in ordering magazines from London so that she could be updated on the latest fashions. After much deliberation with her sisters she decided to order a gown of palest blue silk, modest enough for a clergyman's wife, yet opulent enough be seen in the presence of the Royal family. Charles ordered a new set of vestments for the occasion, and Georgina, Fanny's sister offered to lend them her finest barouche so as to arrive at the Palace in suitable style.

The day passed in a dream for Fanny. Such was her concern for Charles, she clutched his hand throughout the journey to London as he memorised his sermon notes. As they arrived at Buckingham Palace, they were saluted and waved through the impressive gates. Once through the main arch and into the inner sanctum of the courtyard, another check followed by smartly uniformed guards who asked them to certify their reason for the visit.

Relieved that the journey was over without any delays, Charles was now perfectly at ease. He had made subtle enquiries as to the type of sermon the Queen and Prince Consort were expecting. Much to his relief he had been informed that she preferred shorter sermons rather than rambling preaching. Charles determined to keep his sermon to the same format as the ones he preached in his church at Eversley- simple and colloquial.

In the Royal Chapel, Fanny was escorted to her seat by an official in a red uniform along with other members of the congregation. As she waited for the Royal Party to arrive she was spellbound by the elegant surroundings. The other guests, no doubt lords and ladies were regally dressed. The chapel was decorated in the most beautiful shades of blue and gold. A footman had informed her the decorations in the chapel had been the choice of Prince Albert.

Finally the organ struck up and everyone stood to attention. Queen Victoria made her entrance. To Fanny's surprise she was much smaller than she had imagined her to be. Dressed in a gown of dark blue velvet and a lace cap of the same colour, Fanny thought her most becoming. Elaborate pieces of jewellery caught her eye as they glittered in the sunny ambience of the chapel.

Beside her, Prince Albert dazzled in his smart blue uniform. Following behind the royal couple were their eight solemn-faced children. To Fanny's amusement, the youngest, Leopold shot Fanny a mischievous smile as he passed by her. Bringing up the rear, Charles was looking every inch the parsonical figure in his new vestments and red surplice, the colour worn by the clergy on Palm Sunday. Her heart was fit to burst with pride but her nerves were on edge. To her relief, once in the pulpit Charles' delivery was impeccable. There was no hint of his stammer and his sermon was simple but direct and much to the Queen's liking, she heard afterwards.

Later as they rode home in the carriage, Fanny couldn't wait to hear about the conversation that had ensued with the Royal Equerry. Charles leant back on the leather squabs and kissed Fanny's hand. The service had been a nerve-wracking experience and he was exhausted, but he had delivered his sermon, as always, from the heart.

'Well dearest,' he said with a huge sense of relief 'It would appear your husband has found royal favour. According to the Equerry, the Queen and the Prince Consort were most pleased with my sermon. In fact the Queen has requested that I become her Chaplain in Ordinary.'

'What does that mean?' Fanny asked catching her breath.

'It means I preach once a year at the Chapel Royal St. James and I believe there is a small annuity that comes with it as well.'

Over the next few days Mrs. Scrimshaw and Emily tried hard to extract every detail of their trip to Buckingham Palace. They never tired of hearing how their Queen had looked especially after she had given birth to eight children. Did she appear in good health? Did she think her still in love with Prince Albert? Rumour had it that after all nearly twenty years of marriage they were still like two lovebirds. Fanny obliged them by repeating an account of the day. Mrs. Scrimshaw and Emily wasted no time in rousing an audience to embellish the royal experience that naturally put them both very high up in the estimation of the locals. They were now connected to royalty in a round about sort of way. Or so Emily and Mrs. Scrimshaw thought. Not according to Mr. Scrimshaw who advised his wife to tone down her 'tittle tattle'. It would not do to act above one's station in life especially where the Kingsley's were concerned. They were, after all humble in their manner with the local folk and they would not want their encounter with the Royals spoken of outside their home.

Despite the honour of appearing before the Royal family, Charles still had to take care of his parish and conduct three services on a Sunday without the assistance of a curate. Yet he found contentment with the simple day-to-day routine of life within his parish. It seemed the more celebrity status he received the more he withdrew into his familiar world. There was however one invitation away he was more than happy to accept. He travelled with Fanny to the Isle of Wight and there, at Farringford House spent a few days in the invigorating company of Mr. and Mrs. Alfred Tennyson.

Further distinction awaited him when, in the autumn of the same year, he was again invited to preach before Queen Victoria, this time at the private chapel at Windsor Castle. After the service he was presented to the Queen and Prince Consort and to the royal guests, the Crown Prince and Princess of Prussia. On this occasion Fanny stayed at home.

Charles wrote to Fanny that '*after his preaching he met the Queen in a great state of trepidation. Thank Heaven it is all over. After dinner I was presented to the Queen and I had to kneel and kiss her hand. (Colonel Liddell said I did marvellously.) Then she began to talk and I, to stammer. They were most pleased with my books and she liked 'Hypatia' most of all.*

Then the Princess wanted to talk with me and I had to bow to her. She said the Prince had read nothing but my books all through her honeymoon. After, the Prince Consort came up to me and talked for I should think half an hour about my first novel ' St Elizabeth' who is an ancestor of his. I cannot repeat or remember all the handsome things he said to me. I can't see any coldness in him. I should say his face is rather kindly and impressionable. Heaven knows how I got on. I feel I have made mistakes.'

This time however, Charles and Fanny did not share the accounts of the royal event with other parties. On the contrary they spoke to no one about the introductions to the royal family. They both agreed that it was all too sacred and like a fairy tale.

Mrs. Scrimshaw was mightily put out that all the snippets about hobnobbing in royal company had come to a sudden stop. No matter how she tried to entice the Reveren' into revealing details of his royal audience she drew a blank. Even the fruitcake that was now decorated with marzipan and icing, failed to have the desired effect. But it was never lost on her that the family she worked for now had close relations with the royals.

A New Challenge

Life at Eversley was now one of contentment for the Kingsley family. The children were all settled in various schools and despite their busy lives, Charles and Fanny were enjoying a peaceful time. The harmony of the household however was shortly to be disrupted by the arrival of a letter. Charles recognized it instantly as one of great importance. It was signed by the Prime Minister, Lord Palmerston. Charles contemplated the contents for a long while. His delight and excitement were tempered by a fear of the unknown.

He realised he would have to moderate his elation before confronting Fanny. He was unsure how she would react. Taking courage, he decided there was only one way to find out. He lit his pipe and ventured into the garden. Charles found her sitting under the oak tree and, to his amusement, she had nodded off. Looking resplendent in her afternoon dress of rose silk and white lace collar, Fanny was dozing with her mouth wide open. As he approached, she woke up with a start and immediately picked up the novel she was reading.

'The warm sunshine makes it hard to concentrate, does it not my love?' he asked, bemused.

'The book is a little tedious- it would be enough to send the bees to sleep'.

'And into your open mouth, my dear. Do be careful,' he said with a twinkle in his eyes as he sat down on the chair next to her. 'Is this a good time to discuss a matter of some importance?' Charles grew serious and was puffing assiduously on his pipe.

'You appear somewhat agitated. Has anything happened to upset you?' Fanny asked. She straightened up and saw immediately that there was something bothering him. His dark eyes were brooding and he scratched his whiskers with a distinct edginess. Fanny knew only too well it boded a problem.

'If it is the ball at Sir William Cope's next month, please do not insist I attend. I have already agreed to visit Maurice at school that evening,' she said purposefully.

If only, thought Charles, it was a mere matter of one evening.

'No not at all. It is nothing so superfluous as attending a ball. I have received a letter asking me to lecture at Cambridge.'

'Why that is excellent news! When do you they wish you to go? Have they sent you a date?' Now wide-awake, Fanny's grey eyes reflected a warmth and fondness for her husband.

Charles gave a nervous cough and on occasions like this failed to control his stammer. 'It is……' he said between puffs of his pipe 'somewhat m….more than one lecture,' he faltered. 'It is a p..permanent position.'

'Permanent?' Fanny couldn't imagine what position Charles would be asked to hold at his old university.

'I have received a letter today from none other than Lord Palmerston and he has asked me to fill the vacant role of Pr-Professor of History at Magdalene College and he assures me the Prince Consort has given his full support to the matter.' Charles feigned to make light of his words but saying them aloud, he felt a thrill of joy and immense pride.

'A permanent position? Charles, it is such an honour but would it mean us moving to Cambridge? The children are settled in schools and'….she thought for a moment. 'We couldn't possibly move them.'

Charles was instantly deflated. 'Yes, we would have to move but how can I refuse such an advancement?' he asked feeling the anger rise in his throat. He had not expected a favourable response but Fanny was reacting very negatively.

'There are so many things to consider.' Wild thoughts were running through Fanny's head and her heart was thumping. Although the Rectory still needed work and was far from perfect she was happily settled there. The thought of a move away was crushing.

'It is such a huge undertaking,' she thought aloud. In spite of herself, she glanced at Charles. Even at forty-one, his slim figure had changed little since they had first met all those years ago. She couldn't bear to be separated from him but neither could she contemplate a move to Cambridge. Charles remained silent for a few moments then removed his pocket watch from his breast pocket glancing at the time.

'Mrs. Kingsley, I will take this response as a foolish reaction from someone who has just been disturbed from a very comfortable nap and is not thinking straight.' He looked across to the Mount. The trees that bordered it were still dressed in their spring green and swaying in the warm May breeze. 'I'll be away for a stroll. I need fresh air and time to reflect on this response of yours.'

Even with his eyes in shadow, Fanny read the disappointment and anguish written there.

'Charles let us have tea together later and maybe you will have given more thought to this appointment. We need to discuss it at length,' Fanny suggested calmly.

But Charles needed no more time to consider his decision. Having revelled in his student days at Cambridge and reflected on all the happy memories there, he saw this position as a wonderful opportunity to give something back to the university that he had learnt so much from. Only one concern continued to nag at him. Would other tutors and, indeed other academics regard him, as a man worthy of the title as Regius Professor of History? He had not graduated in the subject and it was not one in which he was most accomplished. But he was determined that would not stand in his way.

Later that afternoon Charles returned from an energetic walk to Eversley Cross having visited parishioners on the way. He found Fanny in the parlour.

'Just in time for tea,' she said brightly giving him a warm smile and hoping that the exercise had helped Charles change his mind about his new offer of employment.

Mrs. Scrimshaw having heard the Rector return, gave a faint knock at the door and entered with a tray of tea.

'Thank you Mrs. Scrimshaw. That will be all.' Fanny said in an unusually dismissive voice.

Mrs. Scrimshaw returned to the kitchen out of sorts. 'I can tell you,' she said to Emily with her hands firmly on her hips 'there's going to be fireworks in that parlour before too long. The Reveren' never said a word and he looked as if he'd lost a sixpence and found a penny. There's somethin' goin' on there or my name's not Ellen Scrimshaw.'

Ellen Scrimshaw's predictions were as usual perfectly sound. Fanny was taking long deliberate sips of tea from her china cup whilst Charles having finished his was sitting on the edge of his chair appearing distracted. It seemed an age before Fanny broke the silence.

'Charles – please don't give me one of your hard done-by expressions. ...'

Charles glared at her. It was on rare occasions that they happened to disagree on anything. This sadly was turning out to be one. Charles loathed the confrontation but on this matter of his future he was determined to stand firm.

'Please hear me out,' Charles began, his frustration now getting the better of him. 'Do you not comprehend how important this offer of such a position is to me? Think on it, I will not have to scrape a living at writing anymore. I will not have to bear the humiliation of critical reviews. I can abandon my pen for more worthy matters and I will have a settled position.'

'But away from here,' Fanny pleaded. 'I do not feel strong enough for another move. My health is not as it should be and you are asking me to come and live with you in Cambridge and leave here?'

'Yes. You know how desperately we miss each other when we are apart,' insisted Charles. 'You always fall sick and without me Fanny, you say you feel incomplete-as I do without you.'

'That is perfectly true but as much as I find the Rectory unsatisfactory in the winter, it is where I want to be and remain.'

'But think of the social circles we will be a part of. You've always enjoyed fraternising with lord so and so and lady such and such.' Charles was trying to make light of the problem.

'That is not so.' Fanny appeared shocked at such a suggestion. 'I'm perfectly happy with the village folk of Eversley and I would not feel at home amongst all those puffed up academics!'

'Of which I will soon be one! Is it such an encumbrance for you Fanny to come with me to Cambridge?'

'And for how long will this take you away from Eversley?'

Two years at most, I would think. But the holidays are long and I shall spend at least four months of the year here- and come home at weekends, perhaps,' he added cautiously.

Fanny shook her head and tears welled up in her sad eyes. She stood up abandoning her tea.

'Think of the children, Charles. If I come with you, Baby Grenville will have to grow up in a town! Mary and Rose will be left at home. My mind is made up. I'm sorry but you must go alone.' And with a determined swish of her skirts she left Charles to contemplate his future without his beloved wife.

In November of that year, Charles travelled to Cambridge for his inaugural lecture along with Fanny and Maurice. He had persuaded Fanny to join him for a few days. She had decided it would be a good experience for Maurice who would eventually become a student there. On arrival at the university, Charles was unaware of the stir of anticipation and excitement his arrival in the halls was creating.

'Kingsley's been seen in Cambridge.' Word spread rapidly. 'He's arrived.' 'He's been spotted in hall.' 'His lecture starts in two hours.'

There was an undisciplined early rush to get to the lecture hall. Even before the newly appointed Professor Kingsley had appeared there was a vote of three cheers for the speaker. As he made his entrance to the lecture stand there were more uproarious cheers that only served to make him more nervous. Charles cast his gaze around his audience of expectant students and there sitting with some of the other tutors was his good friend, Mr. Maurice. They exchanged smiles and Charles felt calmly reassured.

His lecture was entitled 'The limits of Exact Science' and much to his relief, it held his audience spellbound. The essence of it was that to understand history one must first understand men and women. *'History is the history of men and women and of nothing else'* he continued in an evangelical tone. *'And to understand history one must study biographies.'* He put forward the theory that history could be discovered through the lives of people. After a two-hour lecture to an enraptured audience, he declared, *'I am here **not** to teach you history- I am here to teach you **how** to teach yourselves history.'*

There was unanimous roar of approval from the floor. The students loved their new Professor and called him a genius and breath of fresh air compared to the staid lectures of the past. Charles however was in a near state of collapse, and Fanny, despite her grave reservations about his new post, gave him as much support as she could muster.

Whilst the students came to regard the new professor as a cult figure seeking out his company whenever possible, there were those amongst the senior dons who decried the choice of his position. One described him as a 'an awkward figure with a rough provincial accent'. Another described him as 'impulsive and illogical'. In sharp contrast, the effect he had on his students more than made up for any criticism from his contemporaries. Where others had failed, he inspired genuine enthusiasm about his subject. He made himself available at all times to discuss different subjects with his students whom he regarded as his equals. And the students loved him for his approachable and boyish charm.

Royal Favour

After a few weeks, Charles had happily settled into university life. His mind was continually drawn back to his student days and the happy memories he had shared with Mansfield. He was lecturing to packed halls and was enjoying the stimulation of young students, eager to discuss history and politics with him.

However, an invitation from Doctor Whewell, the Master of Trinity College to attend his office, cast doubts in his mind. Charles, always the doubter, wondered if his down to earth approach on the lecture platform was causing offence to other dons. Apprehensively he knocked at the door of Dr Whewell's study.

'Come in, Professor Kingsley.' Dr Whewell put emphasis on the word professor and greeted Charles with an effusive handshake. 'I found it takes some getting used to ...the title 'Professor'. Please take a seat.'

A hint of a smile passed Charles' lips. 'I-I t does take a little while. B-b-ut it is such an honour. The title is something I can quickly get used to.' They exchanged satisfactory smiles.

In the dim wood panelled room, Charles hardly noticed the Doctor's immaculately tidy desk. Folders were piled up on the shelves behind him along with rows of leather-bound books that gave the room a very disciplined and learned atmosphere. Outside he could hear the muted footsteps of students hurrying to lectures. Dr. Whewell leant back in his chair and steepled his fingers together.

'Well, Professor Kingsley- Charles- I hope you are not as nervous as the impression you give. There is nothing to be concerned about. On the contrary I have some excellent news for you. It appears you are making a very favourable impression here at Magdalene. I don't have to tell you that judging by the way you pack the lecture halls, we feel privileged to have you at the university.'

He picked up a letter on his desk. 'It seems that you have also found royal favour. I have here a letter from the Prince Consort proposing that you tutor the Prince of Wales on the subject of History. As you may know, the Prince attended Oxford last year, and, I hear, with dismal results. But now the Prince Consort would like him to study here.' He leaned across his desk towards Charles and asked in a conspiratorial tone. 'Personal tutor to Prince Bertie? How do you feel about that Professor Kingsley? Would you accept?'

Charles wiped away the perspiration from his beaded forehead. 'I..I ..it is a huge responsibility the Prince Consort and the Queen have put upon me.'

'Come now, with your enthusiasm for learning and the effect it is having on the students, I can say with all honesty, we haven't had such a positive response for many a long year. I have no doubt the Prince Consort and the Queen have every faith in you.'

Charles considered it for a minute then sat up in his chair a foot taller. 'It will be a pleasure,' he said with a new air of confidence. His eyes glittered in the shadowy office. 'I cannot refuse a Royal request especially from the Prince Consort and Queen Victoria for whom I have so much admiration.'

'It will not be for a few months so you will have plenty of time to prepare and I suggest, we have the Prince in a selected class of eleven other students.'

Charles nodded.

'I am not speaking out of turn,' continued Doctor Whewell, 'when I say, what the Prince lacks in diligence, he makes up for in charm and sociability. The Queen apparently despairs of him and he has a reputation for being lazy. But I feel one has to bear in mind his upbringing. By all accounts it was very harsh so I feel we must give him some leeway. At the age of ten, the boy had a gruelling regime devised by his father. Even his tutors complained he was overworked. Lessons began at eight am and finished at six pm – seven days a week. I think it is understandable the Prince developed something of an aversion to learning. So Professor Kingsley, you have a challenge on your hands.' He smiled and winked at Charles. 'I'm sure the Prince Consort will not be disappointed with your results.'

Charles was in such a state of agitation, he barely acknowledged the students and tutors on his walk back to his house. To be a tutor to the future king of England was surely beyond his qualifications. How did I, a Rector of a small parish of Eversley come to this, was all he could think of.

To add to his worry of these responsibilities, he was also deeply concerned on hearing the results of the Children's Employment Commission. This was a cause very dear to his heart and he was horrified to learn that young sweeps or climbing boys were actually on the increase. With all the large homes being built by the wealthier middle classes, chimneys were even more of a necessity and their owners preferred sending boys up the chimney rather than using the more humane machines. They made a better job of the work. The report found that six was a 'nice trainable age' and since orphans were in plenty of supply, especially in the industrial towns, this cheap labour was in great demand. Charles felt so strongly about the plight of the underprivileged, he preached about it in one of his sermons before the Queen and Prince Albert in the private Chapel at Windsor. He was prepared to take his fight for justice to the highest in the land.

Charles accepted his post as Regius Professor of History to the Prince of Wales and the new student would cycle to Charles' house and attend the lectures that his tutor had carefully put together. He found the Prince's company engaging and a comfortable relationship developed between the two.

'Bertie', as the Prince was known, invited Charles to many social occasions. Charles would write to Fanny and recount the dinner parties he attended with him. Both the Prince Consort and Doctor Whewell wrote letters of congratulations to Charles. It had not gone unnoticed by either party that Bertie had become engrossed in his studies and was producing the best academic achievements of his life.

Although never spoken of directly, there was a rumour that the good-looking Prince had developed the reputation as a 'ladies man'. After a visit to Ireland there was more gossip that he had spent three nights with an actress called Nellie Clifden. Charles and Doctor Whewell met to discuss this situation.

'Sadly, the Queen has gained knowledge about the Prince's philandering,' the Doctor announced. 'It is a very serious matter, as you can imagine, and the Prince Consort has decided to deal with it personally. He is arriving on Thursday morning to discuss matters with his son. I believe there are plans afoot to have the Prince married off as soon as is reasonably possible. It is a sad state of affairs as I can see his time at Cambridge may terminate–and swiftly.'

Charles nodded gravely and, as a sensual man himself, he considered how difficult it must be for the Prince to resist the many sexual liaisons that presented themselves. He saw Bertie as a royal prisoner and this alone, never mind the idea that he was the future king, would entail huge discipline and strength of character.

On the 25th November, the Prince Consort arrived at Cambridge. Charles met him briefly and was shocked by his appearance. Since their last meeting at the Chapel at Windsor, he had lost weight and looked drawn. The gossip surrounding his son's behaviour had exacerbated his poor health. Prince Albert thanked Charles for the progress he had made with his son, adding that the Queen was surprised and delighted that Bertie had taken such an interest in his studies.

Charles bowed and was humbled by the praise. 'I hope that it may continue,' he replied.

Prince Albert declined to answer. Bertie's continued attendance at Cambridge was not something he wished to deny or confirm. He bid Charles goodbye and was escorted to a room to meet with his son. Charles watched this distinguished figure of a man, now bowed with illness yet making every effort to put things right with his son.

After term broke up for the Christmas holidays there was much speculation about the Prince Consort's health. Charles had learnt from Doctor Whewell that father and son had gone for a walk to discuss matters in private. They had been caught in heavy rain and it was assumed this hastened the Prince's debility. On returning to Windsor, his health deteriorated further and there were grave concerns about his recovery.

As with all the other denominations and Churches, Charles led the prayers for his return to health. By December the 14th the nation heard the news that the Prince Consort had died of typhoid fever. The country was plunged into mourning. None of his subjects felt his death more than Charles.

THE WATER BABIES

As with many families throughout the country, the Christmas of 1861 was a subdued affair in the Kinglsey household with the death of the Prince Consort so fresh in their minds. At church, the men wore black armbands and the women replaced their bright festive hair ribbons for black. Queen Victoria made no secret of the fact that she blamed her son for her beloved husband's death and he was quickly dispatched abroad. This brought a premature end to Charles tutoring the Prince and it saddened him deeply. He had embraced his elevated standing at university and it had energized him.

Charles no longer resided permanently at Cambridge and was able to make his visits there less often. One spring morning the following year, the family was sitting around the breakfast table enjoying their father's company. Fanny was never happiest when they were all together. She and Charles had long since reconciled their differences over his position at Cambridge and were once more enjoying a happy and devoted relationship. Maurice was home from Wellington College for the holidays and as it was a Saturday, they were making plans for the day. Rose, now eighteen was going to help her mother decide on some new dress making patterns, Maurice was taking his younger sister Mary, out for a ride on her new pony and on Charles' insistence the gardener's lad, an excellent horseman, was going was to accompany them.

Grenville was happy to stay home and after devoting time to study his latest picture book, he would follow the delicious smell of baking into the kitchen where Mrs. Scrimshaw would be hard at work with her weekly bake. Ostensibly he would be there to help. In Grenville's own mind it was more a question of sampling the different biscuits and cakes as they appeared out of the oven.

After lunch Charles planned to take the children out for a bracing walk to look for spring flowers, newly hatched tadpoles in the ponds and further afield, for trout in the streams up by Eversley Cross. As Maurice was always quick to point out, a walk with Papa was never tedious but enthralling and full of fun. He had been way ahead of his classmates at Wellington on subjects of Botany and Natural History. An afternoon spent with his father in the countryside or seashore meant there were always new things to discover and, following his father's example, delighted in cataloguing all the different species they discovered. Charles created further excitement when he told them the wild orchids might be in flower.

Fanny was about to leave the breakfast table to discuss Sunday's lunch menu with Mrs. Scrimshaw when she sat down again. An idea had come to her.

Charles,' she said warmly. 'Have you forgotten your promise to Grenville?'

Charles gave her a quizzical stare. Grenville was his youngest and, as much as Charles would deny it, he was his favourite son. He could think of nothing he had denied Grenville.

'And what is that, my dear?' he asked, giving Grenville a wide eyed comical glance that made him giggle.

The children's heads swivelled back to Fanny seated at the opposite end of the table.

'A book for Baby Grenville.'

Grenville sat wide-eyed. Whilst he thought himself grown up at the age of four, his parents still annoyingly called him 'Baby Grenville.'

Fanny's face lit up as she continued. 'You have written a book for Rose, Maurice and Mary. Now it is Baby's turn.'

Grenville slipped down from the table, trotted over to his father and took hold of his knee.

'Oh Papa, will you write a book just for me?' His eyes were filled with adoration for his father. Charles gave Grenville's small body a squeeze and ruffled his tousled hair with his large hands. He stood up and, with an enigmatic grin on his face, left the room. The children could hear the study door shut. Papa it seemed had gone to work.

'Father must not be disturbed,' Rose declared importantly. She was very protective of her father. 'He will be hard at the grind,' she said using her father's well-used expression for work.

'How exciting,' Mary chipped in. 'I wonder what he will write for you, Grenville.'

'I expect it will be wonderfully exciting- like his other books,' Rose said thinking of the book of fairy stories, '*Heroes*', her father had written for his older children.

Half an hour later the children were in the parlour sorting out their old reading books. Those they had outgrown, they were bundling up for the village school. They heard the study door open and looked up expectantly as their father came into the room, grinning broadly, and his eyes lit up with pride and satisfaction.

'Here you have it- the first chapter. The story of little Tom,' he announced pleasurably.

'Who is Tom?' Grenville asked clasping at the trouser leg of his father and gazing up at him. Charles slipped his arm around him and Grenville jumped up and down with excitement. 'Who's Tom?' he pleaded. The others stopped what they were doing and waited.

'Tom is a chimney sweep, a hard done by, poor little boy who has a life of servitude climbing chimneys.'

'And what happens to him?' a wide-eyed Grenville asked.

'He runs away from his hard-hearted master and falls into a stream and drowns.'

'Drowns?' the children chorused.

'That's not a very happy story,' Mary ventured, pushing out her bottom lip.

'Aha- don't be too hasty. We could say he falls asleep,' Charles said wagging his finger. He deliberately paused, removed his pipe from his pocket and lit it. The children were on tenterhooks.

'Then,' he continued, puffing vigorously on his pipe, 'he enters a different world, an underwater world where he meets all sorts of wonderful sea creatures. You see, my dear children, he becomes a water baby and lives in a mystical world.'

'Can *we* see a water baby in the river or by the sea?' Maurice asked, ever the adventurer.

'I have never caught sight of one, but their footprints, yes!' Charles declared to his captive audience.

'You have seen their *footprints?*' Grenville asked, his eyes agog.

'I will show you them when we are next at the seashore. They are small and black and look like algae as they stick to the rocks.'

That was enough to satisfy Grenville they existed. Fanny was sitting comfortably by the fireplace in her armchair listening to the animated conversation. 'Can we hear more of what you have written?' she suggested.

Charles picked up his sheaf of papers. 'Here, I have the opening chapter.'

The children settled down, intrigued by their father's wonderful imagination and on this occasion were amazed he had written a chapter of the story so quickly. Charles abandoned his pipe to the mantelpiece and with his audience seated at his feet began.

'Once upon a time, there was a little chimney sweep and his name was Tom. That is a short name and you have heard it before so you will not have much trouble remembering it.' Whilst writing the opening lines, Charles had reflected on the pathos of the little sweep he had meet all those years ago when

he was curate at Eversley. The plight and death of that boy had never left him.

'He lived in a great town in the North country where there were plenty of chimneys to sweep and plenty of money for Tom to earn and his master to spend. He could not read or write and did not care to either; and he never washed himself for there was no water in the court where he lived. He cried half the time and laughed the other half. He cried when he had to climb the dark flues rubbing his poor elbows and knees raw; and when the soot got into his eyes which it did every day in the week; and when his master beat him which he did every day of the week and when he had not enough to eat which happened every day in the week likewise.'

'The story opens,' Charles continued looking at his audience 'early one morning when Tom and his master Grimes set off to Harthover House for their work. He turned his attention to his papers.

'So he and his master set out; Grimes rode the donkey in front and Tom and the brushes walked behind; out of the court and up the street past the closed window shutters, and the winking weary policeman and the roofs all shining grey in the dawn. They passed through the pitmen's village all shut up and silent now, and through the turnpike and then they were out in real country and plodding along the black dusty road, between the black slag walls with no sound but the groaning and thumping of the pit engine in the next field. But soon the road grew white and the walls likewise and at the wall's foot grew long grass and gay flowers all drenched with dew; and instead of the groaning of the pit engine they heard the skylark saying his matins high up in the air and the pit bird warbling in the hedges, as he had warbled all night long. All else was silent.'

Charles almost whispered the words. The children were mesmerized and not one of them spoke.

'Harthover place was really a grand place even in the rich north country; with a house so large that in the riots which

Tom could just remember, the Duke of Wellington and ten thousand soldiers were easily housed therein; at least so Tom believed, and with a park full of deer which Tom believed to be monsters who were in the habit of eating children.'

Charles jumped to main points of the story. 'There Tom gets lost in one of the many chimneys and lands in the hearth of a spotless white bedroom that is Ellie's, a little girl. He is so scared of the consequences that he jumps out of the window and everyone from the great house sets off to find this disgraceful little boy running away from his master.'

'Do they catch him?' Grenville asked.

'No, his feet are swift as the wind. Everybody in the house joins in the pursuit – Grimes the Sweep, the gardener, the groom, the dairymaid, Sir John, the ploughman, the keeper and the Irish woman all ran up the park shouting 'Stop thief'. You see- they all believed he had stolen some jewels. The only one who didn't give chase was her ladyship,' and here Charles reads from his story again. *'My lady did not give chase for when she put her head out of the window, her night wig fell into the garden and she had to ring up her lady's maid, and send her down for it privately.'*

Charles pulled a whimsical face and the children broke into fits of giggles. Fanny looked on as he kept the children spell bound. She was so proud of her husband's talents. Not only was he the most caring and compassionate father, his written word entertained both children and adults.

As Charles recounted Tom's journey across the fells to the stream he portrayed it in a way that only a naturalist can do. He described the insects and wildlife, the colour of the spiders with crowns and crosses on their backs, the lizards, the grouse and *'a great brown, sharp nosed fox with a white tag to her brush.'*

'And so, my children, that is the first chapter of my book for Baby Grenville.' Charles smiled proudly as his children broke into applause. Shuffling his papers together, he turned his attention to the window.

'I see it will be a fine afternoon for a walk.'

The children stayed silent, still absorbing the entrancing story they had just started to enjoy. After a short pause there followed a great chattering and questioning.

'When will father write the next chapter?' Rose asked her mother.

Grenville sat on the rug his face doleful and disappointed that his father had finished. 'I want to hear some more Papa,' he complained.

'Do you think Tom will be eaten by a horrible fish with big sharp teeth?' Mary asked Maurice. At ten years of age she was very impressionable and had a vivid imagination like her father.

And so urged on by the family, Charles continued to write '*The Water Babies.*' When Grenville knew his father was working on the story in his study, he would wait patiently outside the door until Charles reappeared with more of the manuscript in his hand. The topics in the story covered many of Charles' personal foibles. He was preoccupied with cleanliness and when Tom strips off his dirty, ragged clothes, he repeats, *'I must be clean, I must be clean.'* The fairies clean him whilst he sleeps in the water and when he awakes, he is changed into a water baby. Tom is now amphibious. Charles gave his characters names that would intrigue children. *Mrs. Doasyouwouldbedoneby* and *Mrs Douasyoudid* are fairy sisters. Tom meets water-monkeys, water-squirrels and water-flowers and a magical underwater world to fire the imaginations of children. After many adventures, Tom earns a place back in the world of humans. The story has a happy ending when he is reunited with Ellie, the little girl from Harthover House.

The children were so thrilled with this new book they gave their father little respite until he produced the finished work. The atmosphere in the house was one of excitement and the children couldn't wait to tell Mrs. Scrimshaw the latest instalment as it unfolded.

Whilst cooking a supper of fried herrings, Mrs. Scrimshaw was humming to herself as Mr. Scrimshaw came through the back door. He was also in a good mood as he had enjoyed a productive afternoon in their vegetable garden.

'You're in a good mood this evenin', Ellen,' he remarked as he removed his boots. 'Those broad beans are comin' along well.' He peered over his wife's shoulder to see the crispy skins of the herrings.

'Just how I like 'em,' he said as he washed his hands vigorously under the tap next to her and, giving his hands a quick wipe, he sat down at the kitchen table.

'You'll have to wait a moment till I've buttered the bread, Henry.'

'I can do that my love. Now what's made your day? I can see by the smile on your face somethin' good is happenin' at the Rectory.'

'Ooh, it's all a'buzz there with those chil'ren. The Reveren' is writin' this new story and they're so excited they can hardly contain themselves.' She chuckled as she put the plate of bread and butter on the table.

'It's like Christmas all over again,' she said as she served up two herrings on each plate. 'Even our Rose at her mature age talks of nothin' else . She's as bad as young Grenville who the Reveren' is writing the tale for. Sounds to me,' she said as she took a mouthful of bread and butter, 'that book will be one of his best if the chil'rens' fuss is anything to go by.'

'Well you're probably right,' Mr. Scrimshaw replied, as he wolfed down his fish, wishing there were more in the pan.

ILLNESS

The publisher, Macmillan was equally enthusiastic about '*The Water Babies*' and found it needed hardly any corrections. It was one of the easiest books Charles had written and it found instant success with the public. He was desperate to draw attention to the plight of the sweep boys and the publication had the reaction he hoped for.

It was no surprise to Fanny that as his work and social life grew more hectic, Charles was again mentally debilitated. He also suffered from a congestion of the lungs. At forty-four Charles felt old beyond his years. He attributed his poor health to living in Cambridge whose climate he had found unhealthy. Since Charles could no longer afford to keep two houses, he travelled to the university only twice a year and, despite missing the camaraderie of his students, his love affair with Cambridge had waned. He was happy back in the familiar countryside of his beloved Eversley.

But Charles was still working and stretching himself to his limits. He corresponded with Charles Darwin about his book – '*The Origin of the Species*'. He agreed with Darwin's theory that man was descended from the apes and yet well aware it was the antithesis of the Church of England views. Like Darwin, he also believed that the world was thousands of millions of years old, another theory not held by the Church.

One afternoon Fanny went to check on him in his study. Normally she would leave her husband alone to compose his lectures and sermons but she was growing more concerned about his declining mood and the long hours he spent poring over books. Outside it was a bleak wet day. The trees were dripping rain off their leaves and a mist hung over the garden and beyond. The study also had a soulful atmosphere. The energy and vitality of Charles' presence was absent and the room felt like a prison cell.

Fanny sat down next to him. Charles failed to notice her new hairstyle. Her dark hair now peppered with grey was draped in a snood at the nape of her neck. Nor did he smell the liberal dab of new eau de cologne she was wearing.

'Charles, I heard you coughing again. Have you remembered to take your cough mixture?' she asked casually by way of an excuse to interrupt him. She didn't need to tell him that his cough was getting worse. She saw the brown bottle in front of him, 'It's unopened, I see?'

Charles glanced up from his writing. He had been appointed a Fellow of the Geographical Society, and had finished a paper for a lecture he was meant to deliver the following week. Fanny noted that his dark eyes were hooded with fatigue. Two deep lines were etched on either side of his wide mouth. His pallor was grey. Such was his workload, Fanny could see no respite for her husband.

'I'm sorry my dear, what did you say?' Charles leaned back in his chair and pushed his papers away from him. He was unusually vague.

'I'm concerned for you- as we all are. Your health will not improve if you carry on working all hours. And you must take your medicine.'

Fanny looked on helplessly as another coughing fit got the better of him. She was aware of the smoky atmosphere that was now a habitual feature of his study. How was Charles ever going to recuperate if he continued to smoke his pipe? But this was not the time to berate him, she reminded herself. She poured him a measure from the bottle of medicine into a glass and handed it to him.

'If only you looked after yourself as well as you tend to your sick parishioners,' she said gently trying to make light of her reprimand to her weary husband.

'It will pass.' Charles hurriedly swallowed a draft of the mixture then reached for his pipe. Glancing at Fanny's stern face, he thought better of it. After a few minutes his coughing eased but his voice was weak.

Her eyes went to the paper in front of him. At least he was still able to write poetry, she supposed, as she saw the lines of verse.

'Are you going to share your poetry with me?'

Charles leant back in his chair. 'Naturally, my dear. You may not approve of its content though. It reflects my somber mood.'

Charles picked up the sheet of paper and handed it to her.

'When all the world is old lad
And all the trees are brown
And all the sport is stale lad
Creep home and take your place there,
The spent and maimed among
And God grant you find one face there,
You loved when all was young.'

Fanny gave a deep sigh as she read it. 'That is one of the saddest pieces you have written. Were it not for the lung complaint that ails you, I would be concerned that you are having another bout of melancholy.' But Fanny knew only too well this poem reflected his present mood and was written from the heart. He gave her a slow forced smile but his eyes showed the pain of his sore lungs.

'I think it is the same, whether one is a writer, a composer of music or an artist – when the heart feels sad, it speaks openly. How we suffer when the world is not right. There are so many wrongs in the world and I can never hope to right them. If I were to live for another twenty years, my legacy would still be naught compared to what I see every day in the sufferings of others. Such is the state of the world. Man in his greed will always be the oppressor of the poor. '

'You will leave your mark on the world, you can be sure of that, and your verse is beautiful, Charles, but your day is done. Come upstairs and rest. I will ensure the children are quiet. A sleep will help restore your energy.'

'Yes, Mother.' Charles tried to hold back another spasm of coughing. 'I am your obedient servant.' Charles lifted his head wearily towards her. He had no energy to protest.

It was several weeks before Charles regained his health and vitality. He and Fanny discussed his professorship at Cambridge at length and, despite Maurice, their son, being a student at Trinity College, they decided that Charles should resign his post. Letters were written to the Head of Trinity, to the Queen and to the Prime Minister, W.E. Gladstone. They remained on Charles' desk for a week before he made the decision to post them. He agonized over missing the stimulation of student life and his adoring following of disciples but rationalized that it would free him up to devote more time to his parish. His Professorship of nine years was the end of an era.

However, as one door closed another opened. As a great advocate of Charles, the Queen had sought to help him with a higher preferment within the Church, but the government had considered Charles a radical and a threat, and recalling his association with the Chartists had stalled her request. Nevertheless, Gladstone was keen to support his Sovereign and give Charles the recognition he deserved. By chance, the appointment of Canon for Chester Cathedral became vacant.

'I have reached the climax of my career,' thought Charles as he accepted his new position that came within months of his leaving Cambridge. 'And with Gladstone as our Prime Minister, we shall see the whole country benefit.'

To celebrate his new appointment, Fanny organized a dinner with all the family.

'To the new Canon of Chester.' The children and Fanny toasted Charles with glasses of beer as they sat round the table to a large leg of roast pork, apple sauce and dishes of vegetables.

'Papa –it is wonderful that finally you now have the recognition you deserve,' Rose enthused.

Maurice was equally thrilled. Grenville had drawn a sketch of his father in his new Canon's robes and Mary looked on quietly at the family's celebrations. She was worried about the length of time this new post would take him away from the family. Fanny was the most thrilled of all. To have her husband finally recognized by the Church and given a Canonry of Chester was beyond her dreams. If she was honest this meant more to her than all the other accolades that Charles had been feted with. Over dinner they discussed the new post at length.

'It won't mean us moving up north, will it?' Mary asked, her bottom lip in a pout. 'I don't want to move from here.'

'We may have to for a short while.' Fanny was unsure whether Charles would need their company. 'But if we go, how wonderful for us to be a part of a nice old fashioned town like Chester and I'm sure your Papa will enjoy the challenge of preaching in the great cathedral, isn't that right Charles?'

Charles was in a reflective mood yet he was pleased that Fanny was showing more interest in his new procurement that she had given to his post of Professorship at Cambridge.

'Yes, it is true but wherever I go in this hardworking world, I shall take care to have my last sleep in Eversley churchyard. Of that there is no doubt.'

'Dearest, do not think such morbid thoughts in front of our children,' Fanny whispered.

Charles smiled at her as he steepled his fingers over his lips. But his thoughts were elsewhere. A canonry at Chester was an honour he could not refuse. He shared his family's elation but the position did not ease his financial worries. He received a modest income from writing and the £500 a year for his new appointment would hardly allow him enough money to enjoy a comfortable existence. Fanny thought differently. As if reading his mind she touched his arm tenderly.

'Don't be concerned about our income. We shall not do without and I have a surprise for you all,' and here she paused and beamed at her attentive family. 'I'm arranging to have a heating system installed in the house.' Her eyes shone with delight. However her announcement was met with a mixed reception.

'What sort of heating?' Maurice asked. 'We have fires, don't we?'

'It is the latest and fashionable form of heating designed for large houses. It is quite the thing now. In each room there is an iron radiator that is heated by pipes that come from a boiler. Just think of it, children– no more icy rooms in winter.'

The younger children, Mary and Grenville clapped their hands with excitement that their drafty, damp house might be warm. No longer would they have to scurry from room to room along the cold corridor to find a warm fire. Nor hopefully would they have to scrape the ice of the insides of bedroom windows in winter.

A stern look from their father said otherwise. 'I thought we had agreed we could not afford anymore work on the house until the children's education was finished.'

The children's faces dropped as they watched their father 's disapproval. Rose, now twenty-three years, was fast taking over her mother's role as social companion to her father. She was fiercely defensive of him.

'Mama, you know what Father's thoughts are about expenditure. His income cannot warrant such an extravagance. He cannot even afford to fund a Curate, never mind the luxury of a warm house.'

'My mind is made up. What is of more importance –our health or economies to our standard of living? We can cut back on other things.' Fanny's jaw tightened.

Rose was having none of this. She could see how her mother's announcement had unsettled her father and it seemed, he was not about to contradict his wife in front of the children.

'But Mama,' Rose insisted. 'Both Grenville and Maurice are away for most of the time with their schooling. Mary and I are quite happy with our house the way it is. We don't have regular bouts of coughs and colds, do we? We don't suffer from the consumptive illnesses that half the parish have in winter.'

'No,' agreed Fanny 'but your father does. His lungs are exceedingly weak and I think it would benefit his health enormously.'

Charles stood up irritated by the way the conversation was going.

'Fanny, I appreciate your concern and I'm all for women's emancipation but not when I'm still in charge of finances. You have decided that we need this new fangled and, no doubt, expensive heating system,' he said gently, aware that the children were watching him closely. 'We will discuss this later in my study.' And seeing the disappointed faces of his children, his concerned face gave way to a smile. 'Now we have all finished dinner and the discussion about our extravagancies, I am away to my study. Prayers at eight pm, as usual.'

As Charles was about to leave, Maurice stood up and stretched himself to his full height. 'Father, before you go I would like to announce my piece of news, if I may. I was going to talk to you about this later but as you have concerns about the family's finances, my decision seems even more appropriate. I have decided to forgo my university studies and travel the world. I am not much of an academic, as you are well aware, and, in fact, I already have formed a plan to go to Argentina and work on a ranch.' Maurice blushed. He had finally given voice to his plans.

'But why, Maurice? That is impossible.' Fanny said visibly shaken and clutching her napkin to her mouth.

'Why not?' Maurice asked.

'Because they are a bunch of wild Spanish ruffians out there,' Charles said firmly. 'As much as I agree that travel educates the mind, I do not condone Argentina, my lad. Can you not plan to work somewhere safer and nearer to home? Europe has a lot to offer.'

Mary 's bottom lip quivered. 'Oh Maurice! You can't leave the family and go to 'Tim Buck Two'. We shall miss you dreadfully and Mama will spend her whole time worried sick that you might be crushed to death by a stampede of cows.'

Rose smiled. 'I don't think we will be that pessimistic but Father's right. Have you not thought of somewhere closer to home?'

Maurice was adamant. 'I've read about the wilderness in Argentina. There are hundreds and hundreds of miles of pampas grass and not much else. I will live with the locals and herd the cattle like a real cowboy. It will be such an adventure. Please don't stop me, Mama and Papa. Please.'

Charles was thoughtful for a moment. 'I admire your taste for adventure. It would be no mean feat. Just making the journey by boat would be formidable. The seas off the coast of South America can be cruelly wild. But thinking on it, you could write about your travels on your return and maybe sell articles to magazines and you could give talks to the locals about your adventures. My, how fascinated they would be to hear of your tales.'

Fanny looked at him with an amused smile. 'Always thinking about the parishioners', she thought to herself. Then her practical side took over.

'Charles, give a thought to your son thousands of miles away. Suppose he catches some disease out there?' Fanny was dismayed at her husband's reaction but at least Maurice's plans had diverted the topic of heating away from his thoughts. Or so she supposed. She had thought it such a good idea. She said as much when she joined Charles in his study.

'Fanny, perhaps some time you would like to see the houses of the village folk and the conditions they live in. Their houses are permanently damp and many can ill afford fuel for their fires. They rely on wood from the forest to keep their hearths warm. How can I sit in a warm house with an expensive heating system when the villagers are struggling to keep their children from freezing to death in the cold winters? Besides our fires do an adequate job.'

'So we have to suffer because they do? Charles you mix in the highest of circles and your name is known all over the country but do we have to live like poor church mice because the villagers do? Your health is such that you should be living in a warm and comfortable house. Surely, we have tolerated this drafty damp place for long enough?'

After Fanny had gone to bed, Charles lay in his hammock in his study, puffing on his pipe. His thoughts turned again to the folk of Eversley. All to a man, even the children, were hard workers, yet their rewards were few. There was little to relieve their drab, monotonous existence of work and sleep. There had to be something more he could do for them. Eversley School was now filled with the youngsters who were too young to work in the fields or the towns. The evening classes for adults at the Rectory were as popular as ever, but Charles reasoned they should have somewhere to meet on a cold winter's night without having to rely on the alehouse for warmth and company. The idea, when it hit him, was plainly obvious. They could use the schoolroom. It would be warm from the day's use and it would be a respectable place for the women to come to. He would arrange Penny Readings once a fortnight, musical concerts, poetry readings and story telling. Charles imagined the difference it would make. The villagers could look forward to an evening of entertainment in a room that was brightly lit and warm. It would be a far cry from their gloomy, poorly lit cottages. And Charles was already excited at the idea of Maurice, on his return home, entertaining folk with tales of his foreign adventures.

Unbeknown to Charles he was soon to be crossing oceans himself.

INVITATION

Mrs. Scrimshaw was stoking up the range in the kitchen and to her dismay it was 'playing up' in her terms.

'That wood's not seasoned enough,' she complained to Emily who was setting out a tray of cups and saucers. 'It's all very well having fancy heating put in the house but if this 'ere range is out of sorts, the family will go hungry.'

Mrs. Scrimshaw poked the smouldering wood with the metal poker. Sparks flew up as she slammed the door to the fire. 'Well let's just hope it takes a hold otherwise I'll be serving cold beef stew for 'em tonight. There's just enough hot water for you here to make coffee for the Reveren'.

Emily giggled. 'That would never do servin' luke warm stew. You know 'ow particular Mrs. Kingsley is and her fightin' off another cold.'

'Shh Emily. Watch your mouth. If she were to hear it she'd be well put out.'

Emily poured hot water from the iron kettle into the coffee pot and disappeared to the study with the tray for Charles and Rose. Rose was helping her father with his correspondence that was growing daily.

Returning to the kitchen, Emily was open mouthed.

What?' Mrs. Scrimshaw said. 'Has the cat got your tongue?' Emily sat down at the kitchen table. 'Well I'm blowed. Rose is there with him and readin' out a letter 'bout somewhere called Trinidad. And the Reveren' Kingsley is all hot an' bothered and excited like you've never seen. He's like a child at Christmas.'

'So what's so exciting 'bout that then?' Mrs. Scrimshaw was still dwelling on the lack of heat coming from the range.

'Rose was reading that some govern'a of Trinidad has invited them there for Christmas.'

'I ain't heard of the place but if it ain't that far away p'haps they'll only be away for a couple of days.'

'No, Rose is saying they could be away for weeks.'

'That ain't no train ride then- less it's in the wilds of Scotland.'

'Rose was goin' on about the plants and birds and the like. I s'pose we'll get to hear more in a while.'

Whilst Charles was delighted that he should have received an invitation from the Governor of Trinidad to visit the island, he was troubled by the enormity of the trip. Although his appointment to Chester was not until May and he had the winter months free, it would mean leaving the family and his parishioners over the festive period. Fanny however was keen for him to go. She insisted it would be beneficial to his health and it would be an adventure for Rose if she were to accompany him.

'Just think of the vegetation and wild life we shall encounter, Rose.' Charles was poring over the page of the atlas showing the Caribbean islands. 'It will be a dream come true,' he said, his face puckering into a smile.

'And I will bring back a parrot and an animal - an ant eater perhaps.' Rose laughed. 'Oh Father, I can't believe we are going to the Tropics, to a beautiful hot climate, to see exotic plants and trees *and* to be a guest of the Governor. What a wonderful adventure for us.'

Fanny was more practical about the trip. The thought of spending time at sea on a ship in the middle of winter filled her with dread. She would be far happier at home with the children for Christmas. Mrs. Scrimshaw and Emily had been amazed when they heard the length of the journey. Like Fanny, they thought father and daughter were extremely brave to cross an ocean at that time of year.

'You would'na get me on a river in a rowin' boat in December let alone the Atlantic that, I hear, is thousands of miles across. Imagine it,' Mrs. Scrimshaw brooded over a cup of tea with Emily one afternoon. 'Bein' tossed about for weeks and not seein' land and not bein' able to get off the boat. Sunshine there maybe at the end of it all, but that's some price to pay. She's a brave lass that Rose - and the Reveren' come to that.'

An early Christmas was celebrated at the Rectory with all the children except Maurice who was still away in Argentina. They were eager to discuss the details of the journey and had spent many an evening studying the atlas and books about the flora and fauna of Trinidad. Fanny was having reservations about the cost of the voyage and voiced her concerns several times in the weeks before his departure. It seemed unfair that he had made such an outcry about the new heating system yet he could squander money to go overseas.

'I will write articles and send them home to be published and I have a book already planned in my head. That will help towards the expenses. Besides, I think our host will be more than generous with his hospitality,' Charles promised her. Fanny was not so sure.

After they had snuggled up in bed for one last rapturous interlude of lovemaking before he left, he finally allayed Fanny's fears. In the morning he bid a tearful goodbye to her, Grenville and Mary. He was most touched when Mrs. Scrimshaw handed him a beautifully wrapped Christmas cake to be opened when they arrived at their destination.

In early December, Charles and Rose set sail on a mail steamer bound for the Caribbean.

* * *

The Very Reverend Dean Howson sat at his desk in his library overlooking Chester Cathedral and contemplating the heavy fog that lay over the town. Despite the dreariness of the day, the solid structure of the Cathedral in its deep red sandstone hues filled him with warmth. The Cathedral was his lifeblood, his passion and never a day passed when he was not filled with pride at holding a position of such high rank. He glanced at the letter before him and then to his assistant sitting across from him. The Dean scratched his whiskery chin and shook his head. The assistant knew the signs. Whatever the contents of the correspondence, they were not agreeable to the Dean.

'So, we have confirmation from the Reverend Kingsley.' The Dean sighed. 'He has accepted the post as Canon. This is not the news I had wished for, but as the Queen is very much in favour of the appointment, we have no choice. There is nothing to be done.' Dean Howson leaned back in his chair and with a resigned look on his face, waited for a response from his assistant. There was none. The Dean sighed.

'You have a prejudice against this appointment?' the assistant finally enquired.

'Of course,' he snapped. 'Do you not know that Kingsley is a radical? He is totally against my beliefs and those of the Church. He's a Chartist! A Christian socialist! Have you read his books, *Yeast* and *Alton Locke?*' demanded the Dean.
His assistant had read both books but declined to comment how much he had enjoyed them.

'His Christian views are very much open to question. To write such controversial and disputatious (one of the Dean's favourite words) literature - to rouse up the working man is not what we need here in Chester. Respected and well liked by the Queen he maybe, but he is a firebrand and doubtless wholly arrogant. Goodness only knows the effect he will have on our town's people.'

'I believe he is also good friend of the Prince of Wales.' His assistant paused letting the gravity of the comment sink in, 'and we have a request from the Library Committee that the Reverend Kingsley, being the notable author he is, could contribute to their funds by giving lectures. Would that not be a good enough reason in itself to have such an esteemed writer and preacher join us?'

The Very Reverend Howson glowered. 'Mmm, I suppose that has a relevance, but I'm still uneasy about his sermons and their content.' He folded the letter and put it to one side. 'He will only be here for three months of the year so thankfully there will be some measure of restraint on any new ideas he might intend to impose on us.'

AN UNEXPECTED VISITOR

Charles was mesmerised by the earthly paradise of Trinidad and the rich colours of the Caribbean Sea. The warm breezes assailed his senses; the animal and plant life sated his curiosity of this new world. In a letter to Fanny, he wrote that there was so much to see. *'I shall take a full year to assimilate and arrange the mass of new impressions.'*

He was overawed by such a change in his environment. He made copious notes on palm trees - one of his great loves - of snakes, alligators, tropical birds, of the Monserrat Hills and volcanoes. He wrote detailed letters to Fanny extolling the virtues of the climate and comparing the lives of the Negroes who basked in warmth and had little want of anything, in contrast to the drudgery of the workers at home who toiled for little and led such dreary, sad lives.

After seven weeks away, Charles was ready to come home. His time away had refreshed and revitalized him and despite the wintry homecoming on the mail ship, Charles rejoiced at his first sighting of the Needles and Southampton. His home at Eversley, was now not far away.

Nothing much had changed in his absence save for the Rectory itself. During his absence the workmen had demolished half the back of the house, pulled up floors and dug deep holes around the property for the installation of the new heating system. Regardless of all the upheaval, Charles soon set about writing articles for the Penny Readings held in the School. '*Animal life in the Tropics*', was his first and he was pleased with the result. He was sure the local folk would enjoy a temporary escape from the routine of their lives.

As he was putting the final touches to his talk, he was interrupted by the sound of hurried footsteps. Fanny burst in through the door. Her face was the colour of chalk and for the first time since Charles had known her, she was lost for words. She clamped her hands on her cheeks.

'Fanny, what ails you?' he asked.

'We-we have an unexpected visitor. He's waiting in the hall.' Fanny was breathless and near to collapse.

Realizing that something was amiss or maybe the visitor was carrying important news, Charles hastened into the hall, catching a glimpse of several horses outside the front entrance, their uniformed riders bearing the Royal Standard. Who of such importance had come to visit him he wondered?

Emily had ambled across the entrance hall to answer the door. Catching sight of the cavalry of horses she flapped around like a frightened hen.

'We got the soldiers from Aldershot come to see us,' she screeched in a panic to Mrs. Scrimshaw. Terrified, she opened the front door.

'Lord have mercy ...' she mouthed silently. She was staring straight into the handsome, bearded face of the Queen's son. Remembering her position, and with trembling knees, she wobbled to a deep curtsey hoping to hide her blushes. Emily had seen his picture in the newspaper with his mother, Queen Victoria. There was no mistaking the Prince of Wales and dressed as he was, so regally in his red uniform.

Even Charles was taken aback. 'Your Highness, what an honour to have you visit us.' Charles gave a bow of the head as the Prince of Wales greeted him with a warm smile.
Deeply relieved that the Reverend had come to her rescue, Emily turned on her heel and bolted to the kitchen.

'Let us forgo the formalities, Charles. It's Edward to you -please.' He shook Charles' hand with a vigorous grasp. 'And I apologise for so rude an intrusion but we were passing on our way back to our unit at Bramshill Common. It's been a while since we've seen you at Sandringham. The children are always talking about you and they miss you.'

Charles still tanned from his foreign trip grinned broadly. The Prince had never forgotten the camaraderie they had shared during his university days. Not only had Fanny and Charles attended his fairy tale wedding to the Princess Alexandra of Denmark, but Charles had also been a regular visitor to their Norfolk home in Sandringham where he had been accepted as one of the family.

'Come through to the parlour, Sir, and you must update me on how the children are. Please excuse the warmth in here. We have installed new heating which appears to have run amok and is quite out of control.'

They laughed together as Charles hurriedly opened a window to dispel the heat and the Prince removed his topcoat. Emily, who had regained her composure, tailed behind and quickly retrieved it. She gave another curtsey and was backing out of the room when she bumped straight into Fanny who had rushed upstairs to change her dress and was now hoping to make an entrance. The slight altercation between the two went unnoticed by the men.

'Fanny, how delightful to meet you again,' the Prince said warmly. Fanny blushed the shade of her burgundy dress. She was most flattered that he had remembered her name. He gave a short nod of his head and Fanny gave a deep curtsey. Fortunately she had taken extra care with her hair that morning. It was tied back in a snood with two pretty ringlets around the ears. She was relieved her appearance was satisfactory for the royal visitor.

'Can we offer you and your soldiers refreshments?' she asked, her throat suddenly dry. Fanny was so shocked to have a royal visitor in her home her mind was working overtime. If only she had known of his visit she would have spruced up the dark, heavily furnished parlour with vases of flowers, had Emily polish the fire brass until it shone like the buttons on the Princes' jacket and removed the worn hearth rug. Suddenly her parlour appeared shabby and dull. The charisma of the handsome royal visitor filled the room and everything else paled into ordinariness.

'A cup of hot tea would suit me perfectly. Somehow, tea at the camp always arrives lukewarm,' the Prince said heartily.

'Hot tea it shall be your Highness.' Fanny returned his smile and with a pounding heart, hurried to the kitchen to supervise the tea with the best china and silver teapot. And some of Mrs. Scrimshaw's fruit cake.

'Mrs. Scrimshaw! That's my best Coalport – a family heirloom!'

'I'm so sorry Mrs. – I never did the like before.'

Fanny, Emily and a gaping Mrs. Scrimshaw cast their eyes on the ornate gold-rimmed cup that now lay in smithereens on the kitchen tiles. With trembling hands, Mrs. Scrimshaw bent down to pick up the pieces.

'Let Emily do that and attend to the boiling kettle,' ordered Fanny even more flustered than before.

Mrs. Scrimshaw filled the silver teapot with hot water whilst Fanny adjusted the tray with linen napkins, plates, cups and saucers. Cutting thick slices of fruitcake and arranging shortbread biscuits onto another dainty plate, Fanny was satisfied the tea tray was fit for a future king. At the last moment she opened the lid of the silver teapot.

'Mrs. S – there's no tea in the pot- just hot water. Really! Where is your head today?'

Mrs. Scrimshaw looked aghast. 'So sorry, Ma'am. I'm so nervous – I never made tea for royalty before, I don't know whether I'm comin' or goin'.

'Obviously not,' said Fanny checking the water was still boiling hot and spooning out three teaspoons of her best Indian tea into the pot.

By the time tea was served in the parlour, and the soldiers were enjoying the same refreshment in the entrance hall but with the day-to-day china, Emily was doing her best to remain calm. Not helped by Mrs. Scrimshaw's state of agitation, she bustled backwards and forwards, unnecessarily so, attending to the soldiers who, to her mind were the most dashing men she had ever set eyes on. In the kitchen she was begging Mrs. Scrimshaw to find more cake for the hungry men. Much to her exasperation, Mrs. Scrimshaw unearthed the large fruitcake she had been saving for Grenville's birthday.

'They loved your cake – so much so, I promised they could take the rest of it back to camp,' Emily's eyes lit up with delight. She had attracted the attention of one particular soldier of junior rank. Dark haired with bushy eyebrows and brown eyes that made her heart skip a beat, she could hardly wait to present the cake to him. Reluctantly, Mrs. Scrimshaw wrapped up the large cake in a large box.

'Now you can say you've baked a cake for royalty and her Majesty's soldiers,' Emily gushed hoping to pacify her superior. Mrs. Scrimshaw smiled weakly then thought of her new status. Wouldn't she have something to tell the village gossips about her new found fame?

The distinctive clip of the Prince's voice was heard in the hall. The soldiers, having thanked a scarlet-cheeked Emily, returned to their horses. Scooping up the tray of empty cups and plates she scuttled back to the kitchen but not before she had overheard the Prince thanking Fanny for a delightful and most welcome tea. 'And the fruit cake was most delicious,' he added.

'There, now you have the royal seal of approval,' said Emily to a remorseful Mrs. Scrimshaw sitting at the table. Not only had she missed a glimpse of the Queen's son, she was bemoaning the broken teacup that was sitting in her hand. Emily clapped her hands with joy and gave Mrs. Scrimshaw a hug. The normally quiet, reserved maid was a changed person, Mrs. Scrimshaw noted with surprise. The fact that the young soldier with the deep brown eyes had winked at Emily as he left had more to do with her change in mood than the appearance of any royal visitor.

* * *

CHESTER

In May, Charles took up his new appointment as Canon of Chester Cathedral. When he first saw the interior he was lost for words. Its magnificent interior was the most beautiful place of worship he had ever entered. He instantly fell in love with its grandeur, in particular the long nave. The fact that he was now Canon only served to make him more humble and grateful for his calling to the Church all those years ago. Charles found a contentment and peace there that calmed his perpetually overworked mind.

This new placement was also extremely satisfactory to The Very Reverend Dean Howson. He was won over immediately by his new Canon. Despite all his previous misgivings, he was struck by Charles' warmth and affability and had to admit that despite his superior ability and knowledge, Charles had an appealing modesty about him. Not only was he a great success in the pulpit - queues soon formed outside the Cathedral before Sunday Evensong to hear this popular preacher – but he embraced the idea of giving Botany lectures to the young men of the town. Before Morning Service, Charles would visit the Chapter House in the Cathedral. He spent time alone brooding over the problems of his age. With the terrible news that his friend, the Prince of Wales was ill with a bout of typhoid, he said prayers at each service for his recovery. Surely now, he reasoned, this tragedy this would awaken public opinion and the government for the need of clean water and drainage especially in the over populated areas of towns and cities. Only then could these needless deaths be contained.

Whilst back at Eversley, Charles received news that the Prince had recovered and the Queen had instituted a National Day of Thanksgiving. Charles was due to preach at the Chapel Royal, St James, and he decided to make this the ideal opportunity to speak up for his cause to a congregation of the country's nobility. Charles stepped up into the pulpit, aware that this beautiful chapel had witnessed many royal weddings including that of Queen Victoria to the Prince Consort.

'*Let our hearts be bowed as one man,*' he began, his eyes scanning the royal party who were listening intently, '*that as we have the power, that no man, woman or child in Britain be he prince or beggar, shall die henceforth from preventable diseases. Let us act now to remedy the scandalous neglect of the laws of health and cleanliness- neglect that destroys thousands of lives yearly in this country. If his Royal Highness's disease shall bring home to us that this same disease is striking perpetually at hundreds amongst the very lowest whom we leave to sicken and die in dens unfit for men, unfit for dogs....*' Charles paused and his eyes moistened as he recalled the visit with Mansfield to the slums of London. He recalled the foul rank smells of the River Thames and the ditches around the hovels where children drank from the same water as decomposing animals floated. He remembered the slums in his own parish where infants died of typhoid and diphtheria. Charles' deep voice of conviction resonated around the Chapel as he continued.

'*If his illness shall awaken all to a sanitary reform in town and country – if it shall awaken ministers of religion till there is not a fever alley or malarious ditch left, then this fair and precious life of our Prince will not have been imperiled in vain. Generations as yet unborn will bless the memory of a prince who sickened as poor men sicken and all but died, as poor men die that his exertions might deliver the poor from the dirt, disease and death.*'

His sermon was met with a profound silence. Some ladies overcome with emotion dabbed their eyes with handkerchiefs.

The men in their smart suits and neckties flushed under their tight collars. They were listening to man who spoke with more conscience than any clergyman of the day. Naturally they were aware of the plight of the slums in the cities and towns but here was the Queen's preacher spelling it out to them in such a way that no heart was left untouched.

Charles folded his notes and saw the reaction of his listeners. He bowed his head and prayed that his words would have bearing on their lives. He was physically exhausted. The intensity of his delivery was all consuming and drained him. Every lecture, every sermon demanded of him ate away at his reserves of energy. Charles was fighting his own health battles to as well as those of his country.

* * *

Three years had passed since Charles had taken up his appointment at Chester, and although he loved his work, he was troubled with money problems. These were never far from his mind. He spent restless nights trying to determine how to fund his family's expenses. After one such night, he rose and taking care not to wake Fanny, he dressed and slipped out into the wintry February air. Dawn was just breaking behind the Mount. Walking across the fields towards it, he watched as a hazy sun rose above the trees and broke through a lemon sky. It was a typically cold winter light and a frost had settled. Charles shivered as his breath escaped in small clouds and he wrapped his scarf around his chest tighter. The crisp air burnt his throat and his lungs. Fanny would chide him over his early morning stroll, particularly as his chesty cough still plagued him.

It was times like these, he missed his four-legged companion, Dandy, who was now at rest in the garden under a wooden cross that bore his name. He watched as crows stirring from their nests flew silently across the fields. He heard the screech of a jay, the cry of a pheasant. Apart from the birds nothing stirred. The world slept. His feet crunched under frosty grass. Lichen hung in ragged folds from the dormant trees.

As he walked, he brooded on the nagging problem of finance and the possibilities of earning more money. In his darkest moments he longed to give up writing as a supplement to his living. His most recent novel *'At Last'* based on his Caribbean adventures had been received with mixed reviews.

His outgoings far exceeded his income. Grenville was now at Harrow School. Rose was visiting Maurice in America and both children were still dependent on him for money. His brother, Henry, struggling to make ends meet as an author, was continually asking for support. It seemed there was no end in sight to his problems. Deep in thought, he glanced up to the line of trees and caught sight of a mass of snowdrops. Against the bleakness of the dark wood, nestled on a bank was the most wonderful mass of white petals tipped with green. Spring was not far way he reassured himself. Soon the daffodils and primroses would be open, the woods alive with birdsong and the branches showing smudges of spring green. There was hope, and Charles firmly believed that his prayers would also be answered.

'God will provide,' he said aloud with a renewed spirit. He turned for home. Striding out, his eyes went to the tiled roof of his Church now lit with the first rays of sunshine. The gravestones glinted with frost and there next to the Church was his beloved home. Blue smoke from the kitchen chimney spiralled up into the still air. Emily would be up, stoking the range and making a hearty breakfast of porridge for the family.

Charles was right about his premonition. A few weeks later, a letter arrived by special delivery from Prime Minister Gladstone. The contents of the letter were to change Charles' life. He broke the news to Fanny over supper. The canonry at Westminster Abbey had become available and the Queen and

Prime Minister were keen for him to accept it. He was sure Fanny would be delighted.

'Just think, dear wife, this is England's most prestigious place of worship. What higher honour could a mere Reverend of Eversley aspire to? And I have here confirmation it will pay twice as much as Chester.' His face beamed with joy and Fanny could see that for a moment his old spark had returned. Fanny stood up and hugged Charles, a wide smile lighting up her face.

'Oh my darling, I am so pleased for you.' She paused and sat down again. She leaned towards Charles. 'You will be very much missed in Chester since you have made such an impression there – not only in the Cathedral but with the townsfolk as well. It will be a hard wrench for you and them.'

Charles thought about his devoted students who so avidly accompanied him on his field trips. This had soon developed into the Chester Society of Natural Science. Then there were the Geology classes.

'Does Gladstone say how long your duties will be at Westminster?'

'From September to November – a short period but an invigorating one,' Charles replied without conviction.

Fanny realised this new position would sap Charles of the little energy he had left in him. She wrote immediately to Maurice who was now in Mexico and to Grenville, at Harrow, to tell them 'the best news.' But she warned Maurice that on his return home he would see huge changes in his father's appearance. At fifty-three her husband had aged prematurely. His tall erect figure was stooped and his face lined with a permanent look of weariness.

At Chester when word spread round that Canon Kingsley was leaving, groups gathered in and outside the Cathedral to discuss the news. They were deeply saddened and Charles was touched when he received a letter from one of his students saying 'All Chester mourns.'

WESTMINSTER

'Sermons and sanitation are my calling now,' Charles announced proudly to his children over supper one evening when he returned to Eversley for a break from Westminster. His complexion bore a grey pallor and the dull traces of the London air that afflicted its citizens caused by breathing in the persistent smog. Charles had taken a rest from his novel writing. His health was drained enough as it was, keeping up with the new position at Westminster as well as his involvement in sanitation reform. His children were well aware of the effect his new post was having on him.

Grenville was home for half term and Maurice fresh from his foreign travels had arrived back to great celebrations, yet there was an unspoken sadness at their father's deterioration. Fanny had been right to warn them. Even so, Maurice was still shocked at the change in his father.

Rose, now a mature thirty year old, had accompanied her father to Westminster to act as his housekeeper and companion. Their home for three months of the year was in the Cathedral grounds, overlooking a cloister, and was described as one of the most beautiful in London.

After a convivial supper, Charles suggested that the family come to one of his Sunday morning services at Westminster. It would be such a grand occasion to have them there with him. Everyone was very excited at the idea, and Fanny also suggested that Mrs. Scrimshaw join them.

* * *

Mrs. Scrimshaw was extremely proud of her new bonnet. It was the most expensive one she had ever bought and it certainly was not short on flounce. With its feathers and silk ribbons, she felt it most appropriate for her long awaited trip to London. She had been elated when Fanny suggested she might accompany the children to the morning service. At the last minute Fanny decided not to go. The doctor had diagnosed her with a heart problem and she had no option but to stay home and rest.

The family congregated in the hall of the Rectory at an early hour. Maurice, looking tanned and healthy from his trip to South America stood proud and was dressed in a new suit. Mary wore a new silk dress and mantle of deep russet and young Grenville was keen to imitate his older brother and he too was dressed in a smart wool suit. Emily was bustling around making sure they had the packets of sandwiches that Mrs. Scrimshaw had made the night before. Fanny came downstairs to see them off and surveyed the party as she wrapped her bed shawl around her.

'You look a fine family and I do wish I was coming with you. Papa will be so proud to have you there. And send my love to darling Rose. And tell her how much I miss her.'

'Yes Mama,' piped up Mary. 'We have the bundle of your letters here,' and she thought to herself, 'I'm sure you will have written many times how much you miss her.'

'Ladies and gentlemen, your transport is here', Mr. Scrimshaw announced importantly as he strode through the front door. He had volunteered to take the party to the station in a smart carriage loaned by a wealthy neighbour. Mrs. Scrimshaw followed the children and sat on the top of the carriage next to her husband feeling very important to be part of the family outing.

A muted conversation was held on the train. 'And how did you enjoy your first ride on a train, Mrs. Scrimshaw?' asked Maurice as they disembarked at Waterloo, having noted that for once their cook and housekeeper was lost for words and had remained very quiet during the journey.

Mrs. Scrimshaw shook her head. 'If you want the truth, Mr. Maurice, it was a right boneshaker. I'm not so sure I'll be doing that too often. Give me an 'orse and cart any day.' And she took a handkerchief from her reticule and, as if to justify her uncomfortable experience, wiped away the smut that she was sure had covered her face from the smoke and steam that had penetrated the windows. Maurice smiled. He couldn't disagree. The wooden carriages were indeed basic and not built for comfort.

The early hour made for subdued excitement at the prospect of seeing their father at Westminster Abbey. But by the time the children alighted from the hackney cab in Parliament Square, they were full of chatter. Mrs. Scrimshaw stood in awe of the beautiful exterior of the Abbey and the imposing landmark of Big Ben behind.

When the Reverend had told her of his appointment at the Abbey, he had described it as a very hallowed place of worship that had seen a thousand years of history. Grenville was open mouthed as they entered by the large West door. He squeezed Mary's hand as he gazed around at the magnificent architecture and stained glass windows.

The Verger was there to greet them and, dressed solemnly in black robes led them in a dignified manner down the vast nave. Maurice followed behind the family group and watched as the pews either side rapidly filled with eager worshippers. Some had arrived two hours before to get a good seat to hear Canon Kingsley who, according to reports, was a treat not to be missed.

Through an open door the family glimpsed the choir dressed in their robes of red and white. How angelic they looked thought Mary. Then into a small side chapel where they found their father at an altar kneeling in prayer. The Verger left them at the door. Charles turned to see his family assembled before him. His face, though heavily lined was wreathed in smiles. He greeted and kissed them in turn in hushed tones. Then Rose appeared and the thrill of seeing her brothers and sisters dispelled any solemnity that had lingered before. She gave Mrs. Scrimshaw an effusive hug as she took hold of the bundle of letters from her mother.

'It brings me great joy to see you all here,' Charles said quietly and unusually lost for words. Dressed in his clerical robes he appeared to be a stranger from the familiar father figure they enjoyed at home. The fun-loving Papa who always shared a joke with them, the humble man who had wept tears when Dandy his beloved dog had died, the father who loved to march them across the heath land with boxes and butterfly nets, all these memories paled into insignificance as they saw before them a deeply religious man about to preach in the highest Church of the land.

Rose slipped her arm through her father's. Despite his delight and relief at seeing the family, she could tell by the concern in his eyes and furrowed brow that he was anxious. It was quite different preaching at Westminster Abbey compared to the relaxed surroundings of Eversley.

'Shall we take our seats now and let Father collect himself before the start of the service? The Dean has put aside a row for us at the front of the nave. Come now,' she said, as she and Mrs. Scrimshaw led the way.

'Good luck Papa,' each of his siblings said as they filed out. Grenville was last.

'Papa I'm so proud of you and Mama wishes she were here too.'

Charles cupped his son's head in his hands. 'And I'm so very proud to have my family here today, my little Lord Grenville.' he whispered. Grenville, now a proud sixteen year old, gave him a whimsical smile and closed the door gently as he left.

As Charles followed the choir into the main nave, he joined in with the opening lines of the first hymn. The beauty of their crystal clear voices echoed up into the rafters of the great nave.

'Christ whose Glory fills the skies
Christ the true, the only Light,
Sun of Righteousness arise-'

Despite his weariness, the words inspired Charles. His thoughts turned to the countryside at his Eversley home. God's beauty was so inspiring he wanted to proclaim it from every pulpit in the land. He wanted to awaken those sad city souls who only breathed in the smoke and fumes, who saw only the filth of the rivers and streets and the ceaseless noise of traffic and carriages in their every day of their life. Did they know the meaning of the word 'peace' and 'beauty' in their busy lives?

Making his way to his seat in front of the choir stalls he considered how blessed he was to be in the elevated company of so many of England's great writers. Close by him in Poet's Corner, were effigies to Chaucer, Shakespeare, Dryden, Jane Austen and Keats. All held a place of honour. Charles felt a pang of regret to see the memorial of his dear friend, Frederick Denison Maurice whom he had shared so much with the struggle of reform. Close by was his contemporary Charles Dickens, laid to rest there four years ago. Jolted back to the present Charles continued singing heartily the rousing final verse –

'Visit then this soul of mine,
Pierce the gloom of sin and grief-'

Before mounting the steps of the stone pulpit to deliver his sermon, he observed the congregation of several hundred seated before him. He repeated the words that had echoed in his head since waking that morning. 'I am nothing but a priest.'

His children watched their father closely for signs of nervousness. Both Maurice and Rose were aware of the slight tremble of his hands as he arranged his notes. Even though he had preached at the Abbey several times before, they knew that, as the newly installed Canon, their father was under pressure to make a good impression. Charles drew breath and paused. Rose and Maurice exchanged worried glances. If only Mama were here to reassure him. After a hesitant stammer, Charles inspiring words rang out into the Abbey. The children listened in awe as their father's powerful sermon held the rapt attention of his listeners.

At that moment, Maurice had never felt so close to God. Rose, concerned about her father's health hoped this new appointment would not tire him further. At first Mary listened attentively. Her eyes wandered around the great Abbey and suddenly she was lost to its striking beauty and her heart filled with pride that her father was preaching in a place of worship that held so much history. Grenville's eyes never left his father's. He admired him so much for despite his fame and popularity, his father remained firmly committed to his family. Mrs. Scrimshaw sat spellbound. Never had she dreamt she would have the privilege of listening to the Reveren' preach in such exalted surroundings. She brushed away a tear as she thought about the ordinary, homely man she worked for. She was brimming with gratitude that she was in the employ of such a gifted man.

FOREIGN SHORES

Charles completed his three months at Westminster and looked forward to the remaining winter months at home with his family. Maurice, however, was adamant that another English winter would debilitate his father's health further. He and Rose discussed this with their mother.

'This time, I suggest he visits North America, Mama. A long sea voyage and the stimulation of seeing this vast continent would be of great benefit to his health,' suggested Maurice.

'And who better to recommend it than you both?' Fanny looked to her eldest children. Maurice in his three years away had moved from Argentina to work in Mexico, and Rose had travelled to the West Coast to visit him, before going on to San Francisco.

'Oh Mama, it is such a land of opportunity. The people there, the ones I have met at any rate, are delightfully friendly. They welcome you into their homes and Papa would love all of that. Besides, he is already well known there. It makes so much sense for him to go on a lecture tour. He will attract huge audiences and, I have it on good authority, he can command from three hundred dollars to a thousand dollars a week,' added Rose enthusiastically.

'A thousand dollars a week! That is more than the Church pays in a year!' Fanny's eyes lit up. The idea that Charles could embark on a foreign trip and it would be financially rewarding was one she completely approved of. She pondered for a moment. And taking hold of both of her children's hands, announced, 'Let us start planning this straight away. I have already put the thought into Charles' head and he agrees it is an excellent idea. Rose, I will leave you to make all the arrangements. Papa is not up to doing any of this.'

'And what about you, Mama? How will you cope with Papa's absence?' Rose squeezed her hand.

'I will be well looked after here. It will not be easy for either Papa or I to endure a long separation, but you are right about the stimulation of a new continent. It will be benefit his health considerably. I remember how well he was on his return from Trinidad.'

With Fanny's blessing, Rose set about planning a grand tour of North America starting from the East coast.

At the end of January, Charles and Rose set sail for New York, this time on one of the high-speed luxury ships. They arrived to a hero's welcome and were soon ensconced as guests in a beautiful home on Staten Island. Charles immediately wrote to Fanny, assuring her that the *'air is like champagne and I feel well again, my spirits restored.'*

After lecturing in New York, Charles travelled by train to Boston and Philadelphia where he was astonished to find he was addressing an audience of four thousand. The Americans loved him and, despite his occasional faltering delivery, they held the visiting Englishman in high esteem. All the adulation he received was tempered by the fact that he missed Fanny desperately and he wrote to her continually. Fanny who was struggling with her heart problem, wrote back in turn to ask if it would be convenient for him to send home a hundred pounds for house repairs.

At the end of March, Charles and Rose were in the middle of a Canadian winter in Montreal. From the freezing fog of Niagara they headed south to St Louis and Omaha. Their home for a fortnight was a luxury Pullman whilst they crossed thousands of miles of desert and sage scrub to Virginia city and its silver mines, to Sacramento then to Salt Lake city.

Although still attracting large audiences for his lectures, Charles did not have the avid following he had enjoyed on the East Coast. But it was finally on the West coast Charles encountered his 'earthly paradise'.

Their expedition, on horseback, to Yosemite started at six in the morning. Rose was delighted to see her father embrace the long ride through the mountains.

'I feel like a boy again,' Charles exclaimed as he headed his horse up a high pass. The scenery intoxicated him. They rode through passes shadowed either side by snow-clad mountains and pine forests, fording rivers in the valley. Charles was in wild country and loved every second of it. Eagles soared overhead and he glimpsed deer in the forest. Higher and higher their guide led them and as the temperature dropped, Charles embraced the clear air. Finally they arrived at their base for the night, and after a hearty supper, he and Rose sat out under the stars around a blazing fire.

The next morning, the guides told Rose an even bigger surprise awaited them. They were heading to Mariposa Grove, the home of the giant Sequoia tree. Setting off after an early breakfast, they continued their journey until they rode into a vast clearing. Charles was speechless as he dismounted his horse. Before him were the magnificent Sequoia trees.

'Rose, have you ever seen anything so beautiful? Their size and magnificence is beyond description.' Charles stood under the rust red trunk that towered above him to the shimmering greenery adorning its branches. He guessed the tree must be over two hundred feet high and the guide had told him was over two thousand years old. He ran his hands over the deep gnarled grooves of bark. In the unbroken silence, Charles leaned his head against the trunk and had never felt so humbled by one of God's creations. Deeply moved, prayer came to him spontaneously. He prayed that the beauty of God's Earth would remain undefiled, that Man would always respect Nature. His thoughts turned to the stark contrast of the cities at home where the Industrial Revolution was polluting the skies with their factories. The wheels of industry were turning at such a rate and transforming the countryside, Charles wondered if Man, in his desperate ambition to invent and produce, would sacrifice the sanctity of Mother Nature.

Rose left him alone with his thoughts and wandered amongst the trees collecting cones from under the Sequoia trees and carefully packing them in her saddlebag.

'This is indeed the most wonderful work of God,' Charles whispered as they stood in the early morning sun absorbing the silence. Close by were the Douglas firs and pines but it was the Sequoia trees that held Charles rapt attention.

'Can you imagine having one of these trees grow on the Mount and in our churchyard at Eversley? To transport a little of this back to our home counties as an illustrious memory! I can think of nothing better!'

Rose agreed but said nothing about her plan to plant some seeds from the cones on her return.

Charles's good health was not to last. During his stay in San Francisco he caught a heavy cold and this quickly developed into pleurisy. Rose was adamant they follow the advice of a doctor and leave the fog of the city and return to the clear air of the Rockies. After a tiresome journey of four days Charles had no choice but to rest in bed. Six weeks of confinement followed and Charles was ready to leave for home. He wrote to Fanny that once back at Eversley he hoped to *'settle down into an old theologian and never leave her again.'*

It was a hot August day when Charles and Rose returned to the port of Southampton. As they disembarked the ship, a carriage was waiting for them. Charles revelled in seeing the familiar Hampshire countryside as they made their way down the lanes of Eversley and finally to home. The carriage slowed as they passed his Church, his beloved St Mary's and his heart swelled with pride. It stood waiting for him like an old friend in the churchyard that was now neatly and proudly kept by an eager group of parishioners. Its red brick walls radiated warmth that had little to do with the heat of the day.

Leaning forward in his seat Charles saw his first glimpse of the Rectory, the familiar chimney pots, the welcoming windows and well-tended gardens. Despite his tiredness from the journey he couldn't wait to be re-united with his family. Fanny, Mary and Grenville rushed outside to greet the carriage as it pulled up in the drive. There were tears and laughter and whoops of delight from the children, who were thrilled to have their father home. Exchanging no words, Charles wrapped Fanny in his arms and kissed her. Fanny fought back her tears.

'Welcome home Papa!' the children greeted as they hugged him and then fell on Rose with more hugs and kisses.

Mrs. Scrimshaw and Emily hovered in the hallway ready to fuss over him and hoping that their Reveren' hadn't suffered too much after his long journey. Mrs. Scrimshaw had a larder full of bottled raspberries and plums and enough pickled beans to feed the barracks at Bramshill which was just as well as they now had a frequent visitor in the guise of the dark-eyed sergeant who came to call on Emily on her days off.

Mrs. Scrimshaw had prepared a celebration dinner of roast pork with thyme stuffing followed by stewed plums from the garden and a rich custard. They toasted Maurice's marriage to an American girl in New York. They celebrated Charles' return to good health despite his illness on the last leg of his journey. Grenville and Mary wanted to hear all about the winter in Canada.

'How was the winter there? How cold was it?' Grenville asked. He had read about their winters where rivers freeze and people were unable to leave their homes for snowdrifts.

'How deep was the snow? And did you go sledging?' Mary and her brother badgered their father for answers.

Charles delighted them with stories of sledging across the River St Lawrence River and eating moose during his stay there. He described seeing the falls at Montmorency and how they were fringed with icicles fifty feet long. And how he had been amazed at the sight and sound of the grandeur of Niagara Falls in Buffalo. Mary and Grenville had so many questions about America they hardly knew where to begin. But Fanny could see Charles was beginning to tire. Rose volunteered to take up recounting their adventures. They had seen such variations in scenery, met so many wonderful people and collected many specimens of plants and flowers, she assured them it would takes days if not weeks to recount all their adventures.

Fanny was aware that Grenville was fidgeting. His eyes were boring into hers to attract her attention, so she finally nodded to him. 'All right, Grenville, show Papa your new acquisition,' she said with a proud smile. 'But be careful now,' she warned.

Grenville leapt up from the dinner table and whispered gleefully in his father's ear as he left. 'Wait there, Papa I have a surprise for you.'

After several minutes they heard a shout from outside and Rose and Mary rushed to the front door followed by Charles and Fanny.

'Look Papa- I have a bicycle and I can ride it!' Grenville called as he wobbled along the drive sitting on the high wheel of a Penny Farthing. Charles puffed contentedly on his pipe, beaming with pleasure.

'Well done.' He laughed. 'It looks like great fun but I think these bicycles are for the younger generation. I will feel safer with my four- legged transport.'

'It's so easy – once you get used to it,' Grenville called out and waved an arm in the air. Turning the bicycle round with dexterity, he cycled back to the front door and dismounted with aplomb. 'There father, that is my surprise for you,' he said breathlessly, his eyes shining with excitement.

Everyone clapped enthusiastically. Even Emily and Mrs. Scrimshaw had left the kitchen to come and view the demonstration. Over the last few weeks, Grenville had taken many a tumble in his efforts to master the new machine. Much to Fanny's relief he had escaped injury. Not as academically gifted as her other children, nonetheless she was very proud of her youngest son. It gave her great joy to see Grenville impressing his father with his mastery of the bicycle.

Later that night Charles and Fanny held each other in a long embrace, deeply content in their reunion. 'If only, dear one, we still had the physical passion of our younger days, there would be no happier man than I to make love to you, as we used to,' whispered Charles intently.

'Nature has taken its course, husband, and those days of passion are behind us. It is enough that we can hold each other and share the intimacies of the mind. And besides, my weak heart would not take the excitement of our lovemaking. It is enough that we share this bed together, do you not think?'

Fanny nuzzled her cheek under his whiskery chin and realized how much they had both changed since those days of passion. Charles had grown gaunt, fragile even and vulnerable to chest infections. Gone was the strong lustiness they had shared for all those years in the marriage bed that held so many wonderful secrets.

Charles sighed and kissed her tenderly. Tempering his contentment was a nagging premonition their days together were numbered. Fanny, five years his senior would surely die before him with her deteriorating heart condition. It could only be a matter of time. He found the idea frightening. Despite the love and devotion of his children, life without her would be unthinkable. Since he had returned from his American lecture tour with a healthy bank account, he could insure Fanny received the best treatment. With care and rest he was sure she would grow strong again.

The next morning Charles awoke early to open up the Church. It gave him a special joy to return to its comforting familiarity. After all the demanding schedules of his foreign adventures, he found the simplicity of its interior reassuring. He was back to his beloved home and family, to his flock and to his simple Church.

His congregation that still swelled in number was extremely pleased to see him. After his first service, they gathered round, eager to hear about his foreign travels. The youngsters in particular besieged him with questions about America and the land of golden opportunity they could only dream about it.

But duty of a more serious nature called upon him. Sickness was rife in the two hamlets. Charles sadly noted the addition of new gravestones in the churchyard and simple wooden crosses of the poorer folk who had succumbed to fever. He went about his work, visiting the sick with as much energy as he could muster. The days when he strode across the heath land to Eversley Cross with a bounce in his step were long gone. Now he rode sedately on horseback along with his medicine bag. As he observed the barren, scorched fields caused by weeks of drought, he had been relieved to learn the famers had harvested a plentiful grain crop earlier in the month. Finding welcome shade amongst the fir trees, he noticed that even here the familiar birdsong was absent. Nature was struggling to survive in the heat and drought but like all trials of life, he assured himself, they would in the end balance out and return to normal.

Decline

Fanny and Rose were taking tea in the darkened parlour that provided some respite from the sultry August weather. Charles was out on one of his visits to the parish. Angst showed on Fanny's face as she sat in her armchair ignoring the scones Mrs. Scrimshaw had laid out on the tea tray. The room had a gloomy atmosphere. Rose opened the curtains a little to let in more light and sat down next to her mother. For a moment both were alone with their thoughts.

'Come Mama, you haven't eaten since breakfast, do try a scone.'

Fanny reluctantly placed one on her plate. 'Rose, I am so worried about your Papa. Do you think I should accompany him to Westminster this time?'

'Yes, I think he will want you there,' Rose sighed as she stared at the empty fire grate. 'It's barely a month since his return from America and already he has overstretched himself with parish work. I'm concerned about his health and I'm not sure he should go at all. Is he yet strong enough to cope with two sermons a day?'

'He has no choice,' Fanny replied. 'Dean Stanley will be away in Paris next month so there is no one but Charles to take his place. Let us hope this heat dies down. It will be unbearable in the city and will drain his energy even further.'

'If there is any change in his condition, you must summon me immediately and I will come to support you both.' Not only was Rose concerned about her father's health, she was well aware her mother was struggling with her heart problem.

Fanny smiled wearily at her daughter. She knew that she and Charles must make the effort to return to the bustling, demanding world of London.

Reluctantly, Fanny accompanied Charles to their home in the Cloisters. The day of his return, the weather finally broke. Outside, the world was the colour of dull metal as heavy rain hammered against the windows. Fanny's thoughts were full of foreboding. Charles was hunched in a chair in his bedroom.

'Charles?' She leaned over to him, wondering if he was deep in prayer. The notes he had been reading had slipped from his hand. His face turned upwards to her and she could see the pain etched in his eyes.

'What a time to disgrace oneself with illness,' he said. 'I have to preach before a full congregation tomorrow and yet I can barely stand with the pain.'

'Do not even think about tomorrow. Come back to bed and I will summon the doctor immediately.' In spite of Fanny's lack of strength, she helped Charles out of the chair and into bed.

When the doctor arrived, Charles was in an even more exhausted state and his pallor was grey.

'I advise complete bed rest and plenty of fluids,' he advised Fanny not wanting to alarm her about his own diagnosis of his patient's health. Fanny was left to break it to Charles that his sermon the next day was cancelled.

Rose was called urgently to London. This time it was not her father's health concern but her mother's. Fanny was again suffering from a weak heart and was confined to bed. Despite his own debility, Charles tended to her daily and prayed with her in the evenings.

By the end of November, Charles willed himself to take one more service at the Abbey. He awoke to see the storm clouds had gathered and a howling gale was battering London. Looking out to the grounds of the Cloisters and the boughs of the trees bending in the strong gusts, his thoughts turned to Clovelly and the fishermen there. He prayed for their safety recalling the carnage he had witnessed as a young boy when the storm had ravaged the fishing fleet.

He hurried out into wind and rain for an early arrival at the Abbey. The congregation, undeterred by the weather, had turned out in great numbers. Summoning up all his strength, Charles delivered his sermon with all the energy that was left within him. Folding his notes, he bowed solemnly knowing this could be the last time his exhausted body would allow him to perform his duties.

A few days later, he and Fanny returned to Eversley for the Christmas break. Emily and Mrs. Scrimshaw had decorated the house with boughs of holly and ivy. A brightly lit Christmas tree stood in the hall. The glow of the candles on its branches along with the roaring fires in every room gave the house a festive atmosphere. But it was the sight of the ailing couple that brought tears to Mrs. Scrimshaw's eyes. Fanny was immediately taken up to her room and, with a heavy heart, Charles sat alone by the fire in the parlour, drinking the tea Emily brought for him. The doctor's pronouncement was not good. The journey home had weakened Fanny further. She could suffer a relapse at anytime that could prove fatal. Charles sent a telegram to the Queen cancelling the sermon he was due to deliver at Windsor that weekend.

Christmas was spent with subdued appetites and constant attention to the patient upstairs. In the evenings, Charles read poetry to Fanny and together reminisced over their happy thirty-five years together. Facing the reality that Fanny could soon be taken, they discussed her funeral arrangements in detail.

Despite the snow falling in silent flakes and turning the world into a white canvas, the doctor insisted the windows of Fanny's bedroom be kept open to allow her to breathe more easily. A few days after Christmas, Charles climbed wearily up the stairs to see her and shivered as he entered the room. After the warmth of the downstairs, the cold took his breath away.

'How is my dearest wife this morning?' Charles gave her a broad smile as he clasped her icy hand. His smile faded as he saw the torment in her still beautiful face. The years had not aged her but today there were deep shadows under her eyes and her hands trembled. Fanny gazed up at him meekly, her complexion as blanched as the snow-covered fields outside.

'What is it, Fanny?'

Fanny's eyes welled up with tears. 'I am so ashamed that....' She swallowed hard. 'I am so frightened, Charles.'

'What frightens you? '

'Death.' Her answer was barely audible. 'Help me. I cannot leave you. Our time is not over yet. I cannot bear the thought of leaving you, my children, this world and going into the unknown...I am so afraid.' She clutched at her husband's hand.

'It is not darkness you are going to, for God is light,' Charles intoned gently. 'It is not a lonely place for Christ is there with you. It is not an unknown country for Christ is there. Have faith, my dearest, and know we will be together for eternity one day, away from all the toil of this Earth. Sometime soon we will lie in the churchyard together and enjoy our long deserved rest.' And how my heart longs for that time, thought Charles dismally.

Fanny closed her eyes and sank back onto the pillows. Her beloved soul mate had given her the consolation she desperately sought. Charles descended the stairs, his thoughts of Fanny's imminent demise weighing heavily on his mind. He found Maurice dressed in a heavy overcoat and woolly hat about to go up the stairs. He gave him a questioning look.

'Are you going out, son? The weather is not for walking out.'

'Father, I am not about to catch a severe chill by attending to Mama in that icy room. I am properly dressed for it, as you should be.'

Charles gave a weak smile, amused at his son's admonishment. Rose was following behind Maurice carrying a hot water bottle for her mother.

'Father you will catch your death if you persist in staying in Mama's room when it is so bitterly cold. Your cough is getting worse,' Rose cautioned him anxiously.

Everyone is appears to enjoy scolding me today, thought Charles as he entered the kitchen to see Mrs. Scrimshaw busy peeling potatoes.

'Reveren' Sir, you look well chilled and ...'

'Enough,' said Charles holding up a hand. 'Everyone is taking great delight in telling me what to do today.' He gave Mrs Scrimshaw a mercurial smile. 'A hot cup of coffee might restore my blood circulation – and my spirits.'

Charles peered through the steamy kitchen window. The lawn was covered in at least a foot of snow. 'This weather looks set to continue. If the snow persists you must stay the night,' he said, his voice rasping as an attack of coughing halted his words.

Mrs. Scrimshaw nodded. 'Thank you, Reveren'. My Henry will try and get through this snow but if it's driftin' in the lanes, they might be a problem.'

With a concerned smile, she gave Charles a cup of hot coffee and watched as he disappeared to his study. At least he seemed a little more chipper today but his cough was not good, especially with his weak lungs. He was paying too much attention to his wife and not to himself, she thought, as she observed more snow falling onto the window sill.

That night Charles slept fitfully, his continual coughing had left his lungs sore. When exhaustion overtook him he had vivid dreams. He dreamt of Charles Mansfield. They were fishing on the banks of the River Cam. Mansfield landed a huge fish and they embraced each other triumphantly. They laughed and joked and when Charles awoke he desperately wished he could have stayed in the dream with his friend. Those idle days of student life had been good ones. Now he was back to the reality of life - himself a sick man and his wife dying. How he wished it would be quick for both of them so that they could lie peacefully in the churchyard together. He had no fear of death. It was after all only a change of place and a new life that awaited him and best of all -eternal rest. How he wished for that now as a bleak snowy dawn greeted him. How could he face life without Fanny? Try as he might he couldn't find the strength to bathe and dress. Rose came up to find her father lying back on the pillows, his face ashen. He clutched his chest trying to catch his breath.

'Papa, we must call the doctor for you- immediately.' and without waiting for a reply she rushed downstairs and called for one of the stable lads to saddle up and fetch Doctor Samuels in the next village.

'And don't delay,' she added as she plodded through the snow back to the house.

The doctor spent some time with Charles before checking on Fanny. His serious expression told her the worst.

'It is not good news, Rose. Your father has pneumonia. I strongly advise you have nurses to stay with him. You have enough to see to with your mother so poorly. The nurse must monitor his temperature closely and I insist, Rose, that he remains in bed and his room is kept warm day and night. Knowing how close he is to Fanny and how determined he is, he may well want to visit her. On no account is he to leave his room. Only then will he make a satisfactory recovery. I am prescribing him sedatives to ease his chestiness.'

But Charles could not bear the thought of being parted from Fanny. Unseen by his nurse, and trying to restrain his nagging cough, he left his room to see her. Fanny was shocked at the sight of her husband's deterioration and tears filled her eyes.

The wonderful times they had shared throughout their marriage, the home they had made for their children and the lasting mark her husband had made in the world through his books and teachings- loved and adored by so many around the world and now he had come to this. To see this great man bowed by illness grieved her beyond measure. Their closeness and desire for each other had never waned. He had been a devoted husband and now? What lay ahead? Their lives were reduced to two sick rooms.

Fanny opened her mouth to tell him all this but he leaned over her and kissed her icy cheek. 'Don't speak, my love. This is heaven. To see you once more is all I ask for. That we cannot be there for each other breaks my heart.'

Fanny had felt much better that morning and she wanted to tell him that, with God's blessing she might recover, and they could share their fading years together. But Charles was bent over with an attack of coughing and fighting for his breath. He turned and gazed at her fondly before stumbling back to his room. Messages and notes arrived from friends. Mrs. Scrimshaw was kept busy as village folk struggling with the snow drifts came to call asking about the health of the Reveren' and Mrs Kingsley. The parish was in shock to learn that both were taken so poorly. Prayers were said in church for them both.

Mrs. Scrimshaw was in the kitchen helping Rose make up a breakfast tray for Fanny and a warming herbal tea of ginger for Charles. Emily was puffing through the back door with another full bucket of coal in her hand.

'These fires are just eating up this coal,' she muttered as she went through to the study to stoke up the fire 'despite those new pipes Mrs. Kingsley had put in.' she added as an afterthought. She looked around her. Stacks of mail lay unopened on the desk. Alongside were papers and copious notes Charles had written after his American voyage. In amongst them were pressed flowers and glass pots with various dead insects in them. Two fir cones sat on another table.

Emily picked one up. 'Now they would make the fire burn bright,' she said examining the small cone. Replacing one on the table, she changed her mind. After all the study was full of the fruits of their trip. It could be something of special interest. As she finished shovelling coal onto the fire, she stood back and a horrible thought struck her. Suppose the Master never got well again and there were all these notes and books half-finished and there was his 'baccy' jar that had remained unused for weeks. It was a right sad affair. That it was.

Joining the others in the kitchen, she volunteered to take the tea up to the Reveren'.

'Don't worry, Emily, you have enough to do,' said Rose as she added a jar of honey and the bottle of cough medicine to the tray.

'Good honey, that one is too, commented Mrs. Scrimshaw trying to lift the heavy atmosphere that pervaded the house. 'Eucalyptus-it will do his chest no end of good.'

Rose sighed and despondently picked up the tray. She would do anything to get her father well again but she was of a mind that even the Eucalyptus honey and cough mixture would not be enough this time.

Under the influence of the sedatives, Charles had slept well and in his drowsiness he tried to recall his vivid dreams. Rose knocked at the door and nodded at the nurse.

'Thank you, I'll take over Nurse Stowe. There's a hot breakfast in the dining room for you.'

As the nurse left, Rose drew back the heavy curtains and turned to examine her father.

'Papa, did you have a good night?' she asked, hiding her dismay as saw his flushed cheeks and fresh beads of sweat on his forehead. His fever was taking hold.

'Excellent, thank you,' he replied weakly. He blinked as the sun streamed through the window. 'It is another beautiful morning, I see.' He struggled to catch his breath. His heart ached to see his Church nestled in the snow. How he wished it were a normal Sunday. At this time he would be getting ready for his morning service, gathering his sermon notes together and hastening over to meet the bell ringers, the musicians with their trombones and clarinets and the first of his congregation.

He lay on the pillows listlessly as Rose wiped his forehead with a damp cloth. After some persuasion, he swallowed a spoonful of medicine. Rose sat on the bed next to him and helped him sip from the cup of honey and ginger tea. Her father was putting up such a good fight against his illness yet she wondered if he would make it through the worst. She banished the thought from her mind.

'I had the most strange dream last night.'

'Tell me about it,' said Rose gently as she stroked his hand.

'When I was a young curate here, I had a visitor one evening to my cottage. He bore the typical trademark of a sweep's boy –a malnourished body and black filthy clothes. He was a poor mite. We spent an hour or two in the warmth of my parlour.' Charles smiled at the memory. 'He was so famished, he devoured my soup as fast as I could ladle it into his bowl. Some weeks later he died of a fever caused no doubt by lack of proper nourishment. But in that short time I formed a strong bond with him. I was never able to forget him. Last night he came to me in a dream. He was standing across a river and calling to me. It left me with a great feeling of peace. Do you think he is waiting for me?'

'It sounds like your story of Tom in '*The Water Babies*', Papa.'

Charles thought for a moment. 'I have never forgotten him,' he repeated.

'And where is he buried?' Rose was aware her father was drifting off to sleep again.

Charles pointed a shaky finger towards the churchyard. 'There in the furthest corner by the yew tree.'

Out of curiosity Rose went to the window. How beautiful the Church looked dressed in its mantle of white with the black cross poking out from the roof. As she spotted the small mound with the snow covered wooden cross, she saw immediately it was the one her father had pointed out once before. The simple words engraved on the cross had caught her attention. 'Tom-the Sweep'.

'How peaceful it is here this morning,' she said turning back to her father.

'When I see this view with the sun shining on the trees on the Mount and the snow falling off the branches, I can think of no better place in the world to be. In spite of all our travelling, I dream of it constantly, this is home. It is all...' Charles broke into a fit of coughing.

'Papa, you must rest some more,' Rose said as she soothed his clammy forehead. 'Nurse will be up shortly to attend to you and the Doctor will call later. Ah, here is Grenville come to see you.'

Charles saw his seventeen-year old son standing in the doorway, grinning bravely.

'Good morning, Papa. How are you today?'

'Come.' Charles beckoned him to his side as Rose left quietly shutting the door behind her.

'It is good to see such a bright morning. And I do believe there is a thaw on the way. See, the snow is falling off the branches over the firs over there.'

Grenville glanced at the snow scene and saw the trees showing snatches of green. Even though his father was so ill, he never failed to observe the passing moods of nature.

'In that case it should be a good turn out at Church this morning,' Grenville said manfully.

'And will you attend?'

'Of course, and with Maurice, Mary and Rose. Then we can report back to you on the service and the text of the sermon. I'm sure we will all be praying for yours and Mama's recovery.'

'That may be so and let us hope the Good Lord is listening,' Charles said feeling exhausted again. With a huge effort, he sat up and watched as a steady stream of locals file through the lych-gate and up the path to where the Curate was waiting to welcome them. There were his beloved congregation, humble folk most of them leading ordinary lives, but never far from illness such as he was suffering- never far from poverty. It lay at each door. Wearily he thought how much more he needed to do to change the plight of these people who toiled so hard with so few rewards. The church bells were ringing and Charles felt renewed hope.

Grenville was reluctant to leave him but duty called, he explained, and he must be off to join the others. Charles gave a small wave as Grenville disappeared through the door. In spite of the weather it was a normal Sunday morning in January. Life goes on with or without me, he thought. As he drifted off to sleep again he wondered how the poor folk on the heath land were surviving the cold. He must remember to ask the Curate when he came to visit……

After attending church, Rose did not have to wait to hear the update on her father's condition. She could sense he was losing the battle for life and he had developed a calm acceptance of it. She held out two letters the doctor had allowed her to bring up for him.

'Papa, shall I open them? They have the Royal Seal.'

Charles indicated with a nod of the head. The contents brought a wan smile to his haggard face. Rose fought back the tears as she saw his life fading away. Then suddenly there was a glimmer of the 'old' father as she showed him the drawings from the Prince of Wales' children.

'How delightful they have remembered you and sent you such beautiful drawings. And there is a note here from the Prince himself to say he is sending his physician to see you. You will have no better treatment, Papa.'

'And treatment for my dear wife too…. Fanny too,' and he began to pray inaudibly.

Sir William Gull, the Prince's physician was made welcome after his long journey from London in the snowy conditions. He sat with children in the dining room after attending to Charles, and then Fanny. Mrs. Scrimshaw had prepared a dinner of roast pheasant for the important visitor.

'He may pull through but we can't be sure,' he said fixing the children with a stern but kindly eye. 'If he has a haemorrhage, it could be fatal.' He sighed as he took another sip of claret. 'He has taken the time, in his moments of lucidity, to go through the funeral arrangements with me. He has a wonderful simplicity about his views on life and, as you are probably aware, his funeral will mirror this. Such a modest man, yet such great charisma and talent.'

The children were silent as they finished their meal. Rose took a tray of tea to Fanny telling her the news of Charles' condition. Later that evening she sat with her father.

'Dr Gull, come immediately.' she called from the top of the stairs. The doctor was enjoying the company of the two boys by the parlour fire and rushed upstairs to meet her. Blood was oozing out of Charles' mouth, his face ashen. The sheets were spattered with blood. Rose anxiously lit the oil lamp and awaited the doctor's instructions. The sound of her father's shallow breathing frightened her. A short while later she gave the news to the family.

'Father has suffered a haemorrhage. His life is in the balance,' she announced calmly.

One by one they came to see him as he lay in clean sheets and sedated. They were left in little doubt the end was close.

'No one must tell Mama of these developments,' Rose whispered outside the bedroom door. Later that evening she read prayers to her father. In the shadowy twilight of the oil lamp she saw her mother's nurse come though the door. Charles opened his eyes briefly.

'Ah, dear Nurse...and I too have met my end. It is all as it should be.' And the world dissolved before him once more.

Rose exchanged a questioning glance with the nurse.

'Why does he say that? Rose asked.'

'He is of the mind his wife has died.'

Rose let the tears flow. She had held them back for so long, it was a relief to let go of her pent up emotions. Surely, it couldn't be that both her parents would die at the same time. God would spare one of them. Please let not Mother go as well, she prayed.

Rose stood vigil by her father's bedside through the night and dozed in the shadowy light as he slept peacefully. Dr Gull came up at intervals to check his fever and pulse. Assured that he had done all he could, he left the following morning after the family had thanked him for his services.

'The Prince would have wished for nothing less,' he said before he stepped into his carriage.

Another day passed and the family noted how their father still hung on bravely to life. Again that night Rose sat by his bedside and read psalms to him. Once in the night he stirred and she heard him murmur. 'No more fighting, no more fighting.'

'Papa, Papa, I'm here,' she whispered. But Charles was asleep again and Rose watched as the illness and worry lifted from his face to be replaced with a peace and calm.

'He has accepted death and given up his fight for life. He is ready to meet God.' Rose bent over and kissed his pale cheek. 'Dear Father, sleep well.'

Adieu

The next morning shortly before midday the doctor broke the news to the family who were waiting expectantly in the parlour. 'He has passed quietly away without a pain or discomfort.'

Rose was in deep shock. She had witnessed his passing. White as a sheet, it finally hit home that her father had left them. His mighty energy and presence was no longer there. She couldn't begin to imagine the gap in their lives he would leave. She embraced Grenville who was sobbing heavily, then Maurice who, too shocked to move stood rigidly, his head bowed. Mary sat apart, her eyes bloodshot with crying. Mrs. Scrimshaw and Emily having hard the news were going about their morning routines in a dazed state. Neither could speak. There was nothing to say that could bring the dear Reveren' back.

'He's gone to his well-deserved rest,' was all Mrs. Scrimshaw could muster by way of a comment as she and Emily sat down to a cup of tea.

'Who will break the news to Mrs. Kingsley?' Doctor Samuels asked Rose as he was buttoning up his coat in the hallway.

'I will. She must be told soon but how will it affect her health?'

'I would leave it for a few hours. I have given her a sedative. Let it take its course first. I will call by later to attend further to her. She will need a lot of support in the coming days and weeks.'

Fanny sat up in bed, having lived through five days of shock and disbelief. That her husband should have died before her was unimaginable. And how unselfishly he had come to see her whilst all the time fighting his own severe illness. When she felt strong enough to leave her bed, she and Rose had tea together in her bedroom. It was imperative she took charge of the family now her husband was no longer there. She had a funeral to arrange and letters to answer.

Dressed heavily in black mourning, her thoughts drifted back to the last time she had seen Charles, never guessing that he would be taken before her. She owed it to him to be strong in mind and body and to hold the family together in their grief. The late afternoon sun streamed through the bedroom window. Rose sat across from her and poured strong tea from the tea tray Mrs. Scrimshaw had carefully arranged with paste sandwiches and fruitcake. Mrs. Scrimshaw had been firm with Rose that it was of the utmost importance Mrs. Kingsley regain her strength and that her faint appetite was not going to help matters. Rose and Fanny talked for many hours about the loss of their adoring father and husband and his life's work.

'And, Rose dear, you know, Charles even in his forties wished for a release from this life. He felt old before his time. Oh, there was so much energy in him. He swept up people with his ideas and example of how to live a good life but I remember him saying and I quote, because I wrote it down and have memorized it. He said, *'God forgive me if I am longing for this moment of death but I look forward to it with an intense and reverent curiosity.'* So dear daughter, he has gone to the place where he had such curiosity. He will be at peace, for sure, and he has left such a mark on the world that many would envy.'

Not only were telegrams and letters arriving from London but from all over the world, in particular America where Charles had recently made such an impact. Prayers were said at Westminster Abbey and Chester Cathedral. All who knew of Charles Kingsley were affected in some way by his death and none more so than his devoted parishioners for whom he had cared for and nurtured all his years as a young Curate and then Rector.

On the day of the funeral, the cold weather of the past weeks had mellowed into a mild day with glimpses of sunshine. Snowdrops peeped their heads above the hardened ground and in the early morning light, the rooks wheeled around the Rectory. Apart from their cawing, all was silent. Inside the Rectory the family went about their business without any unnecessary conversation. Mrs. Scrimshaw had laid out a cooked breakfast before adding the final touches to the buffet the guests were invited to after the funeral service. The morning passed slowly. From within the house they could hear the tolling of a solitary church bell. All was ready.

The simple oak coffin was covered with wreathes of flowers and a cross of camellias. The local pallbearers assembled, their heads bowed and their attention given to their freshly polished shoes. The lane to the Church was lined with carriages, small and grand, and princely horses. Crowds of mourners queued outside to enter through the lych-gate. In the corner and to the left hand side of the path, the grave of Charles Kingsley was ready and fresh dark soil piled to one side.

With heads bowed, the villagers mingled with the high-ranking officials. The Prince of Wales had sent a representative who filed into the Church alongside the Dean of Westminster and the Bishop of Winchester. There were the smartly dressed officers from Aldershot and Sandhurst, professors and titled men, peers, authors, publishers and huntsmen. Jim Hatchett the wheel-wright arrived with his family. And straggling in at the end of the procession were the 'heathers' the band of gypsies; men, women and children solemnly and awkwardly dressed in their Sunday best.

After the last prayers were said over the grave, the family walked through the side gate to the Rectory acknowledging the reverential nods of the crowd some of whom were openly sobbing. Alongside the wreaths from the family, children from the local school laid bunches of early catkins and snowdrops around the fresh earth beneath which Charles now lay.

It was, as Maurice remarked later to his family, a funeral that reflected their father admirably. He was loved by all and friend to all. He did not hold the poor man lower than the man with great riches. All, in his eyes, and the eyes of God, were the same.

* * *

Kneeling in St Mary's Church in late March, a woman sits silently alone. She strains to recall her late father's familiar voice. She longs to see his tall erect figure stride down the aisle and bow before the altar. After a while the voice comes to her, quietly; the voice that had been heard in far grander places of worship - in the great nave of Westminster Abbey and in the grandeur of Chester Cathedral, in the private chapel at Windsor Castle and the Chapel Royal, St James.

Later the woman pauses in the graveyard and reads the words on the headstone of her father's grave.

'Amavimus, Amamus, Amabimus.
(We loved, we love, we shall love.)

She takes a small package and trowel from the pocket of her mantle, scoops a hole in the soft ground and plants some seeds. Then she crosses the lane, up through the fields to the Mount that overlooks the Rectory and there she does the same. Returning home she finds her mother sitting by the fire.

'All is done Mama. I have carried out Father's wishes and maybe in a hundred years time they will come to fulfillment.'

* * *

EPILOGUE

After the funeral of her father, Rose planted seeds from the Sequoia trees they had collected in Mariposa Grove, Yosemite. Charles had marvelled at their immense height and beauty. One tree now stands in the churchyard of Eversley Church – towering in its glorious beauty above all else. The other stands at the Mount, Charles' favourite haunt across from the Rectory.

Fanny Kingsley lived for another sixteen years and died in 1891 at her home in Warwickshire at the age of seventy-seven.

Writing in her diary on the 23rd January 1875 Queen Victoria commented on the death of Charles Kingsley.

'Poor Canon Kingsley died today and is a sad loss! He was full of genius and energy, noble and warm hearted, devoted, loyal and chivalrous, much attached to me and mine, full of enthusiasm and most kind and good to the poor.'

In the year of Charles Kingsley's death the Parliament passed a law forbidding the use of small boys as chimney sweeps.

Many of Charles's friends had passed away in his last years and he had found solace in composing poetry. In his moods of introspection, his own mortality was never far from his mind.

Drifting Away.

They drift away. Ah, God! they drift for ever.
I watch the stream sweep onward to the sea.
Like some old battered buoy upon a roaring river
Round whom the tide-waifs hang - then drift to sea.

I watch them drift- the old familiar faces,
Who fished and rode with me, by stream and wold,
Till ghosts, not men fill old beloved places,
And, ah! The land is rank with churchyard mold.

I watch them drift – the youthful aspirations,
Shores landmarks, beacons, drift alike.

I watch them drift- the poets and the statesmen;
The very streams run upward from the sea.

Yet overhead the boundless arch of heaven
Still fades to night, still blazes into day.

Ah, God! My God! Thou will not drift away.

Quotes by Charles Kingsley

'Make it a rule and pray to God to help you keep it . . . never, if possible, to lie down at night without being able to say "I have made one human being at least a little wiser, a little happier, or a little better this day.'

About the Author

Sally Armstrong was born in Suffolk but now lives by the sea in Hampshire. Her careers include teaching, working as an airline stewardess on Concorde and a professional yachting photographer. She is the author of two books – one on Formula One motor racing and the second, published in 2015 on Concorde.

Printed in June 2019
by Rotomail Italia S.p.A., Vignate (MI) - Italy